›   ‚Y S,
ARDMHOR

Lea Booth

Copyright © 2022 N Thornely

All rights reserved

The characters and events portrayed in this book are fictitious. Any similarity to real persons, living or dead, is coincidental and not intended by the author.

No part of this book may be reproduced, or stored in a retrieval system, or transmitted in any form or by any means, electronic, mechanical, photocopying, recording, or otherwise, without express written permission of the publisher.

October 2022   V/XXIII

CONTENTS

Title Page
Copyright
Prologue   1
Chapter One   3
Chapter Two   14
Chapter Three   23
Letter One   32
Chapter Four   37
Chapter Five   44
Chapter Six   50
Chapter Seven   60
Chapter Eight   72
Letter Two   80
Chapter Nine   84
Chapter Ten   94
Chapter Eleven   100
Letter Three   109

Chapter Twelve	114
Chapter Thirteen	126
Chapter Fourteen	134
Chapter Fifteen	143
Letter Four	153
Chapter Sixteen	159
Chapter Seventeen	167
Chapter Eighteen	175
Letter Five	186
Chapter Nineteen	192
Chapter Twenty	202
Chapter Twenty-One	209
Chapter Twenty-Two	221
Letter Six	233
Chapter Twenty-Three	241
Chapter Twenty-Four	249
Chapter Twenty-Five	254
Letter Seven	268
Chapter Twenty-Six	274
Chapter Twenty-Seven	282
Chapter Twenty-Eight	289
Chapter Twenty-Nine	305
Letter Eight	314
Chapter Thirty	319

Chapter Thirty-One	328
Chapter Thirty-Two	333
Chapter Thirty-Three	346
Chapter Thirty-Four	350
Chapter Thirty-Five	361
From the author	371
Books By This Author	373

PROLOGUE

The woman stumbled across the room, her hair unkempt, her clothing dishevelled. She moved as if still asleep. Perhaps she was asleep. Most of the world slumbered during the dark hours in the dead of night. It didn't seem as if she was part of the world though. It seemed as if she was elsewhere. As if her body was here, but her mind belonged in some far-off place. Despite that, she moved with purpose. The body and mind might have seemed disconnected, but she knew what she had to do. She was searching for something. Something important. Something she hoped would convey the things she could no longer say.

But she was so tired. Her thoughts gave her no peace, and the only escape from them was darkness. It was becoming more and more difficult to lift herself out of that dark, empty place. It had taken so much to pull herself free that she didn't know if she had the strength to keep moving. However, she knew she couldn't give up. She couldn't let her body sink to the floor as it wanted to. She had to find what she was looking for. It was the only way she could start to put things right.

CHAPTER ONE

Beth wafted the hem of her jumper in a futile attempt to cool down. She could already feel a trickle of moisture making its way down her back, the hair at the base of her neck clinging to her skin. She heard her phone ring and ferreted about in the bag dangling from the pushchair handles, trying to locate it. The ringing stopped the second she liberated it from the cavernous pockets of the changing bag. Displayed on the home screen were the words 'missed call Mum' and the time. Beth registered the numbers with panic. Eleven o'clock! Playgroup finished at half past, and she had only just passed the gates to Ardmhor House, the ancestral seat of the MacAird family and also home to her parents-in-law. It was at least another ten minutes' walk to the church hall where 'Bumps and Bairns' took place and that was on a good day, which today certainly wasn't. She toyed with the idea of admitting defeat and turning around. She could wander down to the pier instead. Rory would probably need feeding soon, anyway. They could sit on the bench tucked against the side of the shop. She'd got some snacks with her, so she could sit and watch the seals as he ate. He was still breastfed, but he wasn't feeding as often since he'd started eating solids, well not in the daytime, anyway. Maybe if he had milk as soon as they got home, he'd sleep after the fresh air, and she could finally get a moment to herself. Then she remembered why her mum had been ringing. She was already waiting for her at the church hall. Beth couldn't just change her plans. She'd have to keep going, no matter how silly she'd look arriving just as the group was packing away.

They should have been in plenty of time for the ten o'clock start. For what felt like the first time since his birth nine months ago, Rory had slept for more than two hours in succession. Beth had been to him when he'd woken at two, practically crawling across the landing to the room he had occupied since he'd turned six months. There was no point in her husband going instead. Although Ali was an amazing dad, he couldn't lactate, and they both knew that was the only thing that would calm the cries piercing the cold night air. They'd hoped that moving Rory into his own room might help him sleep better. They'd reasoned that maybe they were disturbing him, and they'd already tried everything else suggested, but it had made no difference. Really, it had made things worse because there was further to go to reach him now, and inevitably, in the rush to comfort her tiny son, Beth would forget to grab the dressing gown from its hook on the back of the door and spend the next half hour shivering as she tried to nurse him back to sleep.

There had been nothing different about Beth's time comforting Rory in the early hours of that morning. After she'd been wrenched from her sleep, hating Ali as she heard him shuffle into a more comfortable position beneath the warmth of the duvet, she'd lifted Rory from his cot. His soft weight had settled against her as his tears calmed and he started to feed. She'd carefully opened the bottom of his sleeping bag, trying to check his nappy without disturbing him, and was relieved to find he didn't need changing. He seemed to be drifting off as he fed, and she felt her anger towards Ali dissipate. She knew he'd feed Rory if he could. It wasn't his fault Rory wouldn't take a bottle. For a while, Ali had insisted on going to Rory first, so that he could change him and try to settle him, but it had rarely worked. Instead, it felt to Beth that she was just lying there, waiting for the inevitable moment she'd be called in, when all but boobs had failed. It had seemed easier for her to just get up and get each waking over with as quickly as possible, and there was no sense in them both being tired.

This had led to other problems though. Ali hadn't said as much, but Beth suspected he felt left out and a little useless when it came to caring for Rory, and it seemed wrong to complain about tiredness and all the care falling to her, when she had essentially refused his help. She laid Rory gently back into his cot, holding her breath at the crucial moment when his body would feel the change between her warm arms and the now cold sheet covering the mattress. Backing out of his room with the stealth of a burglar, she crossed the landing and fell gratefully back into bed, noticing the time on the clock and wondering how long she'd get before it all began again. If recent nights were anything to go by, two hours if she was lucky, one if she wasn't.

However, she'd woken with a start, finding the bed empty, daylight showing around the curtains, and the clock reading half-past eight. Her first instinct was that something was wrong, and she bolted across the landing to find Rory's cot abandoned. She'd rushed down the stairs, heart racing, only to stop as she registered the smell of fresh toast and the sound of Rory's gentle babbling. She pushed open the door to the kitchen diner and saw Ali emptying the dishwasher as Rory clapped his hands in the highchair, porridge in front of him, under him, and on him.

"I was just going to bring you a drink up," said Ali, pointing at the steaming mug of hot water on the worktop. "We were trying to let Mummy have a lie in, weren't we, mate?"

"When did he wake up?" Beth asked. "I didn't hear him. You should have woken me."

"He only stirred just before eight. I heard him gurgling away as I was creeping down the stairs, so I thought I'd see if I could get him to have some breakfast before disturbing you. He's done alright too, but I don't think I got the consistency of the porridge fingers quite right."

"You have to leave them to firm up a bit first," Beth said with a yawn, pulling out a seat from underneath the edge of the island unit. "So he's really been asleep for over five hours?"

"I know. It's a miracle!" He turned to address Rory instead. "You're a clever little thing, aren't you? Staying asleep for all that time. So how do you feel?" he asked, returning his attention to Beth. "This must be the longest you've slept since he was born."

"I feel exhausted, actually. Worse than I normally do, but..." she paused, a smile forming on her lips, "imagine if this is the start of something, imagine if he starts doing this every night."

So it was a very hopeful Beth who ran back up the stairs to get showered before Ali left for work.

She ate her breakfast at a leisurely pace as Rory played in his activity centre, even managing not to get irritated by the cheery nursery rhymes it played on a constant loop. When her mum had phoned at quarter past nine to offer them a lift to playgroup, Beth had refused. She only needed to brush her teeth and quickly change Rory's nappy, so they could easily be out of the house in ten minutes. That would give them plenty of time to walk to the church hall, and it looked like a nice day.

That was when things went downhill. She'd left Rory sat on his bedroom floor as she went into the bathroom to brush her teeth, the stair gate was closed, so she knew he'd be safe, but in the two minutes she was gone, he'd been sick all down his front and on the carpet. She'd rushed about, changing him and cleaning up, and although they'd miss the start of playgroup, it wasn't a complete disaster. They might only have been half an hour late if she hadn't heard the sound of an explosive nappy fill just as she'd wheeled the pushchair out of the door. It didn't sound like something she could ignore until they reached playgroup, so she'd retreated back into the house and begun her second clean-up of the morning. She'd seen several calls from her mum, who was obviously wondering where they were, but she hadn't had a free hand to answer. Then, by the time they were ready, there didn't seem to be a moment to waste on making a call. Instead, she'd run back out of the door, hot and flustered before they'd even got going.

As she passed the old church and graveyard, where generations of MacAirds were taking their final rest, she heard the shrill cry of a buzzard. Despite her lateness, she couldn't resist craning her head back and surveying the sky. The buzzard was soaring directly above her. In the past, Beth hadn't been a particular fan of birds, but the majesty of birds of prey gliding serenely through the sky couldn't fail to impress. As she watched its progress for a moment, she noticed another slightly larger bird to the side of it; it held its wings flat, unlike those of the buzzard, which were raised into a v shape.

"Look Rory!" she said, kneeling at the side of the pushchair and pointing upwards. "It's a golden eagle. We'll have to tell Daddy when he gets home."

Beth's knowledge of birds was all down to her husband, Ali. It had amused her on their second date, when he'd been bursting with excitement to tell her about the white-tailed eagle he'd spotted that day. Beth had heard of the 'sea eagle', which had been sighted increasingly frequently in the area since being reintroduced to the Scottish islands in the 1970s, and she knew many tourists hoped to see one, but she hadn't thought to keep an eye out for one herself. She certainly hadn't expected Ali, this accomplished man, who'd spent years working in London and then lived halfway across the world, to be bouncing around like a schoolboy because of a bird. At first, she'd wondered if he was teasing her, but after a few romantic walks together, where she'd found herself talking to thin air before discovering Ali a few steps back with his binoculars aloft, she'd realised he was totally serious. She still found it an endearing quirk of his, something that most people outside of the family didn't know about him. He was the life and soul of every party, knew about everything and everyone, and he seemed to be counted as a friend by anyone he'd met. When you coupled this with his tall, muscular physique, his chiselled face, and his intense dark eyes, Beth was always amazed he'd chosen her. He was not how she'd have pictured a bird watcher. The geeky hobby had helped to make him seem more approachable at the start of their relationship. It had been easier to relax alongside his perfection once she had something to tease him about. So now, even though almost five years had passed, she still found herself excited to tell him when she spotted something all by herself.

The eagle sighting had eaten up another couple of precious minutes though. She'd been silly not to have phoned her mum to ask her to come back for them. It was just that the day had started so well. She'd wanted Jean to see how brilliantly she could handle everything. She hadn't wanted to concede any sign of weakness. It was daft because Jean wasn't the type of mum to make you feel you had to prove anything. She was nothing but supportive, but sometimes Beth was her own worst enemy. Since moving from England up to Ardmhor, she'd managed to put aside a lot of the doubts she carried about herself. The job she'd taken on, setting up the museum at Ardmhor House, suited her so much better than teaching had, and meeting Ali had transformed the way she saw herself. But Rory's birth hadn't been easy, and the exhaustion of the time in hospital afterwards had never really lifted. It was like a fog had descended and brought down with it all the fears that used to plague her. Her heart was so full of love for her beautiful sandy-haired baby, with his gurgling laugh and his chubby arms, but she craved time to herself and hated herself for it. When she'd moved to Ardmhor, her parents had been living about six hours' drive away, but last year they'd bought a house just a few minutes down the road, intending to move permanently as soon as David retired. It was the house where they'd holidayed when Beth was a child, and when they'd finally made the move three months back, she'd been overjoyed at the idea of having them so close, but for some reason she was finding the reality difficult.

She wrestled her way through the doors to the church hall, using the pushchair as a battering ram to negotiate the inner foyer door. Beth saw her mum before her mum spotted her. She was at the other end of the hall, enjoying a cup of tea with some of the 'spare grannies': volunteers who liked to chat while cuddling the babies, leaving the mums who'd also got older children free to chase the bigger ones around the room. Beth knew she should be happy that her mum was settling into her new life so well, but instead she felt full of rage. A jealous voice inside her said that this was her place. It was where she had made a life for herself. She had wanted her parents nearby, but her mum had no right to be here without her, looking perfectly at home.

"Beth, you're here at last!" Jean exclaimed as she saw her.

It felt to Beth as if it was one of those moments in a cowboy film, where the room falls silent, and everyone turns to look at the newcomer. Although she'd been coming here ever since Rory was born and she knew each person in the room, she suddenly felt like an outsider. She was hot, she was sweaty, and Rory started to cry. Tears prickled her eyes, and her body screamed at her to run away. She swung the pushchair round and would have made it outside if it hadn't been for those ridiculous double doors. Instead, she felt her mum's arms gently fold her into a hug as the tears began, and she closed her eyes tightly, wanting desperately to believe that if she couldn't see anyone, they wouldn't be witnessing this moment either.

CHAPTER TWO

After her humiliating entrance to playgroup, Beth had been plied with drinks and biscuits while the others in the room fell over themselves to talk about how overwhelming motherhood could be, recounting their own tales of when the simplest things had become near impossible tasks. She allowed herself to accept the comfort meant by their words and tried to fix in her brain that whatever happened she belonged here, that people cared about her. Jean insisted on driving Beth and Rory home, so they strapped Rory into the spare car seat and folded the pushchair into the boot.

"You look exhausted, Beth, so I'm going to come in, make you both some lunch and then I'm taking Rory out so you can have a sleep."

"I can manage, Mum," Beth replied wearily, but with enough exasperation for Jean to pick up on.

"Oh, I know you can manage, sweetheart, but you don't have to. I want to take Rory out. It's a pleasure getting to spend time with him, and it's also a pleasure getting to have lunch with you. I missed seeing you all the time while we were still in England, so I want to make the most of it now."

"Thank you," Beth acquiesced quietly.

"You don't need to thank me. I'm your mum, and I remember what it was like to have no sleep and no time for myself. I think his Lordship takes after you. You were almost one before you slept properly." She paused, and a little laugh escaped her as a new thought occurred. "When you were a baby, we always referred to you as 'Your Highness' or 'Your Ladyship' because you were totally in charge of us, that's why I say it to Rory too, but I've only just thought about the fact that Rory's other grandad actually is a Lord. No wonder he's bossy!"

Beth gave her mum a small smile, but she was too tired to enter into conversation properly. Ali's parents were Lord and Lady MacAird, the owners of Ardmhor House, where Beth had taken a job almost five years ago now. Until then she'd been working in the city where she'd been born and living with her parents in the house where she'd grown up, so moving to Scotland and leaving them behind had been a big step. Ali's parents had been thrilled when Beth and Ali started dating and had always made Beth feel like part of their family. They had also been very welcoming to Beth's parents, having them round each time they came up to visit. But the MacAird's proximity meant that during the first months of Rory's life, Beth, Ali, and Rory had spent much more time with them than they had with Beth's parents. Once Jean and David had completed their permanent move to Ardmhor, family logistics had needed a bit of reorganising, and three months on, Beth was aware of a slight tension as everyone adjusted. Not tension in the vein of anger and bad feeling, more of the sort where no one wants to tread on anyone else's toes. It was clear to Beth that Jean felt they'd lost some of the closeness they had shared, and she also felt her mum was trying not to be put out by the easy relationship she'd built with her mother-in-law, and boss, Angela. Whereas Angela was so keen to involve Jean and make her feel a part of life at Ardmhor House, that she was coming across as pushy. Beth gave a little sigh as she thought how difficult it was to get family right sometimes, and Jean reached over and gave her knee a squeeze.

Jean stuck to her word, and after feeding them all she bundled Rory into his pushchair ready for a walk to the pier and perhaps a trip back to her house, to check whether his grandad was getting on with the jobs she'd left him working on.

"We'll be at least two hours, and I'll phone you

if there are any problems. So finish your drink and then get yourself up to bed." She planted a kiss on the top of Beth's head and closed the door behind her.

Beth sipped her drink and looked around the room. Although she felt tired to her very bones, she didn't want to go to sleep. The prospect of time alone, with no one to be responsible for, was too tantalising to waste. Her eyes fell onto the photographs lined up along the mantelpiece. There was one of Rory, Ali, and herself on the day Rory had been born. Jean had arranged to have it printed, framed, and posted to her as a gift the day after they'd texted it out to announce Rory's birth. It had already been sitting in that spot when Beth and Rory made it home from the hospital, and despite taking hundreds of photos of him since, they hadn't got round to printing or displaying any others. Next to that were a couple of photos of Beth and Ali's wedding. One showed all the guests gathered together, glasses raised, toasting Beth and Ali as they stood in the centre of the group. The other was just the two of them, in front of Ardmhor House, beaming at the camera. Beth picked it up and looked closely at the expressions on their faces. They looked so carefree and so in love. She wondered if they would ever be the couple in the photograph again; she hoped that when Rory was sleeping better, they would regain a bit of what they had been, but at the moment it sometimes felt more like they were two people living side by side than a couple.

The photo alongside their wedding picture was very similar, but much older. This one showed a different couple stood smiling outside Ardmhor House: Beth's great-great-grandmother, Eliza and her great-great-grandfather, Alexander MacAird. Alexander MacAird was Ali's full name as well, and it wasn't just a name he shared with the man in the photo, Ali was Alexander's many times great nephew, meaning that Beth and Ali were already distantly related before they met and married. The last photograph was a wedding portrait of Joseph Turner and his wife Maude, Eliza's parents. Joseph had moved with Eliza to this very house after his wife's death, when he took on the job of factor at Ardmhor. Beth's gran had found the picture amongst her belongings and given it to Beth when she bought the house. When she had first arrived at Ardmhor on a working holiday, Beth had been completely unaware of any family connection. It was only while she was there that her mum and gran had unearthed an old diary belonging to Eliza and the story had been revealed. Beth had become so involved in the diary and felt so at home at Ardmhor that she'd ended up applying for a permanent job there. Eventually, she'd bought the former factor's house, and then she'd fallen in love with Ali.

But the connection Beth felt with Eliza and Alexander wasn't as simple as becoming engrossed in their story through reading a diary. On her first day at Ardmhor, she'd met a man she felt an instant bond with who went by the name of Alex. He had implied that he lived at Ardmhor House, and as they spent more time together Beth had gradually fallen in love with him, believing him to be the son of Lady Angela and Lord James. Alex had made her look at herself differently, but he was reluctant to reveal anything about himself, and Beth had struggled to know whether her feelings were requited. A considerable amount of time had passed before he had told her she needed to know who he really was, and she'd discovered that he wasn't Lady Angela's son after all. He hadn't explained who he was directly, instead he'd led her to the location of an old book, containing a locket, a long-lost letter, and a photograph. The letter had been intended for Eliza, so it hadn't really cleared up Beth's confusion, and then the photograph had made things worse. It was the photo that Beth now had in a frame on her mantelpiece, showing her great-great-grandparents in front of Ardmhor House. However, at that point, although she'd seen pictures of Eliza before, she'd had no idea what her great-great-grandfather looked like. All she'd been able to think as she'd looked at the picture for the first time was how on earth was Alex, the man she was in love with, in a 19th century photograph standing next to her great-great-grandmother? The caption said the photo was of Eliza Turner and Alexander MacAird, and had been taken in the 1890s, but Beth knew it was of the man she'd been meeting. They didn't just look similar, they were clearly the same person. Alex disappeared after Beth found the photograph, and even though no one could come up with any other explanation for who Beth had been meeting, for a long time she'd struggled to accept that what the photo suggested could be true. Even after all this time, with her increased knowledge of the superstitions that surrounded Ardmhor and its 'thin' divide between the living and the dead, she found it surreal that it was a ghost who had convinced her to make her life there. But she did accept it now, and she was more grateful to Alex than she could ever express. He had taught her a lot about acceptance and regret, and he had led her to Ali, the man she'd thought she had been meeting all along.

She stroked Alex's face through the glass of the picture frame and thought about how short and sad his life had been. Since Rory's birth, she had pondered many times on how Alex's mother, Lady Constance, could have lied to him in the way that she had, depriving him of a life with Eliza and their child. No matter how much Beth longed for time alone, she couldn't imagine ever deliberately making a decision that she knew would lead to Rory's unhappiness. However, she had already done things that had upset Rory in that moment because she believed them to be best for him in the long run, like taking him for his vaccinations, so maybe it wasn't as straightforward as she'd thought. Maybe Lady Constance had genuinely believed she was doing the right thing for Alex.

About a year ago, the museum had acquired some letters written by James MacAird, Alex's older brother, which were being auctioned as part of a house clearance. They probably wouldn't have purchased them, but the guide price was low, and the sample shown in the catalogue included a reference to Lady Constance that had drawn them in. A couple of the letters had been written shortly after Alex's death. They mentioned James's concern for his mother as she cleared all photographs and reminders of Alex from the house and pushed the rest of the family away from her. It was hard to know whether her actions were those of a cold woman who simply did not want to think of a son who had disappointed her, or whether they were the actions of a mother who couldn't bear to be reminded of what she had lost. Finding these early stages of motherhood so much more difficult than she had expected had given Beth a bit more sympathy towards Lady Constance. While she still didn't understand her, she no longer simply wrote her off as evil. She was, after all, her own flesh and blood too, and she was learning first-hand now that just because motherly love was supposed to be unconditional, it didn't mean it was straightforward.

She took a sip of her drink and realised it had gone cold in her hand. A glance at the clock told her it was already twenty minutes since her mum and Rory had left the house. Her precious alone time was vanishing, but she was too tired to think how to utilise it. Finally, she took her mother's advice and made her way up the stairs to her bed. At least if she slept, she'd have achieved something. Beth resolved to make more effort not to get irritated with her mum, who was trying so hard to support her and had done nothing to deserve her anger. She knew she needed to apply this to Ali as well. He really wasn't to blame for the things he couldn't do for Rory, and she so wanted them to be the loved-up couple from their wedding picture again. She lay down on the bed and pulled the duvet around her, exhausted, but certain that sleep wouldn't come because of the pressure of the time frame allotted for the activity. Her mind drifted over the people in the photographs and the things that connected them, and she was wrong yet again. Within seconds she was gone, lost in a dreamless oblivion, only stirring when her mum placed a mug of hot water on her bedside table a couple of hours later.

CHAPTER THREE

Almost a week on from the playgroup meltdown, Beth was feeling a little more like herself. She'd had a long talk with Ali, and they'd agreed that they would both get up when Rory woke in the night. Beth would feed him, then Ali would take over changing nappies and settling him back to sleep. She had been resisting this idea because it had seemed like admitting failure. She had thought that because she was on maternity leave, whereas Ali was still working, she needed to handle everything baby related. However, Ali was adamant that he needed to be doing more. He argued it couldn't be right for Beth's life to change completely, but his remain the same. Eventually, Beth had seen that if she clung onto this idea of being a successful mother who did everything, she might end up failing elsewhere. She was simultaneously irritable, mean, angry, and sad. Gradually, she was realising something had to give, before the wonderful life she had built herself came crashing down. Having Ali alongside her as she went into Rory's room, bringing the dressing gown she always forgot and taking away the worry of making a successful transfer from arms to cot, seemed to be making a difference. She didn't feel the panic of needing to grab every moment of sleep, the panic that perversely often kept her awake, and amazingly, the wake-ups appeared to have gone from three to two per night.

It also helped that her parents and in-laws had held some sort of strategy meeting, and one grandparent or other would now turn up most weekday afternoons, ready for their portion of Rory time. Beth had been reluctant to accept this offer of help when her mum first suggested it. It was on the afternoon of the playgroup debacle, and she'd had to summon every ounce of resolve in order to bite down her irritation when she'd realised Jean had been discussing her with Angela. If it hadn't been for the time she'd spent thinking about Alex before her nap, she might not have managed it, but when her anger had surged at the thought of people talking about her inability to cope, some of Alex's words whispered through her mind. He had once warned her she needed to be more afraid of missing out on the life she was supposed to have than she was of failing. He'd been talking about her being brave enough to take a chance and apply for her job at Ardmhor, so maybe this wasn't really the same, but as she heard his words again, it seemed like the same principles applied. If her fear of being seen as a failure prevented her from getting help, she could be putting her family at risk. She needed to be more afraid of that than anything else.

So she'd swallowed her pride and accepted the help being offered, and now, if she was honest with herself, it was those guaranteed hours of time alone that were keeping her going. She wasn't sure whether she was making the best use of them yet, but she had less of a feeling that life was running away from her while she sat trapped under a child. Most importantly, she didn't have that awful feeling of resenting Rory as she tried to entertain him. It was during the fourth of these afternoon slices of freedom that she found herself in the attic. It was perhaps not the wisest choice, as it risked bringing the spotlight back to another bone of contention between herself and Ali. When she had bought the factor's house, she had only been able to afford to do what was necessary to make it liveable. So the roof had been replaced along with the skylights in it, the floors that had rotted because of the holes in the roof had been repaired, and a new kitchen and bathroom had been fitted, but Beth had always had plans for more. She hoped to convert the attic in to one enormous bedroom, with its own bathroom, a luxurious retreat for her and Ali. She also wanted to have an extension added at the back of the house, with a glass fronted living space looking out to sea. They had the money to put some of these plans into action now, but the problem was they couldn't agree on what should happen first. Beth wanted to work on the downstairs, so while she was spending so much time in the house, she could make the most of its position and actually see the sea. However, Ali felt that would be too big a job with a baby in the house, and as they didn't need extra space downstairs, he felt they should focus on creating another bedroom, especially as they'd always talked about wanting two children close in age. Beth could see Ali's point. The huge amount of mess that an extension would generate was probably too much for them now. However, she couldn't help feeling that agreeing to go ahead with the attic conversion was agreeing she was ready to try for another child, and she wasn't sure that would ever be the case. Her best friend from university was expecting her second child any time now, and although Beth was happy for her, she couldn't help imagining how hard it must be to care for two young children. She was relieved it was happening to Lucy rather than to her. She suspected Ali might feel the same at the moment. Rory's sleep patterns had exhausted them both, and she wondered if he was actually starting the conversation about the attic as a way of testing the waters. However, every time he mentioned the idea of another child, she found a way to divert the conversation. She was terrified of discovering that they weren't on the same page after all. She was hoping that starting to clear the attic might be enough to head the conversation off for a little longer.

A lot of the junk that had been in the attic when Beth purchased the house had been thrown in a skip during the initial building work, but she'd hung onto the things that interested her the most. There were some bits of furniture that she was sure she could turn into something fabulous. Some vintage clothes, nothing going back as far as Eliza's time in the house, but stuff that might be useful for fancy dress one day. Some lovely old crockery that she was determined to display when she finally got her extension. And many odds and ends that might find a use one day. However, if she was being realistic, she knew that she'd probably never use any of it and if they were going to convert the attic; it needed to go. Her plan was to work through the boxes and at least thin out their contents.

An hour in, she'd reached her mental limit for sorting through musty paraphernalia. She was just about to make her way back down the stairs when she felt a shift in the atmosphere. The light seemed to alter, and a sense of foreboding settled on her. Some sort of primeval instinct told her she wasn't alone. There was another presence in the attic. Beth had always been easily spooked, and her scalp tingled as the hairs stood to attention. Her fight-or-flight reflexes were telling her to run, and she immediately bolted towards the top of the stairs. But something made her stop. Some force, stronger than her desire to escape the charged air of the attic, made her walk towards one of the boxes of clothes instead. A small wooden box sat in the middle of the pile of clothes. She didn't recall having seen it before, but there was so much up there that it was hard to keep track of everything. Once she had the box in her hand, the atmosphere seemed to shift again. She could hear birds singing outside and a shaft of sunlight slid through the small window in the roof, illuminating the box. She lifted the lid to find a pile of folded, yellowed papers. Taking the first piece of paper from the pile, she slowly unfolded it, but despite the gentleness of her touch, it ripped apart at the fold, leaving her holding two smaller sections instead of the original larger piece. Extra cautious now, she placed the pieces on to the soft pile of clothes in front of her. Almost every inch of the paper was covered in looping black handwriting, and although it wasn't neat, with the lines swooping up and down and the writing changing size and direction, it appeared the writer was sure of what they wanted to say, as there wasn't a single bit of crossing out or correction. But it was the name of the recipient and the date that really drew Beth's eye. The letter was addressed to 'Dearest Joseph, the most special person in the world' and dated June 1864. There was no name at the bottom, it simply ended 'all my love, always'. Beth immediately wondered if it could have been written to Eliza's father, Joseph, and started trying to decipher the next line. It said something about calling on the Turner household and finding his cousins running wild. Even with the unsettling feeling that some other presence had been in the attic, Beth felt a bubble of excitement starting to grow. Joseph's surname was Turner, so it seemed the letter really could belong to him. However, it was impossible to read it properly up in the attic. Even though the sun was now shining, the light wasn't the best for interpreting the jumble of words that filled the page. Also, the feeling of that other presence, the one that had sent shivers down her spine, wasn't something she was going to forget quickly. She decided to carry the box downstairs and enjoy the contents with a nice warm drink and the comforting sounds of the radio.

◆ ◆ ◆

Beth didn't know much about Joseph. She'd

done a bit of digging when she first bought the house. She'd even joined an ancestry website to get easy access to census records and birth, marriage, and death certificates, but she had found out little that she hadn't already known. Joseph had married Maude when they were both twenty, and then Eliza had come along the following year. Maude had become ill and died after a drawn-out illness in 1880, when Eliza was only eight years old. Eliza and Joseph had then moved to Scotland, for Joseph to take on the role of factor for the Ardmhor Estate. Eliza had suffered further tragedy when Joseph died at the age of just forty. At this point, the MacAird family had taken Eliza in at Ardmhor House. The extra details she had learnt were that Joseph had suffered tragedy himself as a child. He had been orphaned at the age of six and moved in with his uncle, who was the vicar for a parish in the countryside surrounding London. According to their marriage certificate, Maude was from the same village, and as they were the same age, it seemed they would have grown up together. A bit more investigation had revealed photographs of the vicarage where Joseph had lived—a grand stone building next to an equally grand church—as well as photographs of Maude's home. Her father was listed as a doctor on the marriage certificate, but he was obviously a very successful one, as the house in the photographs had the appearance of a rambling country mansion. She hadn't been able to find out what she really wanted to know though. Living in the house Joseph and Eliza had shared, she'd wanted to know what sort of person he was, what their family had been like before Maude died, and how Joseph and Maude had fallen in love. It intrigued her to think the answers might have been waiting in the attic all along. Another shiver passed through her as she considered the possibility that Maude had wanted her to find the letters, that she had led her to them. She still preferred to tell herself that ghosts didn't exist, but her own experiences had taught her that some things just couldn't be explained. The kettle reached its crescendo and clicked off, so she filled her mug with steaming water and set it carefully down, keeping it a safe distance from the precious paper. Then she started to read.

LETTER ONE

June 1864

Dearest Joseph, the most special person in the world,

I hope you are counting down the days until school finishes and you are back here with me. You won't be surprised to hear that I have been counting them since the moment you left, and I think your family needs you too. I called in on the Turner household yesterday, and it seems your little cousins are running wild. Your aunt looked on the verge of losing her temper, which you will know is saying something about how riotous the scene was. They need you back to scare them into submission.

How is school? Are you still getting on well with your roommates? I assume you are still sharing with James and Robert, as you haven't mentioned any changes. Have your exams been going well? I know how important it is that you are successful, so that you can study law like your father, but I also know you don't need to worry. You are quite brilliant, Joseph, so I know you will succeed. I have no doubt that you will change the world in all the ways you write about. You've always made my world better.

I simply cannot wait to see you. It will be impossible for the next month to pass quickly enough. It is so lonely here without you. Mother and Father have been away again, so I've been left with just the governess and the staff for company. If they were going to spend so much time away, I wish they'd been good enough to provide me with a sibling for company. We are having at least three children. I am in the process of making one new friend though. A family has moved from London into the old manor house. They have a daughter the same age as us, so I have made it my mission to turn her into the sister I've always wanted. She is a little quiet so far, and I am not sure she is as keen on the idea as I am, but I am certain I will soon manage to bring her round.

Did your aunt and uncle write to you about the village fete? Obviously, they did the bulk of the organising and so much of the work fell to your aunt, but as usual, Mrs Goodall tried to steal all the credit when the day came around. There was a huge drama over the winner of the jam contest, but I know your aunt was excited to tell you about it and I don't want to spoil her fun, so if you don't already know I'll have to leave you imagining the tension and intrigue for now!

The jam contest isn't the only exciting thing I've found out about though. Spending so much time hiding in the kitchen, escaping from the governess, means I've been having lots of chats with Betty, the maid. She told me that Fred from the stables had kissed her and that it had been the best moment of her life. I was intrigued because when I've seen someone kiss my mother's hand she hasn't really shown any change in demeanour. It certainly hasn't looked as if she is experiencing the best moment of her life. Also, on the occasions when Father has kissed the top of my head before he goes off on a long trip, I haven't really liked it. Being so close to him, when he is usually so distant, always feels strange. Anyway, when I said this to Betty, she laughed and said she didn't mean a kiss on the hand or the head, but a kiss on the lips! Did you know people did this? If you did, how did I not? I felt quite embarrassed by my ignorance, so I marched straight off to the stable and asked Fred to kiss me, too. He seemed a little surprised, but I insisted until he did. It definitely wasn't the best moment of my life, although I will admit it wasn't totally unpleasant. Well, it wasn't unpleasant until Betty appeared and slapped Fred right across the face. Then she looked at me and said angrily, 'If I wouldn't lose my job for it, I'd slap you too'. She refused to even look at me for the rest of the day.

Later on, cook took me to one side and said that if I got involved in any more inappropriate behaviour, she would have to tell the governess. I protested that I didn't know what I'd done wrong, and then cook laughed at me, as Betty had earlier. Eventually, she stopped laughing and realised I was telling the truth, that I honestly didn't know why Betty was so upset. Then she softened a bit. She disappeared and came back a moment later with a book which she said might help explain things. Well, the book has been a revelation! I've always known that you are my best friend and that we would get married and have children, but I didn't know about all the things that go with that. The book is about a girl who falls in love with a boy she's not supposed to talk to, so they have to meet in secret. Anyway, when they meet, they kiss and kiss, and she can't breathe because it's so wonderful and they just want to kiss all the time. I can't believe I didn't know about any of this!

You'll be pleased to know Betty is speaking to me again now. I apologised again and again until she believed that I simply hadn't realised kissing on the lips was different to other kisses. Plenty of visitors to our house have kissed mother's hand, so it just didn't occur to me that kisses were supposed to be something special. Since reading cook's book, I feel quite foolish that I didn't already know, especially as Betty is fifteen, exactly the same age as us, yet she was fully aware. I also feel terrible that I hadn't noticed a special connection between her and Fred. I think I get so caught up in my own world that sometimes I don't notice anyone else's.

I so hope you don't write back and tell me you already knew about kissing on the lips. Then I really will feel silly. I'm reassuring myself that you can't have known, as surely if you had, we'd have tried it by now. So, as well as feeling foolish, I'm awaiting your return with even more anticipation than usual. I'm excited to try out this way of kissing with you. I'm sure it will feel just like the book says, and I can hardly wait!

I'm running out of space, so I must go, but hurry back as quickly as you can. I miss you.

All my love,

Always

CHAPTER FOUR

It seemed to Beth that she was going to be granted her wish of finding out more about Joseph and Maude and what sort of couple they'd been, but the letter was not what she'd been expecting. The Maude in the letter could not have been further from the Maude Beth had imagined. The way she talked about kissing and gleefully informed Joseph that they would be doing it when he returned was so different from anything Beth had seen in other letters from that period, or to be honest, in letters from any period. It did sound as if Maude spent a lot of time alone or with the servants, so perhaps she was just as unaware of the expected behaviour for well-to-do Victorian girls as she was of how kissing worked. Her openness about how much she adored Joseph, coupled with her cluelessness about romance, had Beth picturing a girl who was confident and at ease with herself, happy to say whatever popped into her head, with no fear of judgement. The way she had announced that the new girl in the village would become close to her, as if the girl herself had no say in the matter, had made Beth laugh. It was so different to her own apologetic way of being, and so like she had always wanted to be, that she couldn't help but fall a little in love with Maude. She wondered if Joseph's personality had been similar and whether Eliza's confidence had been inherited from both of her parents or if it had been a case of opposites attracting. Beth looked across at Joseph and Maude's wedding portrait, lined up amongst the pictures on the mantelpiece. Maude looked so serene and innocent, it was intriguing to get a glimpse of the person behind that neutral expression.

It was tempting to start reading the next letter in the pile, but there were only a few minutes left before her mum was due back with Rory, so she decided it would be better to return the little stack of paper to the safety of its box.

She heard a cry of "It's only us" and the bang of the door, just as she placed the box safely behind the pictures on the mantelpiece.

"I'm in here," she shouted, just as her mum entered the room carrying a sleepy Rory. He rubbed his eyes and then held his chubby little arms out to her.

"Hello, my sweetheart," Beth cooed, enjoying

his cuddle and wondering how she could ever bear to let him out of her sight. Forgetting for a moment the absolute relief she'd felt when she'd waved him off just two hours earlier. "Has he been alright?"

"He's been an angel, but he hasn't slept a wink, so he must be due a sleep by now. It is tonight you're off to Inveravain, isn't it? Maybe he'll have a nap while you get ready."

"Yes, it is tonight. Angela's booked a table at the Beinn View. She wanted to get everyone together before Jay goes back down to London."

"How long have you got before you need to be out? Do you fancy a drink before you get ready?"

"A drink would be lovely. The table is booked for half seven, so there's plenty of time."

Beth moved over to the kettle, an expert at filling it with one hand now and then reached two mugs from the cupboard, adding a tea bag to her mums, but leaving her own empty.

"Did you get much done in the attic? I'd thought we might return to a hall full of bin bags."

"There were some old cushions that smelt funny, so I've put them on the 'to go' pile, but otherwise all I've done is unpack boxes and then put everything back in them. And then I got a bit distracted..." she tailed off, knowing how much her mum would enjoy the story of her discovery.

"Now, this sounds interesting. Don't you be

going all dramatic and keeping your poor old mother in suspense, Beth Hutton!"

Beth smiled at the fact her mum still couldn't get used to using her married name and handed Rory over to her, before pouring the boiling water. She placed the mugs down on the island in the middle of the kitchen diner and sauntered over to the mantelpiece to retrieve the box, laughing at her mother's eye roll as she dragged out the moment.

"I found this!" she announced with a flourish, placing the box on the table.

"I'd worked that bit out for myself, you daft thing! Now show me what's in it, or I'll have to do it myself and we both know what disaster that could lead to while I'm holding his Lordship."

Beth opened the box and gently removed the first letter, carefully placing the two parts in view of her mother but out of Rory's reach.

"They're to Joseph. This one was written when he was fifteen and it's a sort of love letter, so I'm assuming it's from Maude. I'll take Rory off you in a second, so you can read it yourself, but she is so funny. The letter isn't at all what I was expecting, based on when it was written."

"Oh, this is exciting!" Jean jigged Rory up and down on her lap, as if trying to give a visual aid to her feelings. "And you'd never noticed the box before?"

"No, it was hidden in the middle of a pile

of old clothes. It was weird, actually. It felt as if someone was making me look through those clothes again. I've never felt scared in this house before, but it was as though I wasn't on my own. I'm not sure I'll be able to face going up there again when Ali's out."

"Oh, you're giving me goose pimples, Beth. It's like finding the diary again. Have you only read the one so far?"

"Yes, by the time I'd found them, it was time for you two to be getting back. The pile isn't huge either, so I might try to spread them out a bit. It was really sad when I got to the end of the diary, and it sank in that there was no more to come."

"Well, don't take too long over it. Maude's not just your great-great-great-grandma, she's my relative as well, and I don't know if I've got your patience!"

"Don't worry. I'll probably end up bingeing on them in one go tomorrow, but they'll definitely have to wait until then because tonight's already busy, and I want to enjoy them."

Beth took Rory back from Jean and watched her expressions as she read the letter, knowing her mum would be just as taken with Maude as she was.

"Oh, wow! How could she not know about kissing? She sounds like such a sweetie. It's hard to imagine that she's probably a century older than me, when she's just a girl in this."

"I hadn't really thought about that. She's fifteen in the letter so that means..." Beth stopped talking, trying to do the maths in her head before giving up. "I can't work it out exactly, but she'd be at least 150, probably even 160, if she was alive today, so not a little girl after all."

"No, not at all, and speaking of little ones, it seems as if someone has finally given in to sleep."

Rory had grown quiet and still as Beth held him.

"I'll get off," Jean continued quietly, "and let you get ready for tonight while you've got the chance."

An hour later, Beth wasn't feeling quite so chipper. Rory had woken up the second she'd placed him in his cot, and nothing had settled him. She'd ended up trying to get dressed and sort out her hair while simultaneously balancing an increasingly over tired baby. By the time Ali came through the door, she was in full on panic mode. Rory was now screaming even as she held him. Her hair was half up, and their bed was strewn with potential outfits, all of which had been rejected because they clung to the wrong places or didn't allow access if Rory needed feeding. To top it off, she'd noticed a massive spot which had erupted from nowhere in the middle of her chin.

She couldn't even manage a response as Ali entered the room, surveyed the scene and asked,

"What's up with my favourite people?"

She simply handed him the writhing bundle of his son and locked herself in the bathroom.

CHAPTER FIVE

Ardmhor, 1870

There are many unexpected things about my life. I did not expect to be cradling my second son in my arms before reaching my twenty-first birthday. I didn't expect to find myself living in the wilds of Scotland, and I certainly didn't expect to live with both my husband and his mother. When I married James, his father was still alive, and we were intending to live in London, enjoying all the capital has to offer. However, within a year, his father was dead, meaning James had inherited his title, lands, and wealth. We'd had our first son, and it was somehow decided that we would reside here at Ardmhor, along with his mother, the Dowager. I didn't seem to have any say in the matter, not that I have much say in anything. I am, however, going to have a say in my second son.

Alexander MacAird, born before he was expected, on the seventh of January 1870, is going to be mine. James and his mother might think they can make all the decisions about my firstborn, Little James, the son and heir, but they won't be doing the same with Alexander. Little James is practically still a baby himself. His first birthday has only just passed, but already they have his place arranged at the boarding school James attended, all set up for when he reaches seven. Things are going to be different with Alexander. He is my baby and this time I am going to do things my way.

When Little James was born, his father employed a highly recommended nurse. I cannot fault the job she does, but I feel like my son belongs to her, rather than to me. The nurse fed him and rocked him to sleep, the nurse sang to him, tickled him, and received his first smiles. I only saw him at allotted times, when he was presented to us like a trophy. This is another thing I had not expected. I had not expected that as a mother I would be so distant from my child. I know my parents rarely saw me, but I wanted it to be different for my children. When Little James falls, he wants his nurse to pick him up. When he cries, he wants his nurse to comfort him. I want Alexander to want me. Fortunately, his early arrival means that a second nurse has not yet been obtained, and Little James's nurse is not willing to take on two such small charges, so it has afforded me the opportunity to make Alexander mine, and I intend to grasp it.

I suppose I sound ungrateful. There are probably many women out there struggling, wishing they had a home such as this one or a nurse to handle the tempers of their child. I know I am lucky. It just isn't how I'd pictured my life. I can't deny that Ardmhor is a beautiful place. I'd never seen hills on the scale of the ones here before we made our first journey up to Scotland, and I didn't know the sea could be so clear or appear almost green. When people talk about the importance of fresh air, I imagine that the air here is exactly what they mean. And the house! The house is the epitome of luxury. James's mother oversaw the addition of a whole new wing not that many years ago, and she did not scrimp on a single thing. Since we moved here, a fully plumbed bathroom has been added, with hot water available at the turn of a tap! I cannot complain about the environment I live in, well, I say cannot, but that is clearly not true. I suppose I mean I should not complain.

In each letter she sends, my mother tells me I have everything she ever wanted for me and that she is proud. I am glad of that, for it was trying to make her proud that led me here. If she still found me lacking, I don't think I could bear my situation at all. The night I met James, everyone was trying to catch his attention. There were so many beautiful girls at that ball, all displayed to their very best advantage. It was clear James did not know which way to turn, where to let his attention fall. But I don't think anyone imagined it would eventually land with me.

The area around our village had its share of notable people, but none of the calibre of the MacAirds. Lord MacAird's heir would have been a catch beyond the dreams of even the most ambitious parents in that sleepy part of England. The news that he would attend the summer ball hosted by the Forbes family, the top of the pyramid of the local elite, had spread like wildfire, adding a frisson of excitement to the preparations. There was a sudden rush for local seamstresses to make alterations to dresses previously deemed quite adequate.

I wasn't immune to the excitement. In fact, I found myself quite caught up in it. My mother was so entranced by the prospect of making this match that I became entranced by pleasing her. All my life, I had wanted to make her happy. I craved her praise and attention, so for her to lavish so much time on me, while my dress was fitted or while she schooled me in how to behave, well, it was a dream come true, and I'd have done anything to make it last. I never thought for a moment that her scheming would be successful.

When James proposed, Mother was overjoyed,

imagining the whirl of social events my marriage into the MacAird family would entail. For one short year, the reality met her expectations, but like me, she could not have predicted the previous Lord MacAird's sudden death. Nor could she have foreseen that on inheriting his title, James would withdraw to their Scottish estate and adopt the lifestyle of a virtual recluse. Whether she is disappointed, I don't know. I imagine she must be as the social whirl she longed for came to an abrupt end, but, to her credit, she has not expressed such a view in her letters. I, however, have found it hard. To finally have my mother's devotion and then find myself so far away from her again has been difficult. When I made the decision that having my mother's affection was more important than anything else, I had thought I would get to enjoy it for longer.

I feel it was trying to please my mother that set my life on a path so different to that which I had imagined, and I try to convince myself every day that it hasn't been a mistake. As I've said, my life could be worse. I live comfortably, and James is considerate as a husband. It's just that he doesn't really notice me anymore. Our marriage is not the great love I had envisioned, but I suppose I can't really blame James for his lack of interest in me. If I am honest, I was never particularly interested in him. I only accepted his proposal to please my mother. I desperately want to make sure it is different for Alexander. I don't want a need for affection to force him down the wrong path. It is too late for Little James. He will inherit the title, so it seems impossible that he could avoid the expectations of the family name. Alexander, however, is different. He will grow up knowing that there is nothing for him to prove. He will know that my love will always be there to shelter and protect him, whatever form he should want his life to take. My life is not what I expected, but I believe I can steer it closer to the course I had intended. With my precious new son, I will finally have the love I've spent my life searching for.

CHAPTER SIX

Ali secured the car seat in the back of the car, kissing his now sleeping son lightly on the forehead and shutting the car door as gently as possible, before walking round to the driver's seat.

"You've not forgotten the changing bag, have you?" Beth asked irritably as he turned the key in the ignition.

"No, don't worry, it's in the boot."

"Is blue bear in it? He's not holding it."

"I don't know, he'll be alright without it, won't he?"

"Will you just check? I don't want to take any chances."

"We're already ten minutes late, Beth."

"Fine, I'll check, like I have to do everything else," she muttered crossly as she unbuckled her seatbelt, knowing as she spoke it wasn't really true.

"It was in there," she said quietly, smoothing her shiny pleated skirt underneath her as she took her seat again. It had taken ages to find something suitable to wear, and she wasn't convinced this went with the ankle boots and thick tights she'd added, but the skirt skimmed her tummy, and the short black top could easily be lifted for feeding. She was clutching blue bear tightly and considered briefly whether it really mattered what she wore, it would all be accessorised by baby toys, or a screaming child, for the foreseeable future.

"So are we alright to set off then?" Ali asked, sounding slightly irritable himself now. "It's just we're late."

"I know, you've already said. I suppose that's my fault too, because I can't even look after my own son."

Her tears were back. It had taken nearly an hour for Ali to settle Rory and then coax Beth out of the bathroom when he'd arrived home. He instantly regretted the sharpness of his tone.

"He's our son, remember?" he said more gently. "Not everything has to be down to you. And you're amazing with him. Sometimes it's just hard."

Ali reached for her hand, pulling it to his lips. He turned to her, forcing her to meet his eyes, pulling her into his smiling gaze.

"Don't be getting all Constance on me. I need the normal you with me tonight if I'm going to get through hearing how wonderful Jay is for the millionth time."

Beth managed a small smile. She knew Ali was trying to lighten the mood. It had been one of their private jokes from the early days of their relationship, calling each other Constance if they got a bit unreasonable, in honour of the shared ancestor that neither of them wanted to emulate. It had always seemed funny in the past, not what Constance had done—breaking up her son's relationship and then hiding his letters so that he was unaware of the existence of his own child was hardly a story for a good laugh—but the fact that they shared this distant ancestry seemed to suggest their intense attraction was meant to be. Today the joke didn't feel the same, the last thing she needed at the moment was to be compared to the world's most terrible mother, the woman who deliberately broke her son's heart, even though she knew that wasn't what Ali meant.

The rest of the journey had passed in silence, but at least by the time they pulled into the carpark of the Beinn View Hotel Beth was feeling calm, and Rory was still sound asleep. To Beth's surprise and relief, he stayed asleep as they unclipped the car seat and carried him into the restaurant. He didn't stir as his grandparents and uncle cooed over the beauty of his sleeping face. He didn't so much as give a twitch while Beth savoured her potato soup topped with crispy shallots, actually enjoying it while it was warm. There was no noise from him as she devoured the perfectly cooked salmon with its artistic arrangement of vegetables. By the time she took her last mouthful of sticky toffee pudding, Beth was almost starting to worry. As coffees and drinks were handed out, Rory opened his eyes and held his arms up to her. As usual, her heart melted at the sight of his tiny hands reaching out, her earlier frustration instantly forgotten.

Unexpectedly, it had been a lovely evening; the food had been amazing, and for once she'd been able to enjoy it and concentrate on the conversation. Also, Jay hadn't said anything that Ali could construe as a dig at him. It wasn't that the two brothers didn't get on. When they weren't together, they were quite close, emailing and chatting frequently. It was just that whenever Jay came home, Ali seemed to revert to adolescence, with a constant need to prove he was as good as his big brother, interpreting any praise of Jay as criticism of him. It was the only time when Ali's confident facade slipped. Usually, it made Beth feel protective. It was a side of him he only ever admitted to her. However, she didn't have the energy to bolster Ali's mood right now, so as Rory nuzzled into her and settled down for a quick feed, she was relieved it wouldn't be necessary tonight.

As she drove them home, Beth replayed the rest of the night's events in her head and cursed herself for her earlier complacency. Things were not so rosy hued now. While they were enjoying their after-dinner drinks and a grinning, gurgling Rory was being passed happily between his uncle and his grandparents, Jay had cleared his throat and said he had an announcement to make. Everyone had turned to him expectantly, wondering what he would surprise them with next. Jay made a lot of money working in banking, as Ali had until he'd decided the excess of that world couldn't sit alongside his conscience and moved back to Ardmhor. Elaborate schemes, extravagant travel plans, and big announcements were Jay's calling cards.

"I've decided to follow in the footsteps of my amazing brother and his wonderful wife," Jay began.

"You're getting married!" shrieked Angela.

At exactly the same moment, Jim said, "What, you're having a baby?"

Ali wasn't far behind them. "But I didn't think you were seeing anyone."

"Thanks guys, way to steal my thunder," Jay replied with a laugh. "Dad's being daft as usual. He already knows my plans as I had to sort everything with him. Anyway, what I was trying to say was, I've decided to follow in their footsteps and make a new life for myself here at Ardmhor. I've seen how happy it's made them, and I want the same for me."

Angela immediately burst into tears and pulled Jay into a hug, overjoyed at the thought of having both her boys back home. Jim thumped him affectionately on the back, and Beth felt touched that Jay saw the life she and Ali had built for themselves as something to aspire to. She was certain that Ali would see this as a validation of himself, his big brother saying he wanted to be like him. She was glowing as she looked around the family group, her family, not just linked to her through her marriage to Ali, but by distant ancestors as well. Then she caught Ali's eye and realised she was wrong. Ali didn't see this news as something to be pleased about. She could see he was trying to keep his face neutral, but she knew inside he was seething.

"I'm just taking Rory for a bit of fresh air," said Ali, avoiding eye contact as he carried Rory outside.

"I'll give him a hand," offered Jim, always glad of an excuse to escape sitting around the table.

Beth sat quietly sipping her drink, listening to Jay filling his mum in on his plans. He explained that he'd been feeling unfulfilled in London for a while now. His friends were settling down and having children, and although he was still going out loads, living the high life, he said it didn't feel the same anymore. Beth could sort of relate. Her friends had been moving on and she'd been feeling unhappy at work when she'd made the break and applied for her job at Ardmhor. She'd never lived her life on the epic scale that Jay did, but she understood feeling like things weren't right anymore. It seemed fair enough to her that Jay might want to come back to Ardmhor and live life differently. After all, Ali had done exactly that. It would be unreasonable for him to object to Jay having the same opportunity, but clearly he did. The tables had turned from earlier, and now it was Ali being 'a bit Constance' rather than Beth. But she didn't know how to help him deal with this. As an only child, sibling rivalry was a whole new world to her. She finished her drink and excused herself to check on Rory.

Although it was after nine, the sun was only just setting. It had been a chilly day for May, with almost non-stop rain, the stiff wind only managing to chase the clouds away long enough for fleeting moments of sunshine. However, it was dry as Beth stepped outside. She stopped for a moment to admire the scene in front of her. The Beinn View Hotel was named for its view over Inveravain harbour and out across to a mountain known locally as the Beinn. Despite all the rain of the day, the sun was a glistening ball of flame as it dipped behind the hills, turning the dark clouds that scuttled across the sky purple and tinting the sea with pink. The colours of the sea and sky added a glow to the brightly painted buildings lining the harbour. Beth hugged her arms around herself as she set off in search of the others. The view might be beautiful, but it really was cold. She heard Ali's voice before she saw him.

"It's not that I don't want him here. I am pleased he's coming back. I just don't know where that leaves me. Once Jay's here, doing everything brilliantly as usual, what will be left for me?"

"Don't be daft, Ali. There will always be more than enough for both of you to do here. All the ideas you've had since you came back to help run the estate mean there won't be a shortage of work anytime soon, and you're not kids anymore. You don't need to be worrying about who gets the best toy first. You're both grownups, and you'll work together fine. It doesn't need to be any different from how you work with any other member of staff."

Beth hung back at the edge of the building, her view of them partially obscured by trees. She didn't join them for fear of disturbing what was clearly an important conversation, but she was too intrigued to turn back.

"But he won't be like any other member of staff. He's going to be the next Lord MacAird, so he'll be the one making decisions, and everyone will know it."

Beth's heart contracted a little. It wasn't like Ali to be insecure. She could just make out Jim putting his arm around his shoulders.

"You know as well as I do that the title doesn't mean anything anymore. I don't make the decisions around here now, just as Jay won't in the future. All the immediate family get a place on the trust board, and that applies to you and your children too, even after I'm gone. The rights don't just stay with the title anymore, but the family have no more sway than other members of the board, and the Lord doesn't either. I wish I could make you both Lord MacAird, but unfortunately it doesn't work that way, so we've done everything we can to make sure it won't matter."

"I know, Dad, and it's not really about that. I just feel like I can never match up to Jay, and now I'm going to have to compete with him every day."

"You see, to me, it looks like it's the other way round. I think Jay feels he can't match up to you. You're happy and you've got Beth and Rory, and you always seem to know what you want. Jay might be the oldest, but he was always copying you when you were kids. That's why he's here. It's not that he wants to take things away from you, it's that he wants to be like you. So I suppose you're right, he is always trying to compete, but I think it's to prove he's as good as you, not to show he's better. Just give him a chance. Once things settle down, you might enjoy having him around again."

Beth watched Jim pull Ali, who was still carrying Rory, into a big hug and moved towards them from her hiding place at the edge of the trees. They'd walked back into the hotel together and set off home shortly after. However, despite his dad's words, Ali still seemed unsettled. As Beth steered along the coast road, this time it was Ali instigating the silence, and it was Beth reaching across to take his hand. She wanted to reassure him, even though she couldn't fully understand his fears. Ali had been so successful at Ardmhor, and his ideas were helping to revitalise the estate. Everyone knew how good he was at his job, and Jay being there wouldn't change that. Growing up, Beth had always wanted a sibling, but since marrying Ali, she sometimes wondered if being an only child was a privilege. There had been no one to compete with and no one to compare herself to. The thought crossed her mind that it wasn't just the prospect of more sleepless nights putting her off trying for another child. But then again, why was she telling herself it was just siblings that led to angst? She was finding it hard to readjust to her parents being in her day-to-day life again, and that was something she'd been longing for. Maybe she could relate to Ali's discomfort more than she'd first thought.

CHAPTER SEVEN

There had been little opportunity to talk on the night of Jay's announcement. Ali had been reluctant to discuss anything on the drive home, and after Rory's long, late nap, it had been a nightmare trying to settle him to sleep. When Beth came downstairs the next morning, wrapped in her dressing gown, with Rory tucked under her arm, Ali was already gone. She placed Rory in his highchair and set about making breakfast for the two of them. It was playgroup again, and she wanted to make sure they were ready in plenty of time after last week's debacle. She'd accepted her mum's offer of a lift this time, but even so, she didn't want to take any chances. The sun was shining, and the kitchen felt warm. Beth opened the window to let in the breeze and turned the radio on as she made porridge and stirred in fruit puree. Rory sat bashing a spoon on the tray of his highchair, laughing as Beth tested the temperature of his porridge and pulled a face at him. I've got this, she thought to herself. Just call me Supermum.

It seemed as if her life was currently a landscape of peaks and troughs. She was never just meandering slowly and happily, following the course of a stream through the gentle comfort of a valley. She was right on top of a mountain, feeling like she could do anything, or she was hurtling down the other side at a sickening pace, falling into a deep pit of despair, certain that nothing could save her from a painful landing. Right now, she was back on top: Rory had eaten more porridge than he had ended up wearing, she'd got both of them washed and dressed without any disasters, and now he was playing happily while she quickly tidied up before her mum arrived. Yes, this morning was a mountain top morning, but it was hard to get comfortable when you weren't sure how long you'd got until you slipped again.

Unlike the previous week, Beth and Rory were amongst the first arrivals at 'Bumps and Bairns', and without the need of the pushchair, thanks to Jean driving them, they'd even made it through the complicated double doors without incident. Beth was thankful that no one mentioned her behaviour at the previous session and finally relaxed. She watched her mum heading into the kitchen to help serve the drinks and was relieved not to feel the bitterness she'd experienced the week before. Today, instead of feeling pushed out, it felt good to see her mum being accepted as part of the community. Feeling annoyed with her mum was not something Beth enjoyed. She was so grateful for all the help and support she gave her, but she didn't seem to have control over her emotions anymore. She thought about Ali's reaction to Jay's news the night before. Had he responded that way because he was also struggling with the huge adjustment to parenthood? Was he simply too tired to adapt to any other change? Or was it something bigger than that? She really hoped it was just tiredness and that things would settle down. Ali was always the positive one of their partnership. He was the cheerleader that got them through any difficulties. That was his role, and Beth liked it that way. She already felt that a split had opened between them since Rory's birth, only a tiny crack, but none the less it was a fissure in something that had been totally solid. She didn't know how they would fare if she had to play the part of cheerleader instead.

Jean stopped off at her house on the way back from playgroup. They were going to pick Beth's dad up and then go on for lunch together. Jean said she wouldn't be long, but Beth got herself and Rory out of the car anyway. She loved any opportunity to go to her parents' house and relive the happy memories it contained. Although they had not owned the house for very long, it had previously been a holiday house, and Beth and her parents had stayed there several times. It had partly been the memories of those trips that had encouraged Beth to come on the working holiday at Ardmhor. The house was in a beautiful location. It sat on a headland, overlooking first the sea and then hills and mountains beyond. Stunning views characterised the area as the coastline wound in and out through a chain of peninsulas. It meant sudden glimpses of sea just as you thought you were heading inland, or spectacular backdrops of mountains, when you'd thought there should be nothing in front of you but sea. A twisting path led from the garden to the seashore, and although it was a public space, a lack of easy access points meant it usually felt as if the house had its own private beach. Beth had loved that rocky shore, with its dragon's caves, islands of rock, and the sandy section that appeared at low tide. It still seemed amazing that she could now come here whenever she wanted. At the back of the house was a large byre, which Beth had never seen the inside of during their holidays. Her dad was busy converting it into a home for the miniature railway he had always dreamt of building. Jean kept rolling her eyes at the time David was spending out there, but as they retrieved him and reminded him of their lunch date, Beth couldn't help noticing that some buildings being added around the track bore more of her mum's hallmarks than her dad's. She doubted she'd be able to keep Rory away from here in the future. Between the beach, the trains, and the couple of ruined croft houses in the garden, it was a child's paradise. When she considered that his other grandparents lived in what was basically a castle, she wondered if Rory would want to spend any time at home in the old factor's house.

They ate lunch in the café at the end of the pier. It was a favourite with all of them, partly because of the amazing seafood rolls they served and partly because of its location. If you looked one way, you could study the hustle and bustle of the ferry traffic, watching as passengers rushed between the gift shops, hurriedly making purchases before they needed to board. However, if you looked the other way, there was the peace of the sea and the chance to watch curious groups of seals as they bobbed amongst kayakers from the activity centre or basked on the rocks. In the three months since Jean and David had moved permanently to Ardmhor, they had eaten there almost every week, and today didn't disappoint. For Beth, the peak of the mountain was almost feeling secure.

It was only when she arrived home that she slipped back over that edge again. Usually, when she got home after playgroup, the house was empty. Even allowing for the time she'd spent having lunch, there should still have been a couple of hours before Ali was due home from work, so Beth was puzzled to see his shoes abandoned by the stairs as she shut the door behind her. Rory had nodded off on the short drive back from the pier, so she set the car seat down gently on the floor and wandered off in search of Ali. She tried the office first, the room where in the past the factor had carried out estate business and where Ali now liked to tie up any loose ends he hadn't finished during the day, but she found it empty. He wasn't in the kitchen either or the little sitting room at the front of the house; not that she'd expected to find him there—it only really got used on winter evenings when the fire was lit. She returned to the hallway and picked up the car seat again, before heading up the stairs to continue the search. She found Ali lying on their bed, fully dressed in his work clothes but with the curtains tightly shut. He had his back to her, and at first, she thought he was asleep, but then she noticed the glow of the phone screen he was holding in his hand. She placed the car seat down on the floor and climbed onto the bed behind him.

"Hey sweetheart, are you okay?"

"Fine," came a muffled reply, with no attempt to look away from his phone.

"It's just you were out early this morning and you're not usually back at this time."

"I saw a text first thing saying that Jay wanted to call a meeting, so I got in early. Then after the meeting I didn't feel like hanging around, so I came home. That's it."

His tone was agitated. He spoke the words as if they were a warning not to pursue the topic further, rather than the start of a conversation. Beth backed away. This wasn't what Ali was like. He was always open and positive, and she didn't know the right way to react.

"Okay, well, Rory's asleep in his car seat, so I'm just going to leave him in the corner while I make a drink. Do you want one?"

There was no proper response, but Beth took the quiet grunt from the other side of the bed as an affirmative and set off down the stairs.

When she returned five minutes later, with a cup of tea for Ali and hot water for herself, Rory was still fast asleep, but he was no longer in the car seat, instead he was lying in the middle of the bed, and Ali was gently stroking the top of his head. She walked round the bed, placing Ali's tea on the bedside table next to him, before taking her place at the other side.

"Shall we start this conversation again?" she ventured.

"Yes, sorry," Ali responded, looking at her with the beginnings of a smile. "It's not been the best day."

She reached for his hand. "I'd sort of gathered

that already."

"Before you came outside last night, I was talking to Dad about Jay coming back, and he said that Jay wasn't out to change everything, that he just wanted to show he could do things as well as me. I didn't believe him. I mean, I do love Jay, and we can get on, but he always has to win. Dad reckons Jay feels like he's second best, whereas to me, it seems like he's always trying to show me up and prove he's better. Anyway, today he calls this meeting to announce his big new idea for the estate. So I was right, and Dad was completely wrong."

"And what is it? What's his big idea?"

"He wants to set up a complex of self-catering lodges in the fields towards the back of the coach house."

"They'd have a great view from there," Beth started to respond, before a glance at Ali's face told her to stop talking.

"That's not the point. He's already had some people out doing a preliminary survey of the site. I've no idea how nobody noticed them. He's got a feasibility study all written up, and he's only been working here for one day. Everyone was so enthusiastic. It was all 'Jay this, Jay that, oh it's going to be so wonderful having you working here Jay'. He always has to come along and do whatever I'm doing, but better than I'm doing it. It's like when I wanted tennis lessons. I was going for ages and thought I was getting really good, and then Jay decides he wants to come too and within a couple of weeks, he's beating me every time. There's no way he's ever felt second best. He can't get enough of proving how superior he is."

Beth weighed up her words carefully, trying to think how to phrase what she wanted to say without annoying Ali even more.

"I suppose your dad could still be right. Jay might keep trying to prove he's superior because he starts off feeling second best. Like he sees you have a good idea, whether it's tennis, or trying to revitalise the estate and he thinks to himself, why didn't I think of that? Why is Ali so much better at ideas than me? And then he has to go all out to top you, to prove he's just as good."

"Well, why ever he does it, it makes me feel about this big every time it happens," Ali responded, holding his thumb and finger a millimetre apart.

"I can imagine. So, what are you going to do? Do you think his idea is something that could work?"

"I do. They're only preliminary sketches, but they look fantastic, and the projected costing is nowhere near as high as I'd have thought it would be. Like you said, there are amazing views from up there, so I think they'd let really easily. Also, as well as the revenue from the lettings, the people staying there would spend money in the area, so it'd benefit everything else as well. There's not really a downside."

"Well, apart from it being Jay's idea," said Beth, meeting Ali's eye and holding his gaze.

"Yes, apart from that."

"So, what are you going to do?"

"What can I do? I'm going to have to suck it up and get behind him because it's the right thing for the estate. I just don't think I can do it yet." Ali paused for a minute. "Beth, I need to ask you something, but I don't think you're going to like it."

"Okay," she said, concerned now.

"The company that we worked with to develop the wind farm has been wanting us to consider expanding our site. They've been on at me for a while to visit a site they've already developed that's on a similar scale to what they'd like to do here…" he tailed off, looking at her expectantly.

"So, you could do that. There's no harm in looking, is there?"

"Well, no, but the site is on Shetland. By the time I travel there and look at everything they want me to see, it's going to take at least four days. I didn't want to leave you on your own with Rory for that long, so I've been putting them off."

"But now you want to go so you can escape from Jay?"

"Yes, that pretty much sums it up."

Beth sat silently for a minute. She didn't want to be handling every sleepless night and every never-ending day that followed by herself, but on the other hand, it was work, and she could see how much Ali was struggling.

"When would you go?"

"I made a quick call before I left work and if I can make it up there by the day after tomorrow, that'd work perfectly for them."

"Wow, that soon." Beth felt like her fall from this morning's mountain top was speeding up by the second. "Well, if you need to go, we'll manage, but isn't there a chance you might feel more left out by the time you get back?"

"Possibly, but I think by then the novelty will have worn off Jay and his amazing ideas a little. Also, I'm hoping the wind farm will give me a new focus of my own. If nothing else, at least I'll have had time to get used to the idea of him being around without having to see him every minute."

"Right, well, I suppose we'd better get you packed," Beth said, with more conviction than she felt.

"How was I lucky enough to end up with you?" Ali said, reaching over and pulling her into a kiss that could still make her melt.

She relaxed into the moment, responding to the touch of his lips on hers, feeling his fingers work their way into her curls, but then a noise from the bed in between them broke the spell. It was a cry that grew persistently louder, and it brought them back to reality with a bump. As she picked Rory up and tried to work out what he needed, Beth felt a rising sense of panic. How was she possibly going to manage by herself?

CHAPTER EIGHT

Beth went from wistfully waving Ali off, thinking how much she loved him and how much she'd miss him, to cursing his very existence within the space of about ten minutes. Rory had started screaming for no discernible reason the moment Ali disappeared from view. The house looked a mess with breakfast pots still strewn about the worktop, but if she tried to put Rory down to tidy up, the screaming intensified. She glanced at the clock. It was only an hour since Ali had left. It felt as if time was stretching out. All she could see in front of her was a non-stop torture of noise and frustration until Ali returned. Although that would only be in a few days' time, it might as well have been the end of eternity. She usually loved being in their house, with all its history and original features, but right then it felt dark and depressing, and she knew she needed to get out. Despite the drizzle that had persisted throughout the morning, she fastened Rory into the pushchair, wrestled the rain cover into place and put on her own waterproof coat. They needed to be anywhere but there.

After wandering aimlessly along the road for half an hour, Rory had fallen asleep, and Beth was feeling weary too. The low hanging mist obscured the hills, reducing the views to an angry grey sea, which merged into a heavy grey sky. Her hands were stiff from gripping the pushchair handles. Continuing to walk wasn't an appealing idea, but she didn't want to go home either. If she did that, Rory would probably wake up, continue his screaming, and she'd be back to square one. She headed towards Ardmhor House instead. There would be shelter from the rain and maybe she'd find some company as well. While on maternity leave, she'd largely kept away from Ardmhor House during visitor hours. At first, she'd popped into the museum regularly, but it was unsettling seeing other people taking charge of her creation, and she'd eventually realised it was easier if she didn't go. She'd still been to the house many times, after all, it was where her parents-in-law lived, but she usually avoided times when the museum was open.

The carpark wasn't busy as she negotiated steering the pushchair from the road onto the drive of the house. Visitors had more than likely been put off by the miserable weather.

She nodded hello to Callum in the ticket office and made her way through the gates, turning to follow the path to the viewpoint. It was the place where she had first met Ali and the site of all her encounters with Alex. She found it calming to sit there and remember how Alex had believed in her. It also made her thankful for how her life had changed since she'd met him. She might feel sorry for herself now, but she had to remind herself this was nothing compared to the miserable state of her life then. The viewpoint worked its magic to an extent. It was good to remember that she had coped with worse before, but although she knew what Alex would say to her, it was her own voice saying the words in her head now. She couldn't hear Alex speaking anymore.

With the drizzle not showing any sign of relenting and the view non-existent, she decided maybe today was the day to brave a visit to the museum. If nothing else, it would be a dry space to wheel the pushchair around while Rory slept.

As she manoeuvred the pushchair through the museum door, she collided with a fast-moving figure travelling in the opposite direction. She had already begun her apologies when she realised the figure belonged to Eilidh. Eilidh had taken Beth under her wing when she'd first moved to Ardmhor, and they had become close friends. In fact, other than her friend Lucy, from her university days, Beth would describe Eilidh as her best friend. They hadn't seen much of each other over the last few weeks though. Eilidh was busy planning her wedding and trying to avoid spending money, and Beth hadn't really been up for nights out either. It was a pleasant surprise to find themselves in the same space as each other.

"Hello stranger!" cried Eilidh, pulling Beth into a hug and then quickly releasing her when she realised how soggy she was. "And hello tiny man," she said to Rory, trying to peer through the fogged-up rain cover. "Have you got a bit of time to spare? I was just heading to the café for an early lunch. Do you fancy joining me?"

"That sounds fantastic," Beth replied, smiling for the first time since she'd shut the door behind Ali.

The café was in a converted outbuilding, known as the coach house, at the start of the drive to Ardmhor House. It was warm and welcoming, with the smell of food wafting out to meet them. Eilidh found them a table, with room to park the pushchair and went to place their order, while Beth removed the rain cover with the dexterity of a surgeon.

"How are you?" she asked Eilidh as soon as she returned to the table. "It feels like ages since I've seen you."

"It has been ages, but don't worry, I know your

hands are a bit full. And I'm fine, stressed but fine."

"What's stressing you out? I don't think I've ever seen you worried."

"Oh, nothing really. It's just making decisions for the wedding. Everything's so expensive, so I want to get the decisions right, but you have to decide so far in advance that I don't know if I'll still want the same things by the time the wedding comes around. And then I think to myself, should we just get married now, rather than waiting longer so we can save up? Do we even want a big wedding? I just don't feel like I know the answers."

"It's not just you, Eilidh, it is a lot of stress for one day. I remember agonising about ridiculous things before our wedding, things that I bet no one else noticed."

"But are you happy with the choices you made?"

"Well, there are probably things I'd do differently now. I think I'd choose a different dress, and there are things we spent money on that we didn't really need to bother with, but it was perfect for us at the time. Whatever you do, you'll have a brilliant day, but no matter how great it is, a few years down the line you'll probably be able to think of some things you'd do differently because tastes change all the time."

"I suppose so. I think it's the money that's

freaking me out as well. We saved for so long to buy the house. It seems frivolous to spend such a lot on just one day."

"It's your money though, Eilidh, and if you want to spend it on a big wedding, that's okay. And if you decide to run away and just have a couple of witnesses, that's also okay. Whatever you choose to do will be amazing because you and Rich are a great couple, and everyone loves you."

"You soppy thing," Eilidh chided, while simultaneously looking slightly misty eyed. Fortunately for Eilidh, who wasn't usually one for displays of emotion, Sally, the café manager, interrupted them as she placed two steaming bowls of soup on the table. She stopped to say hello and coo over how big Rory was getting before heading back to the counter. "Oh, and I'm annoyed about your brother-in-law," Eilidh continued, after a slurp of soup.

"Well, you're not the only one there. What's he done to upset you?"

"They've taken me off some of my usual jobs to assist him with his big proposal for the self-catering village. I know I'm paid to do whatever I'm asked, but I had all my work organised, and now I've had to drop everything because the future Lord's back and we all have to dance to his tune."

"You sound like Ali! He's so annoyed with Jay

that he's swanned off on this research trip and left me on my own with Rory."

"Yeah, he didn't look happy during the meeting yesterday. Surely Rory's no bother though? Look at him sleeping away there. He's like a little angel."

"Well, yeah, he is an angel and I love him to pieces, but he wakes up so often in the night, and half the time I can't work out why he's upset. Then by morning I'm too tired to deal with anything. I never thought being a parent would be so hard."

"You're selling it well, Beth," said Eilidh, laughing. "It's a good job me and Rich aren't planning on children, or you'd be putting me off!"

"You'd be an amazing mum if you wanted to be. You're basically unflappable, whereas we both know that's not the case with me. Don't pay any attention to me moaning. You know how useless I am at most things."

"Beth Hutton MacAird!" Eilidh said in exasperation. "I thought we'd got you past this 'I'm no good at anything' business. You are a successful woman who is just going through a difficult patch. I've read that sleep deprivation is used as a torture technique, you know. Everything's going to get easier as he gets bigger."

"I really hope you're right," Beth said with

a small smile, using a chunk of bread to mop up the last of her soup. But she did feel more hopeful. Chatting to Eilidh had given her a bit of perspective. Everyone had their own things to deal with. Sometimes it helped to realise you weren't the only one struggling.

It had stopped raining by the time she left the café. The mist had lifted, and the hills had been restored to pride of place on the horizon. The sun was doing its best to make its way through the higher-level cloud, occasionally managing enough strength to scatter sparkles across the sea. Beth felt as if her mood had improved with the weather. As she reached the house, she remembered the box of letters on the mantelpiece. Rory had woken up before she'd left the café. He'd devoured the remains of her bread roll and enjoyed some pieces of fruit, so she was hopeful he'd be happy to play with his toys on the floor for a bit, while she found out more about Maude and Joseph.

LETTER TWO

September 1867

Dearest Joseph, the most special person in the world,

I've written that same phrase at the start of every letter I have sent to you. I've meant it every single time I've written it, and I still mean it now. From the moment we met, I knew we were meant to spend our lives together. Do you remember that first summer, when you didn't know anyone and kept lurking just out of sight, watching us play by the stream? I finally dragged you out of your hiding spot and made you join in. Then, do you remember a few years later, when the other boys said girls couldn't join in anymore? You threatened to take down the rope swing you'd built if they didn't let me play. And do you remember the first time we kissed?

We were sitting in the shade of the willow tree, with the stream tickling our feet. I remember every single moment that we've spent together and every moment that I've suffered when we've been apart. For me, you are the most special person in the world. Everything feels right when I'm with you. My question is, do you feel the same about me?

I've always thought you did because how could I feel all these things if you didn't? So many times I have written to you about my feelings, and you have never expressed any views to the contrary. I have always believed that you want the same as me, a house together, filled with children, filled with love. Time and time again, I've told you of these dreams, and from your replies, I have taken them not just to be my dreams, but ours. So if I am right, if I am the most special person in your world, then I need you to fight for me. I need you to tell my parents that you want to marry me. I need you to show them that we are meant to be. Please Joseph, I'm begging you. If you don't speak to my parents, our dreams will disappear.

I realise that my actions recently might have led you to doubt whether my feelings still held true, so I will try to explain myself. The night of the ball, everyone was swept up in the excitement. There wasn't a soul alive in this parish unaware you were bringing James

MacAird, the heir to a fortune. I was only aware of him as your roommate, but obviously I couldn't fail to notice the whispers, the gossip, and the sudden rush to the dressmakers. It's true that I couldn't wait for the night of the ball, but that was because it would finally be time for us to be together again. I wasn't excited about James being there at all. I was worried he might be in the way, a stranger in our little friendship group, but I was enjoying the excitement his attendance was causing. There wasn't a parent present that night who didn't hope their daughter would catch the eye of James MacAird. Which is why I never gave the idea that he might be interested in me a second thought. I also thought that as your friend, he would understand our connection. I assumed that any attention he paid me was only friendly. Perhaps it was precisely because I didn't seem interested that he felt the need to win me.

I promise you I have never given him any reason to believe he is special to me. I have never shared any dreams with him or felt his lips against mine. Honestly, I have not encouraged his attention, but he will not disappear. There are cards each day and visits every other. Although I have not encouraged him, my parents cannot fail to notice what an advantageous marriage it would be, and I fear that should he ask for my hand, they will expect me to say yes.

While it feels as though I cannot escape James

MacAird, you, on the other hand, seem to have almost disappeared. Perhaps you feel you are being a gentleman, stepping back and allowing me to move on to a grander future. But that is not what I want. What I want is to tell my parents to give up their dreams of me as the future Lady MacAird because I will be marrying Joseph Turner, but how can I do that when you haven't asked me?

I don't want to force your hand, Joseph, although I suppose it wouldn't be out of character! But if you want me, if you want our future together, you need to act. Think of every moment we've shared, the children we've imagined, the kisses we've tasted. Think of never having those again. Please Joseph, please speak to my parents. You can make everything right, just like you always have. Nothing has been decided yet, no one has asked any important questions. There is still time.

Do this for me, my one true love and my most special person. Do this so I will know that I wasn't wrong about us. Please do this so that my dreams, our dreams, can come true. I'm begging you, Joseph, please do this for me. Do this for us.

All my love,

Always

CHAPTER NINE

Wow, Beth thought to herself, what a letter! No wonder Joseph had kept it safe, and no wonder he'd done what Maude had asked and made her his wife. How strange though that Maude could have ended up married to Alex's father. Eliza's diary had spoken of the connection between her father and the then Lord MacAird, but it hadn't mentioned that Maude had known him too. Perhaps Eliza was not aware that her guardian had wanted to marry her mother. Maybe Constance knew though, perhaps that was why she found it hard to accept Eliza. Beth knew from their photos that Eliza and Maude looked alike, and maybe that had made Constance jealous.

It occurred to Beth that if the Lord MacAird of all those years ago had succeeded in his pursuit of Maude, Alex would not have had to suffer Constance as his mother. But that would surely also mean he would never have lived, which was too high a price to pay, even to be free of Constance's interference. Beth wondered whether she would exist if Maude and Joseph hadn't married? Would enough time have passed for the components of her to have come together anyway? Or would that one change all those years ago have ruled her out of existence?

It scared her to think that every decision you made could have repercussions for years to come. Alex had tried to teach her it was better to accept opportunities than to live with doubt and regret, but it was still hard to know which opportunities were right. If Maude had viewed marrying James MacAird as too good an opportunity to pass up on, Ardmhor would still be here, and the factor's house would be here too, but all the people closest to her would never have been. It was a sobering thought.

◆ ◆ ◆

The next morning was sunny and bright, a complete contrast to the previous day, and Beth hoped it was a good sign. After his screaming fit when Ali had left, Rory had been as good as gold for the rest of the day. He'd played happily as she read the letter, he'd eaten his tea rather than simply smearing it over his highchair, he'd babbled on demand when Ali rang to tell them he had safely arrived at his destination, and best of all he'd only woken once during the night. If this continued, Beth thought to herself, she might make it through the next few days after all.

It helped that she had something nice to look forward to. Bob and Mary, a couple who had been on the working holiday which brought Beth to Ardmhor, were coming to visit. They were on their fourth working holiday when Beth met them, and had done another couple since, but the year before last Mary had suffered a hip injury, and although she had recovered well, they had both decided working holidays were no longer for them. However, neither of them wanted to stay away from Ardmhor, so they still made regular visits. Today was only a brief stop, breaking up their journey to a murder mystery event being held at a hotel further up the coast. The plan was for Beth and Rory to join them for lunch with Angela, in the private apartment at Ardmhor House. Rory was napping, and Beth was showered and ready to go. The weather definitely seemed to foreshadow a good day.

"Hello sweetheart, you answered quickly!" said Jean as Beth swiped the screen of her phone to accept the call. She had practically leapt from the settee to the kitchen island, where her phone was buzzing noisily.

"Rory's asleep. I didn't want the phone to wake him."

"Oh sorry, is he okay?" Jean lowered her voice

to a whisper, as if she was in the room with them.

"You weren't to know, and he didn't stir at all, so don't worry. What are you and Dad up to today?"

"Well, your dad's got a busy day planned in the byre. He's building a mountain for his miniature cable car to run up. I know you said you were having lunch with Bob and Mary, and I was wondering if I could join you. I've heard so much about them, but I've never actually met them, and I could be an extra pair of hands in case Rory gets fractious."

Beth hesitated. If her mum came, it wouldn't be the same as their usual catch ups. She'd be looking out for her mum and trying to keep her involved, rather than just enjoying it. But how could she say that without hurting her mum's feelings?

"The only thing is we're having lunch at Angela's, and I don't know if she'll have got enough food in for an extra person."

There was silence for a second before Beth's guilt got too much and she hastily tagged on, "I could ring her and check though."

Jean picked up on the reluctance in her daughter's voice. "No, don't do that. It'll be too late for her to change what she's planned, but she might feel like she needs to agree anyway. I don't want to put her in an awkward position."

"Well, if you're sure Mum," said Beth,

experiencing guilt and relief in equal measure.

"Yes, totally. Give Rory a kiss from me and have a lovely time. I'll see you tomorrow."

By the time she hung up, it was predominantly guilt Beth was feeling. Angela would have had no problem with her mum joining them for lunch, and Bob and Mary would have loved meeting her. But it wasn't how Beth had been imagining the afternoon, and when she'd been put on the spot, it had seemed important that things stayed as planned. Now she'd had a bit of time to think, whether her mum joined them didn't seem such a big deal. She looked over at Rory, who was sleeping peacefully in the Moses basket he was really far too big for but still sometimes took naps in. He was growing so fast, eventually the time would come when he didn't need her. It was just difficult to imagine at the moment, when it felt as if her life was on hold for him. She wondered if her mum had felt the same. Was the reward for all this exhaustion and worry simply to be your children finding you irritating and trying to avoid you? She didn't want to imagine Rory feeling that way about her. Her guilt level increased further. Jean certainly didn't deserve her thinking like this. She was so supportive and helpful, and Beth had always felt they were the textbook example of a perfect mother and daughter relationship. She didn't know where these new feelings had come from, and she didn't like them one bit. But she didn't pick up the phone and call Jean back.

◆ ◆ ◆

As she pushed Rory along the road towards Ardmhor House, Beth tried to stop worrying about how Jean was feeling and focus on enjoying the afternoon instead. She always loved visiting her parents-in-law at their home. The private apartment at Ardmhor House managed to be both impressive and cosy. Large windows flooded the rooms with light and gave views over the gardens down to the sea. It was furnished with a mix of antiques, that had been in the house for longer than anyone could remember, and pieces that Angela and Jim had chosen themselves. Everything worked together to make a luxurious but homely setting.

Bob and Mary were thrilled they were meeting at Ardmhor House. They loved having a connection to Lord and Lady MacAird. In fairness to Bob and Mary, there were still moments when Beth herself marvelled that the MacAirds were now her family. From the day she'd arrived at Ardmhor and met Alex, she had fantasised about being Angela's daughter-in-law, she just hadn't imagined it would ever come to pass, especially after she found out Alex wasn't actually real. No, she thought to herself, she might have daydreamed about being part of the MacAird family, but she couldn't have contemplated it being reality.

The only dark spot in the afternoon was when Mary enquired after Beth's parents, asking whether they'd made their permanent move to Ardmhor yet. When Beth confirmed they had, Mary said how much she'd have liked to meet them, and Beth's guilt rose back to the surface. After they said their goodbyes, Beth began collecting the toys Rory had strewn across the floor while Angela gathered up the remains of their meal.

"I should have thought to ask your mum and dad. It just didn't cross my mind," said Angela as she carried a tray of cups and saucers back to the kitchen.

Beth waited for her to reappear before answering.

"Don't feel bad about it. Mum asked me this morning if she could come, and I put her off."

"Oh," was all that Angela came up with in response.

"I don't know why I didn't tell her to come. It just felt like things wouldn't be the same. But I feel really mean about it now."

"I think it's normal to be wary of something changing dynamics you've already got used to, and I'm sure you won't be offended when I say you're not a natural with new situations!"

Beth smiled. "Well, that's definitely true, but this feels like more than that. I keep getting irritated with my mum over nothing." She felt almost traitorous discussing this with the other mother figure in her life. "Did you ever go through this with your mum?"

"We had our moments, but I was only a teenager when she died, and my dad was gone as well by the time I met Jim, so we never had to deal with any grown-up stuff together."

"Oh, I'm so sorry Angela. I should have thought. I know you lost your parents really young and now I'm being ungrateful for mine."

Angela waved her hand dismissively. "Don't worry, Beth, it was a long time ago, and I'm pretty sure I'd get annoyed with them at times if they were still here. I know for definite that after the boys were born, it took quite some time for me to feel like myself again. In fact, I don't think I ever went back to being quite the same person. Jim and I certainly had our struggles at that point, and I imagine it would also have led to a bit of readjusting in the relationship with my parents."

"I just hate feeling like this. My mum and dad were literally the most important things in my life until I moved here, and I usually love seeing them. What if Rory feels this way about me one day?"

"I don't think you need to worry about that

just yet! And I think part of your answer might be in what you've just said. The last time you were all living near each other, your mum and dad were everything to you. Now that you're all back together, you've got Ali and Rory as well. Your focus has changed, but theirs won't have in the same way. It's bound to take a while for everything to settle down."

"Do you think?"

"I really do. It's obvious how much you love them. I just think you're exhausted, and you're all getting used to totally different lives from those you had before. You'll get there. Just try not to overthink everything."

"Easier said than done," Beth replied quietly.

"I know, sweetheart," said Angela, pulling her into a hug. "Everything will be alright though. Maybe give your mum a ring on your way home, tell her about the afternoon, make her feel a part of it."

Beth thought about telling Angela about the letters before she left. She hadn't thought to mention them when the whole family was out for dinner the other night and she'd not really seen Angela since, but then she reconsidered. Maybe it would be good to keep this as something special between her and her mum for a while instead. However, she did follow Angela's advice about calling her mum, and they ended up having a lovely chat about the contents of the second letter. She told her mum that Mary had been really keen to meet her too and promised to do a better job of arranging things next time they came to visit. Jean talked her through the progress of the miniature cable car, making it sound as though helping to install it had been all she'd ever wanted to do that day. However, her mum's efforts to take away her guilt didn't have the intended effect, in some ways her kindness made Beth feel worse, but she was glad they'd talked, and she was determined they would navigate their way through this unchartered territory in their relationship.

CHAPTER TEN

Ardmhor, 1876

Ardmhor House seems incredibly quiet. Our family here has dwindled from six down to three. The first loss was James's mother two years ago. I feel as though I should say her loss is a heavy burden, but truth be told, it was a relief. She never warmed to me, and I'd spent most of my marriage trying to please her but never quite managing it. No, I do not mourn her passing. In fact, the house seemed to come to life a little after her death. I am finding our more recent parting, albeit not of such a permanent nature, much harder to bear.

A little over two months ago, on an August day when the rain never stopped, we had to wave goodbye to both James senior and Little James. Little James reached the great age of seven last

November, so it was time for him to set off for England, to be educated at the same school his father had attended. He looked so small and uncertain as he climbed into the carriage to start his journey, but there was to be no delaying the event. It had been agreed almost since the day of his birth. I could see his bottom lip trembling, and for once I was glad of his attachment to his nurse. She accompanied him to his school before taking up new employment in England. At least she was there to dry his eyes and settle him into his new life. I am not sure whether he realises she will no longer be here when he returns, but hopefully, over the course of the year at school, he will have forgotten how much he cared for her. My husband also accompanied them, in order for him to attend to business in London. It would have been nice if we could all have made the journey. I would have loved to see London again, but James felt it would necessitate more stops if we were all travelling. I had to concede that the length of the journey is arduous. Alexander might have coped, but Flora is not yet three and it would have been difficult for her. There is talk of a railway eventually reaching all the way to Inveravain, which would suddenly connect Ardmhor to civilisation, but I have little expectation of seeing it in my lifetime.

Now just Alexander, Flora, and I remain here, rattling around this enormous house with only the staff for company. There are other families of good reputation in the area but all are a long carriage ride away, and visits seem to stop when Lord MacAird is not in residence. I have yet to gain an agreement from James that Alexander will not be going away to school, but these last two months have made me more determined than ever. Alexander will also be seven by next summer. I will not have myself and Flora left behind while they all disappear to England. It is not just that I dread being abandoned. I cannot bear the thought of my beloved Alexander being torn away from me. His hands still show the soft dimples of babyhood, clinging to me as I kiss him goodnight. The idea of those hands being pressed against the windows of the carriage, pleading to be released, well, that thought is more than I can stand. I picture him looking back at me as the carriage takes him away from everything he loves and all he has ever known, and I know I wouldn't be able to cope with that. The mere thought of it is enough to break my heart.

I realise Alexander cannot remain solely mine forever, that he needs to become his own person. He already works with a tutor each day and has made excellent progress. I hope to convince James that Alexander can learn everything he needs at Ardmhor. Although there aren't many children of a suitable calibre for him to mix with up here in the wilds, I have made significant effort to find friends for him. It has been heart wrenching at times. It was disconcerting when he first expressed a desire to spend time with Bertie, the vicar's son, rather than with me. However, I am glad that he is getting to experience the strong bonds of early friendships. When I think of my own childhood, fetes, balls, and trips to London were all so easily accessible. That makes me wonder if the best solution would be to persuade James to move us all to the London house. If we lived there, Alexander would be nearby even if he is made to attend boarding school, and Flora would have so many more opportunities available to her.

Yes, that could be the answer. It should be easy to convince James of the benefits of a childhood like my own. Indeed, with the passage of time, I could almost convince myself that it had been totally idyllic. I had a beautiful home, my family had plenty of money, and I had access to every entertainment that money could buy. The only thing I lacked was love, and even that isn't strictly true. I did have plenty of love. It just didn't come from my parents, the source of affection a child should be able to depend on. Instead, it came from the staff and my friends. In that respect, I was very lucky. I had two close friends, one that I had known from the earliest days of childhood and one that had become like a sister to me. Our early meetings weren't so promising. It took a while to overcome our different natures when we first found ourselves living in the same village, but we soon came to realise that we understood each other. We both spent our time trying to please our distant parents, and we realised we could pour that affection into each other instead.

I try not to think about those happy times now. Thinking of what I had makes my current loneliness harder to bear, but I know without a doubt it was the night of the ball that changed everything. That was the night I first met James. We were so excited about that ball. It wasn't usually a grand affair, but it was held at the start of the summer, when the boys of the area who had been away at school would return, so it meant we would all be together again. When the whispers began that James MacAird would be attending, the excitement reached dizzy new heights. He was one of the most eligible young men in the entire country, and it quickly occurred to both our mothers that marriage to him would bring significant advantages. We were eighteen, exactly the right age to be finding husbands, and I think we both allowed ourselves to get swept up in the preparations our mothers were making. There were dress fittings, experiments with hairstyles, and discussions about suitable conversations. It was like a game, and although we were opponents in it, we did not think there was any danger of it coming between us. We already had our own loves and dreams. James MacAird only interested us as a way of finally impressing our mothers. We believed our sisterhood was stronger than anything, but we were wrong.

When James singled one of us out, it changed everything. Jealousies we didn't realise existed came to the surface. Although neither of us had wanted him, when one of us was basking in the glow of parental approval and the other wasn't, he suddenly seemed more important. He saw the competition between us before we did, and he made the most of it. We lost sight of each other for a while, and then it was too late.

I realise I'm making James sound like some sort of monster. He isn't. He has been a fair husband, and although we live as he chooses, he does take the time to listen to me. I cannot hold him responsible for the loss of my childhood loves. He is a charismatic man, and I underestimated his pull. I allowed myself to get swept up in the desire for something I'd never wanted, and as much as it would soothe me to blame someone else, I know I made my own decisions. That is why I cannot lose Alexander. I knew from the moment they handed Little James to his nurse that he wasn't truly mine, but Alexander belongs to me. If they take away my precious boy, I won't be able to keep up the pretence any longer. I won't be able to tell myself that winning the game was worth everything I lost.

CHAPTER ELEVEN

Beth heard the alarm ringing and knew she had to get Rory to safety. No one else could help. They were on their own. She had to reach him quickly, but her feet wouldn't move. She summoned all her strength, willing her legs to travel more quickly, but it was as if they were making their way through quicksand. Her panic intensified as the ringing grew louder. She wouldn't be able to keep him safe, she was going to lose him. As she surrendered to the wave of despair, she noticed a tingling sensation in her arm and tried to work out what it meant. The ringing continued, but it didn't sound like an alarm anymore. In fact, it sounded more like her phone. Concentrating on her arm, she realised it was resting on something. Her mind finally started to make sense of the situation, she wasn't in her room, desperately trying to cross the landing and reach Rory—instead, she was sitting on his bedroom floor, her arm stuck awkwardly through the cot bars. It was dark in Rory's room with the blackout curtains at the window, so it was difficult to know how long she'd been asleep, but the stiffness of her body told her it had been a while. Patting the floor in a bid to find her phone, she remembered she'd left it charging downstairs. She'd been bored without the ability to scroll mindlessly through social media as she waited for Rory to succumb to sleep. She unravelled her aching body from the floor, standing up tentatively while awaiting the rush of pins and needles in her legs. Cautiously she moved towards the door, not wanting to stumble and undo her good work settling Rory. Then she made her way downstairs to find out who had been calling.

When she reached her phone, she saw three missed calls from Ali. As she pressed to ring him back, Beth realised how much she was missing him—and it wasn't just because she wanted someone to help with Rory during the night. She pictured them curling up on the settee together, opening a bottle of wine and choosing a film to watch. Hmm, wine, she thought to herself, as the phone continued ringing at Ali's end. She had barely drunk any alcohol recently because she was still breastfeeding Rory, but now there were bigger gaps between feeds, the odd glass of wine wasn't a problem. She wondered if they had a bottle in. A drink would be lovely right now. Before she made it to the cupboard to check, a weary sounding Ali answered the call.

"Are you okay?" Beth asked. "I'd fallen asleep settling Rory, so I missed your other calls. It's a good job you rang actually, or I might have been on the floor by the cot all night."

"I bet Rory would have loved that. Was it the phone that woke you then?"

"Yeah, I was dreaming the house was on fire and the phone was the smoke alarm."

"Well, it's probably good I woke you up and helped you escape then. Maybe I could be on one of those half-dressed fireman calendars," he added with a laugh.

"I think that'd be in your dreams, Ali," she replied smiling, thinking that he'd actually fit in quite well amongst a group of toned, topless fire fighters. "Also, I probably wouldn't have been dreaming about fire alarms if it hadn't been for you ringing."

"Good point. So apart from escaping burning buildings, have you both been okay?"

"We're fine. He's been great all day, so I'm expecting he'll make me pay tonight instead."

"There's got to be a first time for a good night though."

"True, and at least you'll be home soon. Rory's

missing you."

"Just Rory?"

"Well, maybe I'm missing you a bit as well. Are you okay? You sound tired."

"I am," he said, giving an apologetic laugh. "You'll probably want to kill me, seeing as you never get the chance to stay in bed for a full night, but I haven't slept well at all while I've been away. I don't know if it's missing you two, or thinking about Jay being back, but my mind just hasn't been able to switch off."

"Well, only two nights to go and Rory will exhaust you into sleep again," Beth replied happily.

She really was looking forward to him being back. It might have felt like they were drifting apart a bit recently, but him being away had brought home to her how much she relied on him and how much she enjoyed just being near him.

"The thing is though, Beth," Ali began quietly, "there's another site they've suggested I visit on the way home. But it'd mean another night away, maybe two."

It took a moment for Beth to reply. She didn't want to sound pathetic and needy, especially as she was coping fine, but she really didn't want to spend an extra couple of nights alone. However, she didn't want to make Ali feel worse. He was clearly struggling with Jay being home, which was totally out of character for him. Ali had encouraged and supported her ever since they'd met. What kind of person was she if she couldn't at least try to do the same for him?

"You do what you need to," she said after a moment. "We'll be fine, and we've got plenty of people we can call on if we need help."

"Thank you, sweetheart. You're a total legend."

"I know," she said with a smile, wishing she believed it herself.

Beth was in for more disappointment as she opened the cupboard door. She was in search of the wine she now definitely felt she deserved, but all she could see was a bottle of whisky. No matter how much she fancied a drink, single malt would never be her choice. As she was weighing up her limited options, she thought she heard a quiet knock at the door. She listened and there it was again, a very gentle tapping. She opened the door to see Eilidh clutching a bottle of wine

"I thought you might need company and maybe this," Eilidh whispered, holding the wine aloft.

"It's like you read my mind, but why are you whispering?"

"I'm trying not to wake Rory up."

"It's okay. You're safe for now. It isn't until after midnight that the trouble usually starts."

"Oh, that's good because Rich has gone to the pub with Andrew, and he wanted to know if they could call in later. I said I wasn't sure if it'd be too noisy for Rory, but I'll tell him it's okay, shall I?"

The glug of wine transferring from bottle to glass had never sounded more satisfying to Beth. It was a mild evening, so they slathered on some midge repellent, grabbed the baby monitor, and settled on the bench at the side of the front door, where they could enjoy the evening sun and a view of the sea.

"So how's it going on your own?" enquired Eilidh as the magic of the wine worked its way through them.

"Not as bad as I thought it'd be, actually…"

"So, story of your life really!" Eilidh interrupted, totally straight faced.

"Oi, don't be mean," Beth replied, mock hurt. "Although it's probably true, you know me too well."

"You're so much more confident than you used to be, but you're bound to find things harder at the moment. You just need to be kind to yourself."

"I know," Beth took another sip of her wine, thinking of Alex, who had given her the same advice so many times. She didn't mention him now though. Eilidh was one of the few people who knew the whole story of Alex. She'd been fascinated by Eliza's diary and had never shown any sign of doubting Beth's experience, but Beth didn't like to bring Alex up too often. It still felt odd to chat about meeting a ghost as if it was a normal event. However, thinking of the diary did bring her discovery of Maude and Joseph's letters to mind. They spent the next hour warmed by the late sun, discussing the letters and their contents, talking through Eilidh and Rich's wedding plans, and generally putting the world to rights. As the sun finally dipped behind the distant hills and they were contemplating heading inside, they heard voices approaching from the direction of the Ardmhor Hotel. Gradually, the figures of Rich and Andrew came into view.

Beth always felt a little self-conscious around Andrew. Although it was getting on for two years since he'd been back in Ardmhor, and she'd seen him around many times, she couldn't quite get past the fact that they'd had a brief fling before he'd left for Mexico. Even at the time, it hadn't been serious; Andrew was a bit of a ladies' man, and for Beth, it hadn't been anything like the connection she'd felt when she finally met Ali, so she knew that bumping into him shouldn't be a big deal. There had been plenty of nights out with her and Ali, Eilidh and Rich, and Andrew and whoever his latest girlfriend was, but she still found herself initially tongue tied, every single time.

"So how's the activity centre going?" she ventured as she found herself next to Andrew in the kitchen, looking for more glasses.

His time in Mexico had been spent working at an outdoor activity centre, and he had opened his own when he returned to Ardmhor.

"Yeah, good. We've got lots of bookings for high season already. It's just a bit patchy right now. We need to find a way to spread things over the year a bit more. How's things with you? When are you back at the museum?"

"I've got another month or so before I'm officially due back. I'm not totally looking forward to it, but I suppose I need to get back to being me again, instead of just Rory's mum."

"I bet you'll enjoy it more than you think. And I'll definitely welcome the return of the old Beth. I don't know if you're aware, but I really liked the previous version of you. You know, before you got all old and domesticated."

Beth knew not to take Andrew seriously. Flirting was how he communicated, and she knew he had a girlfriend at the moment—one that had lasted longer than usual; however, she still hoped no one noticed her blush as they joined the others at the table. It surprised her to hear another knock at the door a moment later, and she was even more surprised when Eilidh said, 'that'll be Jay' and jumped up to answer it. The last time Beth had spoken to Eilidh, she'd sounded pretty fed up with being pulled from her normal duties to work with Jay, so she hadn't expected her to be inviting him along on nights out. Jay was his usual effervescent self and soon had everyone laughing at his ridiculous tales, giving Beth no chance to quiz Eilidh on her change of heart. By the time Beth waved them all off from the doorstep, the wine and company had done their job. She fell happily into bed and drifted off to sleep quickly, not even looking at the clock or thinking how long she might get before the next wake up call.

LETTER THREE

October 1880

Dear Joseph,

I used to call you the most special person in the world, and although time has moved on, and our circumstances have certainly changed, it is still the truth. That's why I need to write this letter. I cannot leave these things unsaid. For me, it is impossible to be around you and pretend everything is fine. I can't exchange pleasantries with you on the way into church as if you are just another member of staff. It may seem wrong that I am telling you this now. I understand how difficult your life is, and my worries must seem trivial in comparison. Perhaps I shouldn't be adding to the burden of a man deep in grief, but it doesn't feel as if I have a choice. I am truly sorry for your loss, Joseph. I would never want to see you in pain. However, I can't help the feeling that you have been lucky. Not in the loss you are feeling now, but because you have been so loved. You have enjoyed a bond of such depth that its passing leaves you bereft. I can only imagine the joy that such a relationship would bring.

For years, I would dream of seeing you. I would imagine all sorts of convoluted scenarios that would bring us back together. Then, as time went on, I thought of you a little less. There were still moments when a sight, or a sound, or a smell, could unexpectedly transport me straight back to you, but gradually their frequency diminished. I'd reached a sort of peace with the past, but now, you are suddenly part of my present again. However, it is not in the way I had hoped, and it is much harder to cope with than I had imagined.

After I wrote to you all those years ago and begged you to fight for me, I waited. I waited with total certainty for you to approach my parents and ask for my hand in marriage. You wanted the same as me. There was no question in my mind. I had complete faith that you saw us growing old together, surrounded by our brood of much-loved children. That certainty made the realisation you weren't coming all the more devastating.

I know I cannot hold you responsible for the fact that I accepted James's proposal. But when I realised you didn't want me, there seemed little point holding out for anything else. James MacAird represented the pinnacle of my mother's ambition. If I couldn't have my happiness with you, I thought why not let my mother have her happiness instead? You probably find it hard to imagine me accepting what someone else wanted. Maybe you still picture me whirling through life, bending everyone to my will. But once I understood that the only thing I truly wanted was unavailable to me, I changed. There no longer seemed any point in trying to exert control. I've been going along with the plans of others ever since. Firstly, I did what my mother wanted, and since then I've accepted whatever James has demanded. I live here in the wilderness, and my boys live hundreds of miles away. It is so very far from what I had planned.

So what I want to know is why? Why did you not fight for me? And if it was because you had never loved me, why did you let me believe you did? Why didn't you tell me I had got everything so wrong?

I also need to know when you fell in love with Maude. For a long time after I wrote you that last letter, I existed rather than lived. I went through the motions of being a wife and then of being a mother, but I didn't feel those moments. Then, when Alexander was born, I saw a future again.

I thought someone would finally love me. The thought of that unconditional love healed me a little. I felt strong enough to try to repair the bonds I'd broken when I married James. I wrote letters to both you and Maude. I asked you, much as I'm asking now, for an explanation of why you abandoned me, but I also offered my forgiveness; as much as you'd hurt me, I wanted us to be friends again. In Maude's letter, I apologised for accepting James when I'd suspected she held hopes of a future with him. However, both letters found themselves consigned to the flames of my bedroom fire. Before I had chance to send them, I heard the news that the two of you had married. The shock was indescribable, imagining the two of you together broke my heart all over again, and bitterness stole my resolve to make amends.

I started to wonder how long you had known of your feelings for her. Had you known from the moment I introduced you? Were you both laughing at me? Had you been thinking—'silly Constance, forcing us together in her pretend family'—while secretly wondering how to get rid of me? I have learned to control the hurt that those questions cause me, but they haven't gone away. Far from it, they still circle my mind in the depth of the night, and I still need to know the answers. So I'm begging you again, Joseph. I know life is hard for you now, and I understand how much you must miss Maude. I've been missing both of you for the last ten years, and the knowledge that it is too late for a reconciliation is a bitter blow. But please find the strength to answer my questions. I can't carry on without knowing the truth.

Yours, as ever,

Always

CHAPTER TWELVE

Beth was reeling as she put the letter down on the kitchen table. It appeared she hadn't been learning about Maude and Joseph's relationship after all. But even if she had known the letters weren't from Maude, she would never have predicted that Lady Constance MacAird was their author. It hadn't occurred to her that the 'Always' at the end of each letter might not simply be a loving sentiment, that it could actually be a name. Constance, constant and always. That part made sense, but little else did. Beth had always known that Joseph Turner and James MacAird attended school together, and she'd recently discovered that Maude had known James MacAird as well, but she hadn't realised that Joseph had any previous connection to Constance. From what she'd read in the diary, it seemed Eliza hadn't been aware either. It just didn't seem possible that the woman in the letters, who was so honest and open, could be Constance. The Constance MacAird that Beth had got to know through Eliza's diary was scheming, volatile, and primarily concerned about appearances. Surely she couldn't have written these words.

Beth reached into the box containing the letters, desperate to learn more. She unfolded the next piece of paper, but the date was earlier. It was older than the first letter she had read, written when Constance was only twelve. It was still addressed to 'Joseph, the most special person in the world', and signed off by 'Always', but it was more childlike. It was full of descriptions of village events and accounts of what Joseph's young cousins had been up to. The next piece of paper revealed a letter written at a similar time, as did the next and the next. A couple were from slightly later, but none were written after 1880, the date of the letter she had just read. They were all fascinating, with their details from a long-vanished world, but Beth couldn't help feeling disappointed. She wanted the answers to Constance's questions. She wanted to know why Joseph hadn't asked her to marry him, and like Constance, she wanted to know whether Joseph had been in love with Maude all along. But the answers certainly weren't in the box of letters, and she didn't know where else to look.

Rory was out for the afternoon with Angela and Jim, so Beth summoned her courage and ventured back into the attic for a search. She didn't think there would be more letters up there, but she hadn't noticed these until the previous week, so anything was possible. It turned out to be a futile hope though. All she unearthed was more dust and junk.

"Where are the rest of the answers?" she demanded of the empty space, scaring herself by trying to invoke whatever presence she'd felt the week before. But there was no shift in atmosphere today. All that she felt was a sense of futility as she sat on the floor. She was both overwhelmed by the mess she had created and frustrated that she hadn't found any answers. Although the attic roof lights were small, she could see it was bright outside. An urge to escape engulfed her, and she decided she didn't want to waste any more time in this gloom. The cleaning up could wait. She needed to be out in the open.

Without a pushchair to constrain her, or the weight of a baby to carry, she could roam wherever she wanted. Finding her hiking boots in the cupboard under the stairs, shoving her waterproof jacket, phone, and a drink into a rucksack, she locked the door behind her. She was going to let the great outdoors clear her head. Heading through the woodland which began at the border of their small garden, she walked roughly in the direction of Ardmhor House. The climb took her through the fields where Jay was proposing the self-catering lodges. The outlook from there really was stunning. Beth knew she couldn't say this to Ali, but she wondered why none of them had thought of doing something similar before. Looking around her and taking in the view, it seemed like an idea that couldn't fail. Instead of continuing into the gardens surrounding Ardmhor House, she turned and headed up the hill, aiming for a path that would lead her out in the opposite direction. She felt as if she was being pulled towards where the scenery got wilder, the places where it was too hard to walk with Rory in tow. She wondered whether Constance had ever walked out here. Previously, she would have said a definite no. The Lady Constance MacAird she had created in her head didn't go traipsing about the hills; she gossiped with important ladies and always maintained decorum. But the Constance she had seen in the letters might have done. This version of Constance was a different person; she was passionate and desperate to be loved—she wasn't going to be held back by convention. Beth could picture this version of Constance hiking her way up to some hidden spot and giving vent to her frustrations, rallying at the injustice that her life wasn't how she had planned. What Beth couldn't imagine was how this Constance had become the one from Eliza's diary. She had fallen for the girl in the letters, whereas she'd always seen the other Constance as a villain.

The higher Beth climbed, the more the view opened up. She could see the ferry in the distance making its way out to the islands. The village scattered below her looked tiny now, the miniature houses and the matchbox sized cars reminding her of the world her dad was creating around his train set. It all looked so insignificant against the scale of the mountains and the sea. She walked on, drawing level with the outdoor activity centre Andrew had set up, then heading out towards the point of the peninsular. She checked the time, mindful of the fact that however far she walked she'd have to cover that distance home again as well, but it was still quite early, and looking at how far she'd covered already, she was confident she'd have time to head down to the lighthouse and then walk back along the shore.

As she reached the lighthouse, she leaned against its smooth white base, enjoying the coolness against her back. She'd walked at quite a pace, and the breather was welcome. Closing her eyes, she tilted her face towards the sun, while the breeze drifted over her skin. The waves breaking below and the gulls calling overhead were the only sounds until she was pulled her from her reverie by a voice shouting her name.

Opening her eyes, she saw Andrew waving as he made his way over.

"Hi Beth, I thought it was you. Lovely day, isn't it?"

"Yes, gorgeous. I thought I'd make the most of it, seeing as I've got the afternoon to myself. How come you're not working?"

"We've not got anyone booked in for the afternoon, and I was feeling sorry for myself. I thought a walk might clear my head."

They fell into step together, heading along the path down to the shore, which would eventually lead back into the village.

"I somehow never associate you with feeling down. What's the matter?" asked Beth.

"Nothing really. It's like I was saying last night, the centre is well booked for high season, but we're not operating at capacity now, and we struggled over the winter. I'm just getting concerned about keeping it all viable. I don't want to be forced to let any staff go."

"I think it's fair enough to be worried about that, Andrew. It's a big deal being responsible for other people's incomes."

"And Leonie finished with me when I rang her at lunchtime."

"Oh, I'm sorry. You'd been seeing her for a while, hadn't you?"

"A few months, which I know isn't that long

for most people, but for me it's ages."

Beth smiled. "Yeah, for you, it's almost like you were married!"

"Kick a man when he's down, why don't you!"

"Sorry, Andrew," Beth replied, blushing slightly at her inadvertent rudeness. "I'm not used to you being serious when you're talking about relationships."

"Don't worry," he said, flashing her his usual grin. "I've only got myself to blame for that."

"So, what happened? I mean, only if you want to tell me."

"It was my fault. She's been dropping lots of hints about taking things further, maybe moving in together, but I just wasn't ready. I kept avoiding the conversation, or changing the subject, and I guess she got fed up with it."

"I'd thought that maybe you were considering settling down this time. I mean, you've said yourself it's unusual for your relationships to last longer than a couple of weeks."

"I think maybe I was, I mean, it's what I want —to find someone. It just didn't feel quite right. It's difficult, you know, since Ali snapped up my ideal woman while I was out of the country."

Beth laughed and gave him a shove. "We both know you're only saying that because I'm unavailable. Your problem is that you can't give up the thrill of the chase."

"I think you might be right, but I need to sort myself out. I see you and Ali sometimes, out and about with Rory, and it just looks perfect. I really want that, but it never feels how I'm expecting it to."

"Well, you're welcome to borrow Rory whenever you want. I could do with a good night's sleep."

"You know what I mean though, Beth, I want to feel I belong with someone."

"I know," she replied.

They walked on in silence for a while until the ringing of Beth's phone broke the peace. It was Angela, asking if they could keep Rory out for a while longer. They'd bumped into friends who'd invited them for something to eat. Beth was happy to agree, knowing that Rory would be fine. She'd packed plenty of milk in the changing bag and he was eating more 'proper food' each day now. It also meant that she didn't need to rush back, she could relax a little.

"Everything alright?" asked Andrew as she put her phone away.

"Fine, Angela just wanted to know if they could keep Rory out longer. It'll be nice not to have to rush or worry about getting his tea."

"So you're at a bit of a loose end for the next couple of hours?"

"I suppose so. Why?"

"I was wondering if you fancied a quick trip

to the pub. We could have a drink and grab some food. You could cheer me up, and I could keep you company."

"I don't see why not," she replied. The idea of someone else cooking and clearing up for her, along with an adult to talk to, was very appealing. Beth smiled as they picked their way along the shore back into the village. She was looking forward to the next few hours.

As she settled into the corner table, watching Andrew getting their drinks, Beth felt a wave of nostalgia wash over her. It took her back to when she had first arrived at Ardmhor. Andrew had worked behind the bar then and had flirted with her every time she came into the pub. She reached out her phone and opened the group chat that the volunteers had set up before the holiday ended. It had miraculously kept going over the past five years, although that was probably because of the number of relationships that had been formed before everyone left. Mary and Bob had been a couple for many years before they first came to Ardmhor, but the other five volunteers who had spent the full month on the holiday had made their own connections as well. Fraser was the heir to a vast estate in England and had fallen head over heels for Olivia, a petite and perfect student studying estate management. Just over a year ago, they had married in a beautiful ceremony, held in the private chapel at Fraser's family seat. Olivia had looked simply stunning in a fitted silk gown that skimmed over her tiny frame, with an antique veil that trailed behind her. Although Beth had been rather taken with Fraser when she first met him and therefore uncharitably resentful of Olivia, she had felt nothing but happiness for them as she watched them exchange their vows. She had Ali by then, and she had learnt to be much less critical of her own flaws. The others brought together by the holiday were Megan and Steve. Megan was an American divorcee looking to reconnect with her Scottish roots, and Steve was a university lecturer. Over the course of the holiday, they had discovered they didn't want to live without each other, so they had relocated to Edinburgh together. As Beth had stayed in the area and all the couples saw Ardmhor as playing a special role in their lives, they had maintained a connection. There wasn't the intensity of messages there had been straight after the holiday ended, but they were all still in touch most weeks. Beth took a picture of the inside of the pub and sent it to the group with the caption 'wish you were here'.

Andrew arrived back from the bar carrying their drinks and a couple of menus. He settled into the chair opposite Beth as she read through the familiar list of pub classics. After both settling on burgers, the conversation turned to the activity centre.

"We struggled to bring in enough visitors when we first began opening the museum over the winter," Beth was saying as her food was placed in front of her. "We had to think really carefully about ways to bring in different groups, rather than relying on passing tourists."

"So what worked?" asked Andrew.

"Well, we get a lot of business through schools. I sometimes go out taking artefacts to them, and other times they come to us. It's great for schools to visit in the off season as they can have the whole place to themselves. We've also advertised in ancestry forums and offered packages helping people research their family trees. We only do that over the winter, when we're not so busy, but it's proved really popular."

"School parties could work really well for us actually," mused Andrew. "We could offer discounts over the winter, and maybe we could put together some activities to take to them."

"You could do corporate team building sessions as well," Beth suggested. "You could team up with local accommodation and offer packages."

"That could really work. It's just knowing how to go about it all and get the word out."

"It's not my speciality or anything, but I've had to put together quite a lot of promotional materials for the museum. I could have a go at making something for you, if you thought it might help."

"That'd be amazing," Andrew responded with a grin.

They ate their meal chatting about prices, discounts, and what the centre could offer to school parties or large groups. Beth noted down lots of details on her phone and was already working through ideas for how to present them. By the time she arrived home, she wasn't thinking about Constance MacAird at all. And she wasn't thinking about missing Ali, or about how many times Rory might wake up that night. Instead, she was feeling excited about planning ideas and helping to build something successful. It was an excitement she hadn't felt for a while, something she hadn't realised she'd been missing.

CHAPTER THIRTEEN

Ardmhor, 1880

I'd thought of Maude as my sister. I loved her completely, showering her with the affection I so desperately wanted to receive from my parents. Her death has come as a great shock, but I think I have coped with the news of her death better than I coped with the news of her wedding. Perhaps the intervening years spent trying to banish both her and Joseph from my thoughts have helped. When I received the letter from Mother all those years ago, casually mentioning that Maude and Joseph had married, the shock forced me into my bed for weeks. Everyone thought I was ill, that I'd exhausted myself by insisting on caring for baby Alexander without the help of a nurse. But that wasn't it. The problem was the torture of imagining the two people I'd loved the most united without me. It cut at my heart to think of them living out my dream, especially when my reality was so very far from it. It was like a gaping wound that I refused to let heal. I pictured them setting up their home together. I saw their smiles as they chased cherubic children round the hallways. And I heard their laughter when they remembered me, the silly girl who had forced them together. It was a terrible time, and I wondered if the darkness would ever loosen its grip on me.

Alexander's birth had reawakened hope in me, but Maude and Joseph's marriage almost stole that away. Although I was never physically apart from Alexander, it took time for me to really see him again. Eventually, I began to feel the warmth of his small body in my arms. I smelt the gentle perfume of his downy hair. I saw his eyes searching mine, and I knew I had to bring myself back to reality. Over time, I put up barriers to keep Maude and Joseph from my thoughts. A few years down the line I had reached a place where if one of them sneaked under my barricades, it was only a sense of mild sorrow I felt, rather than the pain of a stab to the heart.

I realised I couldn't blame them for wanting to be happy. They weren't the only ones capable of putting themselves before others. After all, I had married James. I made that decision despite believing that Maude also had her sights set on him. So although she and Joseph had moved on without me, and perhaps they had been laughing at me all along, I could hardly claim to be perfect. I reached a place where I regretted, rather than hated.

At some point, things changed again. Dreams crept up on me of a day when we might be reunited. I wondered whether we could restore the bonds that had been so strong in childhood. But then I heard of Maude's death and those fragile dreams crumbled. The shock and disappointment I feel is different this time. I think the news of their marriage changed something inside me forever. The barriers I built to protect my heart mean I am no longer capable of that depth of feeling. This time, there is just an aching sadness. A sorrowful acceptance that we can never put things right.

When I think back to the night of the ball, the night when everything changed, it doesn't seem important enough. One night, one insignificant gathering, can't have been enough to change my life in the way it did. That doesn't mean I wasn't excited about it. I admit that the anticipation as the footman opened the doors was quite overwhelming. Maude was at my side, clutching my hand as we climbed the steps to the ballroom.

I think we both felt beautiful that night. The silk and taffeta of our dresses danced around us as we moved, whispering promises of what the evening might hold. Our mothers had primed us with weapons to engage the heir to the MacAird fortune. James MacAird was the prey for every parent in the area, and their daughters were to be the hunters. Maude and I had enjoyed the attention lavished on us as we prepared, but we both knew those attentions were in vain. At least, I thought we did. The eldest son of a family like the MacAirds was hardly going to be interested in the daughter of a doctor or the daughter of a low-ranking member of the aristocracy. And he was Joseph's roommate, he would know the relationship that Joseph and I shared. I was absolutely certain that nothing would happen between me and James MacAird, and I thought Maude knew he wouldn't consider her either. I thought we were enjoying the fuss, safe in the knowledge nothing would change.

As it happened, both Maude and I danced with James MacAird many times that night. However, those aren't the moments that have lived on in my mind ever since. My memories of that night all centre around Joseph. Nothing has dulled the sensation of his arms around me as we whirled across the floor. I have never fitted so well with another person. I still believe we were born to be together. This seemed so obvious to me that I thought it would be obvious to everyone else.

It therefore came as a surprise when, in the days following the ball, James MacAird kept calling.

My mother could hardly contain herself, and I must admit it was flattering to think I was being singled out. However, Maude was always present, as was usual at our house, so I couldn't be certain that his visits were entirely for my benefit. Maude clearly enjoyed his company too, so I was always careful to make excuses to give them moments alone together. To begin with, I didn't think he was seriously pursuing either of us. I thought perhaps he was expecting Joseph to be with us as well, that maybe he wanted to become a part of our group. But Joseph stayed away. After a week, I began to worry. Joseph had still not appeared, but James had called every day. His words became more personal, and I finally realised he might have serious intentions towards me. Things felt different with Maude as well. She grew cold, and I saw then that perhaps she hadn't considered the plans to win James futile from the start.

However, I still thought I could make everything right. I reassured Maude that I had no interest in marrying James MacAird. I told her I was certain that once Joseph asked for my hand in marriage, James would ask for hers. Although Joseph had virtually disappeared, the problem didn't seem insurmountable. I still believed I could bend things to my will, I was used to people dancing to my tune. I wrote to Joseph begging him to act. It had occurred to me he might think I had changed my allegiance, so my words were chosen carefully. I did not want him to have any doubts about my feelings. I told him again and again how much I loved him and that all my dreams revolved around him. Then I begged him to speak to my father and ask for my hand in marriage. The envelope bore my kiss as a seal, and I gave it to Maude to deliver. I couldn't entrust its delivery to anyone else. I had to know for certain that Joseph had received it.

Then I waited. I waited, and I waited, and I waited some more. The days passed, but I was still certain that Joseph would appear, that everything would be alright. It took me a long time to accept that he wasn't coming. By then, Maude's visits had dwindled too. There was only James appearing day in and day out. So even though I knew I didn't love him, and I knew that perhaps Maude did, when James officially asked for my hand, I said yes. We were married only a few months after his proposal. I didn't see Maude again after I told her I'd accepted James's offer. She was angry with me, and I was angry with the world for denying me my dreams.

Neither Maude nor Joseph attended our wedding. The night of the ball was the last time I saw Joseph. Those glorious moments when he led me round the floor were the last I spent with the love of my life.

I don't think that James loved me either. He found me attractive and entertaining enough, but I don't believe there was any great depth to his affection. I wonder now whether he saw winning me as a way to show his roommate just who was best. Perhaps pursuing me was no more than an outlet for adolescent rivalry. Although Joseph was absent from our wedding, and he and James no longer sought each other out, they were still connected through mutual acquaintances. They heard occasionally about each other's lives, but James never mentioned Maude and Joseph's wedding. I only learned of it from my mother. Therefore, it came as a shock when James informed me of Maude's death; I hadn't heard her name from his lips during the entirety of our marriage. One of their fellow schoolmates had included the news in a letter, writing that Joseph had not coped well with her illness and was struggling with her death. Even after all that has happened, my heart aches for him. And it aches because the damage caused to our little group can never be repaired. Our made-up family had meant so much—Joseph needed it because he had no parents, and Maude and I needed it because our parents were so disinterested—yet it crumbled with no resistance.

The sadness I feel seems understandable. In fact, it almost feels honourable because it shows

I have forgiven Joseph and Maude for how they hurt me. However, I also feel a sense of disgust, and the reason for this is difficult to admit. Amongst the sadness, a part of me is glad. Maude and Joseph are no longer revelling in their own happiness, and that makes me happy. It pleases me that they are no longer together, living my dreams and excluding me from them. So I'm disgusted with myself because I know no one should ever feel this way, especially not about people they claim to have loved, but that seed of happiness is still there, and I can't resist watering it, trying to make it grow.

CHAPTER FOURTEEN

Beth had been so fired up after her trip to the pub with Andrew that she'd got the laptop out to work on ideas as soon as she arrived home. She hadn't really considered that she could be missing work. When she had been teaching, she'd looked at colleagues about to start maternity leave with total envy. She hadn't been able to understand the concerns of those who worried they might be bored. Even though things had changed since then and she loved her job at the museum, she still enjoyed days off even more. So the idea of all that time to spend exactly how she wanted, coupled with her excitement about becoming a mum, meant it hadn't crossed her mind that a year off could be too much. She'd long since realised how naive she had been about the idea of time to spend exactly how she wanted, but it hadn't occurred to her that perhaps she wanted to be working again.

When she had confided in Angela about getting irritated with her mum, Angela had mentioned that it could be hard to remember who you were once you became a parent and that subsequently everything needed time to readjust. Thinking about that now, it made sense that focusing on something she was interested in, rather than making everything about Rory, could be helpful in lots of ways. While Rory had his morning nap, Beth spent more time on the marketing materials for the activity centre and found the time had flown. After that they had both walked up to Ardmhor House. Rory spent an hour with his grandad, while Beth and Angela looked through the school bookings the museum had over the next couple of months. They decided Beth would run each of them as a way of easing back into work.

When Ali had first told her about his research trip, Beth had been dreading the time on her own, but she had to admit now it had been good for her. Apart from that first morning, when Rory wouldn't stop crying and she'd felt overwhelmed by the idea of coping alone, everything had gone really well. It had helped that Rory had slept a bit better, and Beth was well aware that there were no guarantees of that continuing, but she really did feel more confident about her ability to cope. The idea of getting back to work and having another focus again was also making her feel pretty excited, something she could not have imagined thinking five years ago. But none of this compared to the bubble of happiness that swelled inside her when a text popped up from Ali saying 'see you in a few minutes'. Rory was already tucked up in bed and the delicious smell of lasagne, Ali's favourite, wafted from the oven. Beth poured herself a glass of red wine and sat by the window, watching for the car pulling up in front of the house.

She thought over the worries she'd been harbouring that they were drifting apart. She knew she loved Ali and that there was no one else she'd rather spend time with, but recently she'd been so exhausted that a good night's sleep was as far as her fantasies in the bedroom went. So when he stepped out of the car, she was relieved to feel the same explosion of butterflies that she used to feel when they first met. She ran to open the door and threw herself at him, knocking his case out of his hand in the process.

"I'll have to go away more often if this is the way I get welcomed home," Ali said into her hair, not releasing her from his grip.

They stood for a while, both unwilling to break the spell of being together again, until Beth finally stepped back.

"And it gets even better," she said, as Ali retrieved his case from the floor. "The lasagne should be ready in about twenty minutes, Rory's fast asleep, and there's a big glass of wine waiting for you."

"Just hang on," said Ali, with a glint in his eye. "You're saying Rory's asleep, and we've got a spare twenty minutes? What could we possibly do to fill the time?"

Then he raised his eyebrows and led her to the stairs. In the end, the lasagne was slightly on the well-done side, but neither Beth nor Ali noticed. They were too wrapped up in being together, feeling everything was right with the world.

◆ ◆ ◆

By some miracle, Rory only woke once in the night and slept long enough into the morning that both Ali and Beth were showered and dressed by the time he stirred. It was a much happier Beth that kissed Ali goodbye that morning than the Beth that had waved him off on his trip a week earlier. Unfortunately, the Ali that arrived home from work later in the day was not a happy one at all. Beth was balancing Rory on her hip, trying to hold him tight with one hand and load the dishwasher with the other, when she heard the door slam and Ali kick his shoes off with considerable force. She looked up in surprise. It wasn't like Ali to be so heavy-handed.

"Are you alright?" she called out to him, putting Rory onto his play mat as she made her way into the hall.

"Why didn't you tell me you'd had a party here while I was away?"

"Because I didn't," Beth replied, confused. Then it occurred to her what he meant. "Oh, you mean when Eilidh came round? It wasn't a party, and I just didn't think about it. By the time I spoke to you, my mind was already on other things."

"But it wasn't just Eilidh, was it? Jay was here too, wasn't he? And Andrew."

"Yeah, Rich and Andrew called on their way back from the pub and then Jay arrived. Actually, I don't know why Jay turned up. I meant to ask Eilidh about it because I didn't think she liked him much, but I didn't get the chance and I've not seen her since."

"And then apparently you went out for a meal with Andrew the other night, which you didn't mention either."

"I told you about doing some marketing materials for the activity centre though, didn't I? I forgot about going to the pub when I spoke to you because I was more excited about using my brain again. I bumped into Andrew while we were both out walking, and then your mum rang and asked if she could keep Rory for a bit longer.

Anyway, Andrew said why didn't we call in the pub, as we were both at a loose end?"

"Oh, so everyone knows apart from me then?"

"Ali, what's going on? Why are you being weird about this?"

"I'm not being weird," Ali responded, his voice rising. "You know I've been feeling a bit freaked out about Jay being back, and now I've got him telling me he's been hanging around here while I've been away. Then some of the other blokes tell me about you spending the night in the pub with your ex. I don't think it's weird that I'm pissed off."

"Well, I do," Beth hissed back. "Firstly, Jay hasn't been hanging around here. He came round for a short while one night with a group of others, and it wasn't me that invited any of them. Secondly, Andrew is not my ex because we were never going out, which you already know. You're the one with loads of ex partners."

"But I haven't been going out on cosy dates with any of mine."

"And neither have I. Once again, Andrew isn't my ex, and it wasn't a cosy date."

Ali looked at her and shook his head.

"I can't deal with this right now. I'm going out."

But Beth was quicker than him.

"Don't you dare," she said, shoving her

feet into her boots as she opened the door—desperately fighting the urge to shout and only managing because she didn't want to scare Rory. "If anyone's going out, it's going to be me."

Then she shut the door behind her with as much control as she could muster.

◆ ◆ ◆

Half an hour later, Beth was pacing the end of the pier. She was still seething, but she'd calmed down enough to at least see where Ali was coming from. Any interaction with Jay seemed to reduce him to the level of a hormonal teenager. When that was limited to them playing the occasional video game together over the internet or chatting about the ridiculous TV shows they'd been obsessed with as kids, it was sort of endearing, but it didn't transfer well into everyday adult life. She could see how Ali would have been blindsided by Jay announcing they'd been spending time together, and she imagined Jay had mentioned it to Ali in a manner deliberately designed to wind him up. Although Beth had no experience of siblings, she knew only too well how it felt to be the outsider in a group, to feel like second best and wonder if you'd only been invited because no one else was free. She suspected that was how Jay left Ali feeling, whether or not he meant to. Then, when someone else teased Ali about seeing her in the pub with Andrew, it probably hadn't felt like a bit of banter as it usually would. It had probably felt like everyone was laughing at him. She was still angry. It wasn't her fault Ali was feeling this way, and he shouldn't be taking his frustration out on her, but she could see why he'd reacted as he had. The idea of him feeling humiliated made her heart ache. So she decided to go home and sort things out. Also, it had started raining, and in her rush to leave, she hadn't picked up her coat.

Beth arrived back to an empty house. There was just a note on the table saying, 'Taken Rory to Mum and Dad's.' It was getting close to Rory's bedtime, and she didn't know if he'd had anything to eat yet, so she phoned Ali's mobile to see where they were up to. There was no answer, so she tried Angela's number instead.

"He's not here," Angela replied when Beth asked if Ali was there. "He said something had come up and asked if I could watch Rory for a bit. Is everything ok?"

"Yes, fine," Beth lied, not wanting anyone else to know they'd argued. "Shall I come and get Rory now?"

"Well, I've just made him something to eat, so shall I give him that and then Jim can drop him back round to yours in a bit?"

So instead of sorting things out, Beth spent the next hour getting more and more cross. She was grateful it was Jim dropping Rory off rather than Angela, as she knew he wouldn't ask questions. Then, after Rory was home and another couple of hours had gone by, Beth had moved from anger to worry. What if something had happened to Ali? What if he'd done something daft? But just as she was contemplating what she ought to do, she heard the front door open and slam shut again. Then she heard someone bumping along the walls as they made their way into the kitchen. She heard the fridge open and the TV go on, and all the anger came back. She didn't go downstairs to try to make things right. She didn't see why she should. So the night passed with Beth staring at the ceiling, simmering with resentment, and Ali dead to the world in front of the blaring TV.

CHAPTER FIFTEEN

There was no loving doorstep farewell the next morning. Beth pretended to be asleep when she heard Ali come into their room in search of clean clothes. She only moved once she heard the front door shut and was sure he had gone. Downstairs there was the stale smell of alcohol and evidence of drunken snacking. Beth looked around her with a sigh. This was unchartered territory for them. They never argued, and she felt devastated. Although she knew Ali was in the wrong, in the cold light of a new day, she also knew she'd do whatever was needed to make things right. She didn't know why she hadn't told him about Eilidh and the others coming round, or about the meal with Andrew. It hadn't been a conscious decision to keep quiet, but maybe she had been holding back, subconsciously punishing him for leaving her on her own. She just wished she could go back in time, do a few things differently, and make sure the row never happened. With that an impossibility, she settled for sending a quick text instead. After typing out multiple messages, she decided to keep it short and sweet - 'I'm sorry I upset you. None of those things were secret, they just didn't seem important enough to mention. I love you.' With that done, she changed her focus to clearing up and sorting out Rory. There wasn't anything else she could do for the moment.

The first of the museum sessions Beth had agreed to lead was taking place mid-morning, so after breakfast, they set off for the short walk to Ardmhor House. A text arrived from Ali just before they left. It was only brief, simply saying, 'I'm sorry as well. Love you so much', but the relief it brought Beth was immense. They were going to be okay. She was grateful for the distraction of the museum, and she was also grateful that Angela didn't pry about what had gone on the previous night. Despite it being obvious that something was wrong, Angela didn't question Beth when she said everything was fine. Not for the first time, Beth thanked her lucky stars that her mother-in-law was far removed from the horror popular culture suggested she should be.

Beth nervously watched the school party

filing into the museum, but within minutes she was back in the swing of things. It was satisfying to own her space again, and it was fun to see eyes light up as imaginations were sparked. She was buzzing as she walked out of the museum to be met by Angela, Rory, and her mum.

"We decided we'd all take you out for lunch, to celebrate your first day back at work," Jean explained. "So, have you got any preferences? It's between here, the pier, or the pub."

"The pier?" suggested Beth.

"Sounds good to me," replied Angela and Jean at the same time.

So the four of them set off to stroll down to the pier. The sun came out as they walked, warming the air and requiring them to squeeze their coats into the basket under the pushchair. They found a table outside the cafe and settled themselves in. Rory clapping his hands with glee at the antics of a gull busily screeching and flapping on the shore.

"Have you told Angela about the letters you found?" Jean asked Beth while Angela was placing their order.

"No, I wanted to tell her when you were here as well."

"This sounds intriguing," said Angela, picking up on the tail end of Beth's words as she sat back down.

"Oh, it is," Jean began. "Beth found a box of

letters in the attic at her house. Eliza's mum, Maude, wrote them to Joseph, her husband, the one who moved up here to be the factor."

"Didn't Eliza and her dad move here because her mum had died?" asked Angela.

"That's right," Jean confirmed. "So there wasn't much about Maude in the diary, and no one in the family seems to know anything about her either. But from reading these letters, she doesn't sound like your average Victorian lady."

"No, the writer is much less reserved than I'd have expected," Beth interjected. "But I don't think it was Maude that wrote them anymore."

"Oh!" said Jean, surprised.

"Yes, I haven't had a chance to tell you about the last letter I read. It was written much later than the first two. In this one, the writer talks about her marriage to James MacAird and how hurt she was when she heard that Joseph and Maude had married. So the writer can't be Maude, it has to be Constance. Which also fits with all the letters being signed off 'Always', it was a play on Constance's name."

"Wow!" said Angela. "I knew James MacAird was an old acquaintance of Eliza's dad, but I'd assumed Constance only met Joseph when he moved here to become factor. I'd love to see the letters. I've never really been able to understand Constance and why she acted like she did. Those letters we bought a while ago, the ones her older son wrote, didn't really help that much, so it'd be brilliant to finally see something which sheds a bit more light on her." Angela paused for a moment. "Didn't you say the letter writer isn't as reserved as you would have expected? I have to say that doesn't sound much like Constance. In the diary, she's pretty much as uptight as they come."

"I know. From the first few letters I read, I would never have expected Constance to be the writer, but it seems that she and Joseph had been sweethearts since childhood. There's a letter where she begs Joseph to intervene and ask for her hand in marriage when James MacAird starts pursuing her. However, for some reason, he didn't, and he married Maude instead. I think it devastated her. The last letter was written when Eliza and Joseph first arrived at Ardmhor. It's basically Constance questioning him about why he abandoned her. The problem is that all the other letters in the box are earlier ones, so now I've got all these questions and no way of finding out the answers."

"We don't have anything else connected to Constance in the archive, do we?" Angela queried, not really expecting a response because she already knew they didn't.

"No, nothing," Beth confirmed. "Which is so disappointing. I'm absolutely desperate to know more."

Angela and Jean shared her frustration, but neither of them could think of a way forward.

◆ ◆ ◆

Although the food at the pier had been as good as ever and the clouds stayed away, Beth's heart wasn't in the outing. She'd enjoyed surprising her mum and Angela with the news about Constance, but her mind kept wandering back to her argument with Ali. Deep down, she wanted to be home with him and feel that everything was normal again. It seemed that Ali wanted things back to normal as well. Apart from the long, intense hug they'd shared when he first came through the door that evening, neither of them referred to the events of the previous night. Rory was fussing and demanding attention, so it was easy for them to go through the motions of their evening routine and avoid any proper conversation.

After his improved sleep of the previous week, Rory chose that night to return to his usual pattern of waking. This resulted in a bleary-eyed breakfast where the elephant in the room, otherwise known as the argument, could still be ignored. It also meant there hadn't been an appropriate moment for Beth to mention the text she'd received from Andrew, which asked if they could meet up to go through her marketing plans for the activity centre. She absolutely knew she needed to tell Ali, but as the proposed meeting wasn't for a few days, it didn't feel like that rushed and tired morning was the right time to bring it up.

❖ ❖ ❖

It was later on, as she was walking back from her parents' house with Rory asleep in the pushchair, that she bumped into Andrew. She'd spent a lovely afternoon enjoying the holiday feeling she got every time she visited her mum and dad. They'd been down on the shore, helping Rory to paddle at the edge of the sea. Then they'd spent some time in the byre with her dad's miniature train set. Rory was still too young to appreciate the intricate settings David was building, but he absolutely loved watching the train speed round and round the track, squealing with joy each time it passed him. Beth had just reached the turning to the proposed holiday village when she spotted Andrew. He was jogging and she couldn't help but notice how toned his legs were in his running shorts. His hair had curled up wildly because of the warmth and exertion, and as he slowed down to say hello, he wiped his sweatband over his forehead. Beth told him not to interrupt his run, but he reassured her he needed a break and slowed down to a stop. They talked for a few minutes about the ideas she'd come up with, and she promised she'd email them through to him. Then they chatted about inconsequential things for a while, with Beth enjoying the uncomplicated, light-hearted banter—something that was in short supply at home right then. She knew it wasn't really fair to compare this brief meeting to the previous evening with Ali. Andrew's easy, flirtatious manner only worked because she didn't share a life with him. You couldn't have the connection she had with Ali and still exist purely on banter and superficial chats. But she was glad she'd seen Andrew, having had the chance to explain her ideas meant there was no need to meet up in the next couple of days, which also meant there was no need to mention it to Ali. She felt it would be better for restoring the peace between them if they avoided talking about Andrew for a while.

What Beth didn't know was that while she was enjoying a relaxed chat with Andrew, Ali had been up at the proposed holiday village site, looking at plans with Jay. She didn't realise that Jay had nudged Ali and said,

"Isn't that Beth down there on the road? Who's she talking to? It looks a bit like Andrew."

She was unaware that Ali had stood watching her laugh at some silly joke Andrew was telling. She didn't know he'd winced as she shoved Andrew playfully when he reached the terrible punchline. She couldn't know the sinking feeling that had developed in the pit of his stomach as he thought to himself that they didn't joke like that anymore.

◆ ◆ ◆

Beth was surprised how subdued Ali seemed that evening. She knew things were still strained between them, but she'd hoped they were settling down. Unfortunately, it seemed as if they were actually becoming more fraught instead. So she didn't object when Ali said he might go to the pub after Rory had finally settled to sleep. If she was honest, she felt relieved at the idea of being alone. Her eyes fell on the box of letters as she pottered about the kitchen, stacking the dishwasher and wiping down the sides, getting things ready for the next day. After pouring herself a hot water, she placed the box on the table in front of her, ready to read the letters again, wondering if there was anything she'd missed before. As she carefully opened each letter and spread them out on the table in front of her, it became apparent that one letter seemed much thicker than the others. On closer examination, she realised that two letters had become stuck together. Very carefully, she separated the two pieces of paper, slowly trying to prise them apart, anxious to avoid causing any damage. After a tense moment or two, when it looked as if the ink had fused the two letters together, making separation impossible, they finally gave up their hold on each other. Miraculously, neither letter seemed damaged, the words still looking clear on both, but what really thrilled Beth was the date she had noticed at the top of the previously hidden letter: it said November 1880, the month after the letter full of Constance's questions.

LETTER FOUR

November 1880

Dear Joseph,

Your answers to my questions only seem to have extended the list of things I need to know. I am finding it difficult to believe that you didn't receive the letter I wrote before James proposed. And I can't agree with you that none of this matters anymore. It certainly matters to me. Your lack of response to that letter changed the course of my life. I took your silence as an admission you no longer wanted me. Had I known it never reached you, I would have behaved differently.

But I can't understand how you failed to receive it. I didn't entrust that letter to any old source of delivery. I gave it to Maude to pass on to you. It was too important to risk it going astray. This isn't a case of a postal failure with unexpected consequences. Maude told me she passed the letter into your hand. That's why I don't understand. Maude told me she gave you the letter, whereas you say you know nothing of it. Both these things cannot be true, but the only person who could explain is no longer with us. I don't want to accuse Maude of deliberately withholding the letter from you, but I can't think how else to explain events. It can't be that she simply forgot because she remembered well enough to tell me she had delivered it. Perhaps the letter was damaged and she didn't want to tell me, but she knew the importance of its contents, so that wouldn't make sense either. Therefore, I can't agree with you that the past is the past and should be forgotten. I can't move on without knowing the truth.

You also say it doesn't matter at which point you and Maude fell in love. In the grand scheme of the universe, you are probably right, but again, it matters to me. Why would I ask if it didn't? So I am truly grateful that you indulged me. It means so much to know that you did once share my feelings. To have it in writing that your love for Maude only developed after my marriage to James eases my mind immensely. The thought that I had misjudged our connection, that it hadn't meant to you what it meant to me, plagued me for many years. Knowing that fear was unfounded has lifted an enormous weight from me.

However, it also stirs up other emotions. It means that if you had received my letter, everything would have been different. You would have asked for my hand in marriage, and I would never have accepted James's proposal. We would be together, watching our children grow, just as we had planned. That's why I feel I must know what went wrong. Maybe this is what you meant about some things being best left in the past. Knowing your love was real is like a balm to my heart, yet it makes me feel more keenly than ever that my future was stolen from me. In the past, I could blame you, but now I don't know where that blame should lie.

Then there is our meeting the other day as you left James's office. The look you gave me as you pulled me into the shadows was a look I recognised so well from all those years ago. It was the look you always had when you so desperately wanted us to be alone, when you wanted us to be taking pleasure in each other's kisses but other obligations got in the way. You write that what we shared is in the past, but your face said something different. The urgency with which you repeated the words you had written, wanting me to know without doubt that you hadn't received my letter, gave me hope. Does a part of you also wish we were still together? Believe me, I am not trying to belittle the importance of your life with Maude. I simply mean that perhaps we both still feel our connection. And who could blame either of us for wanting to act on it?

Which leads me to my most important question. Why don't we act on those feelings? I understand you will have reservations. You are an honourable man, and I am married to your employer. Although I would be happy to accept the shame of the situation, I don't doubt that your conscience would not allow an affair. So let me be very clear, I would willingly leave James to be with you. He has already taken my boys from me by sending them to that school so far away. Although being denied access to their lives completely would be devastating, I don't imagine the pain of it would be much greater than the loss of them I already feel every day. My husband would not be saddened to lose me. There is neither hatred nor love between us, and as we are so removed from society up here in the wilds, I am sure we could avoid a scandal. Perhaps James would allow me to keep Flora if he got to keep his heirs. I have jewellery that I could sell, and you have skills that are always in demand. We could leave and start afresh, choose new names and begin again. We could live the life we had always intended. I understand that more change might be difficult for Eliza, but I know I would love her dearly, and I would do all I could to make her happy. And one day, once they'd finally finished at school, surely my sons would seek me out. Perhaps we'd be lucky enough to have children of our own. I'm not under any illusions. I know this would be a hard path to follow, but just imagine how it could be. Imagine us finally living those dreams we shared for so long.

I promise I will not make your life here difficult. If you don't share my enthusiasm for this plan, I won't keep writing to you, and I'll endeavour to keep my distance. I will not embarrass us both by pressing this issue, but I'll first ensure that it is not another miscommunication keeping us apart. If you don't respond to me, I'll approach you once about the contents of this letter. That way, I will know for certain how you feel.

Hopefully, you can now see why I needed my questions answered. It is because I have never wanted to be with anyone else. My love is still strong enough that I would leave everything behind to form a new world with you. Don't dismiss what I am asking as a flight of fancy. Really think about it. Imagine us together, building the life we used to dream of. Imagine that it doesn't need to be a dream. I suppose, when I think about it properly, you are right, lost letters and past mistakes don't matter anymore. The only question that needs to be answered is whether you will leave with me. That will tell me

everything I need to know.
   Yours, as ever,
   Always

CHAPTER SIXTEEN

Beth couldn't help feeling sorry for Constance as she placed the letter carefully back in the box. As there were no more letters, and Constance was still married to James MacAird at the time of Joseph's death, it seemed Constance hadn't received the answer she wanted. Twice she had put her feelings on the line for Joseph Turner and twice he had let her down. The first time was arguably not his fault, but there could be no excusing his rejection of her this time. It must have been very hard for Constance to recover from.

Once again, Beth saw Constance differently, and there were also questions to be asked about Maude. The letter Joseph denied knowledge of was preserved in the box in front of her, along with his other letters. If Joseph had received it when Constance first wrote it, why deny that now? Maybe he was trying to deceive Constance and excuse himself for the way he'd rejected her; however, all accounts suggested Maude's death had broken him—it didn't fit for him to tell a lie which would cast her in a bad light. But he'd obviously come into possession of the letter at some point. Had he found it after Maude's death, but not wanted to dishonour her memory by admitting that she'd concealed it? Beth looked at Joseph and Maude's wedding picture on the mantelpiece. Maude and Eliza were very similar, and some of that family resemblance had made its way down to Beth. Since reading Eliza's diary, Beth had been proud to think she was like her. These letters had then made her feel the same about Maude. It had been hard enough having to accept that Constance was the real author, having to accept Maude as a villain would be even worse.

A glance at the clock showed it was getting late, and Ali still hadn't returned from the pub. Beth considered waiting up for him, wanting to clear the air and get things back to how they'd been the night he'd returned from his trip, but she was also tired and had another school session booked at the museum in the morning, so she made a drink to take up to bed instead. Pausing at the bottom of the stairs, she put the box of letters into her bag, ready to show Angela.

She was hoping that after her session in the museum, they might have a trawl through the old MacAird family photo albums. It was a long shot, but perhaps they could offer some more insight into Constance.

◆ ◆ ◆

Angela was only too happy to oblige with Beth's request to look through the albums. By the time Beth had finished the school visit in the museum, Angela had reached out each one from the 1870s until 1900.

"I know we've looked through them all before, but sometimes you spot something you've missed when you're looking at it from a different perspective," Angela said as she opened the earliest album.

She had carried the pile of them up to the apartment. That way, they could keep Rory entertained more easily than they'd be able to down in the old estate office.

"I totally agree," said Beth, taking a sip of her drink before placing it safely out of the way. "Last time we looked through them properly, we were focusing on Alex and Eliza. I don't think we really bothered to look out for Constance at all."

"Plus, it's a great excuse for another nosy," Angela said with a smile. Her pride in the family albums was no secret.

They leafed through several albums, finding

nothing of particular interest, breaking off occasionally to distract Rory with different toys. It seemed Constance hadn't been keen on appearing in front of the camera. There were a couple of stiff images of her and James in front of the main entrance to Ardmhor House, but there was no life in them, no connection between the two people in the picture. Angela thought they must have been taken at the start of the 1880s, putting Constance in her early thirties. The same age as me, Beth thought to herself. Constance sounded such a sour old woman in Eliza's diary written just ten years later, it was hard to imagine how young she'd really been.

A little while later, they found a more interesting image of Constance. This was also taken on the front steps, but they must have posed for it in the summer, when the boys were back from school, because it was a family portrait instead. It was still a very formal picture, with the two boys and little Flora in front of their parents. There wasn't any of the heads leaning together, arms around each other that you might expect to see in a modern family photograph. The boy stood in front of Constance was much smaller than the other, so he had to be a young Alex. Beth shivered to see him in such an old image. Even though she'd now had years to grow used to the idea, she still found it hard to believe that Alex had lived here well over a century ago. It was difficult to accept him as a Victorian gentleman when she had met him as a contemporary. But it wasn't only Alex that interested her now. The Constance in this image differed greatly from the one in the portraits of just her and James. In this picture, she was absolutely alive. She wasn't staring into the camera as she was in the other photographs. This time, her head was tilted down, her gaze focused on the young boy in front of her, her hand resting protectively on his shoulder. There was no doubting the love radiating from her. For the first time Beth believed the inscription on Alex's gravestone, it seemed he really had been the beloved son of Lady Constance MacAird. But in the letter Beth had read the previous night, Constance was offering to leave Alex behind to start a new life with Joseph. She did a quick calculation of the dates. Constance must have written that letter at a similar time to these pictures being taken, so maybe the camera lied. Beth couldn't imagine a woman so in love with her son being willing to leave him, and she knew enough about Victorian divorce laws to know that if Constance had gone through with her plan to leave James, no court in the land would have allowed her access to her children.

"It makes no sense that she'd be willing to leave them for Joseph. She's so different in that photo. The way she's looking at Alex is pure love," Beth said, voicing her confusion out loud.

"I agree. It is a different Constance in that picture. It's beautiful. But I suppose we need to remember that with Alex now away at school in England, the only time she would have had with him were those few weeks in the summer. Maybe that wasn't enough to get her through the loneliness she felt the rest of the time."

"I suppose so. I just can't imagine anything that would make me willing to leave Rory behind."

"Apart from him waking up every hour," Angela replied with a wink.

"Well, maybe I might have considered it for a moment," Beth said, rolling her eyes at her mother-in-law. "But I wouldn't seriously have done it."

"I know," Angela said, reaching for her hand, "and beautiful though Rory is, his sleeping patterns could try the patience of a saint. You've been amazing. But being serious, one thing that comes through in all of Constance's letters is that she really wanted to be loved. She wanted to be surrounded by children, but in the last letter, it sounds like she feels her sons have already been taken away. The early letters make her sound like someone who had to control things and make them happen, but now she's saying her life is nothing like what she'd planned. The Constance in those early letters wouldn't have let her husband send her children away to school, so she must have been very low to allow James to do that. Maybe leaving everything behind, even if it meant giving up her children, was the only way she could see to make things better."

"It's funny," Beth started, trying to think how to explain what she meant. "Constance is Eliza's total enemy in the diary, but they're actually quite similar. They both feel they can't control their lives and neither of them finds a way to be with their first love."

"You're right. You can't help thinking that if Eliza had known about all this, she might have seen Constance differently. Perhaps she'd even have confided in her. I wonder if that would have changed the ending of Alex and Eliza's story?"

"I just wish there was a way we could find out more. I want to know how Constance goes from being willing to give up everything for love to being willing to thwart her son's chance of happiness," said Beth.

Then another photograph caught her eye. This one showed a large group arranged on the lawn in front of Ardmhor house. The caption written above it stated 'Birthday Celebrations'. Underneath the picture, the names of the people captured in the image were listed row by row. Beth couldn't see the two MacAird boys, although she thought Flora was one of the children at the front, but she spotted Constance with ease. She was near the centre of the group, at the side of her husband. Once again, Constance wasn't looking at the camera, but neither was she looking at her husband. This time, she gazed intently at a man slightly in front of her, a little to her left. The man must have moved as the image was taken because his features were blurred, but Beth already knew who he would be. Sure enough, as she ran her finger along the names, her thoughts were confirmed. Constance MacAird was staring straight at Joseph Turner, and her expression was identical to the one she had worn when looking at her son. It was a look of pure love.

CHAPTER SEVENTEEN

Ardmhor, 1881

I can't pretend it's been easy having Joseph and his daughter living at Ardmhor. I'd wished for him to be back in my life for such a long time, but I'd wanted us to be together. I'd never imagined us as passing acquaintances. When I asked him to run away with me, I'd convinced myself that he would agree. I knew I would lose a lot. There would be no more glorious reunions with my precious boy. But I reasoned perhaps I could live with that pain if the rest of my existence would be happier. After just a few years of boarding school, Alexander has already changed. It takes longer on each return for him to become my boy again. I think I'd decided that if I was going to lose Alexander anyway, I might as well lose him now, while there was still opportunity to find a different happiness. However, Joseph didn't agree to my plan, so there was no choice to make. Alexander and Flora are the only chances I'll ever have to be truly loved. I make it my mission now to ensure Alexander wants for nothing when he returns home, to make sure he becomes my boy again before he returns to school.

While I love my boy ferociously, I struggle to find any affection for Joseph's daughter. I know I am being unreasonable and that it is not really her fault, but I can't help blaming her for the fact Joseph and I are not together. When no reply came from Joseph, I stuck to my word. I skulked around the house, lying in wait for him, looking for an opportunity to question him, to check he had read my proposal. I honestly hoped his lack of response was down to another error in communication—as if such a thing could happen twice! As most reasonable people would have assumed, that was not the case. He looked at me with the same sort of passion I'd seen during that other whispered conversation in a shadowy corner, but his words told a different story. He said that it didn't matter what his feelings were, he couldn't put Eliza through any more upheaval. And that is why I blame her for my unhappiness. I know it's not really her fault. If Joseph loved me enough, he would find a way to make things work. But even though I know this, I can't ignore the little voice in my head. The voice that keeps telling me, 'If she didn't exist, you'd be together.'

It doesn't help that she is so like Maude. Eliza's voice and expressions are so similar to her mother's that sometimes it is as if Maude herself is right here. That should please me. When I married James, I was almost as sad about Maude's disappearance as I was about the loss of Joseph. However, that was before. It was before I found out that Joseph had not received my letter. The only plausible explanation for that is that Maude chose not to pass it on. She told me she had placed it in his hand—yet he never saw it—and that lie rules out any other possibility. So it is hard to care for Eliza when I am struggling to find forgiveness for Maude.

To prevent myself sinking down again, like I did when I heard about Joseph and Maude's marriage, I tried to pretend he wasn't here. I tried to make myself believe that the new factor was just someone who reminded me of him, but the more I tried to avoid him, the more present he seemed to become in my life. James seems energised by renewing their boyhood friendship. He invites Joseph and Eliza to dine with us almost every night. It takes all my strength to make polite conversation. Inside my head, I'm reaching out and shaking him. I'm shouting,

'Why, Joseph? Why have you done this to me again? Why won't you ever fight for me? Why am I not enough?' Obviously, I don't say those things out loud, instead I smile serenely, and I compliment the housekeeper on the food or comment politely on the mild weather we're having.

I try so hard to be pleasant to Eliza during these occasions; I don't want to feel such animosity towards her. I compliment her clothes, and I ask how she is managing as mistress of her father's house; I've even offered to help with her embroidery. However, it doesn't seem to help matters. She answers my questions with as few words as possible and she declined my embroidery offer with visible disdain. All of which makes it even harder for me to like her. However, I am determined to try. The problem is that aside from her keeping Joseph away from me, and the issue of her reminding me of my traitorous best friend, we are very different. She is quite bookish. Ladylike entertainments don't really interest her. Whereas I am frivolous and emotional. I love to create beautiful things, whether it is outfits, hairstyles, or embroidery. I like to chatter, and sing, and dance—not that I get much opportunity for singing and dancing here. However, I can see those things do not appeal to Eliza. I thought perhaps I could reach out to her through Flora, but although there is little more than a year between them, Flora is still in the stage of fairy tales and dolls, which Eliza has long moved on from. Thus, I am quite at a loss with finding an interest to connect us.

Actually, that is not quite true. I know that we both love Joseph, but how can I possibly share that with Eliza? I have also noticed that she is increasingly fond of Alexander, just as he is of her, but I fear he is something I don't want to share. She already monopolises the first love of my life and I am wary of her taking the second. Alexander is so kind and caring—I see him making sure that Eliza is part of the children's games after church, pulling faces at her across the dinner table, or asking about her favourite books. Eliza deserves to be loved, just as I longed to be, and I tell myself that I should be able to share a love of Alexander with her. Alexander could be the way to bridge the gap between us, but that little voice in my head is still there—it says again and again, 'She's taken Joseph, she'll take Alexander too.'

Joseph himself hasn't made things any easier. If I'm honest, when I said I had hoped to avoid him, I was lying. Not intentionally, but I was lying to myself. Despite knowing it would be better for me not to see him, I longed to anyway. Yes, it is agony to sit around the table with him, but it is a delicious agony. It was easier when he was just a memory, but I couldn't carry on without his presence now. I am addicted to the sight of him. I am intoxicated the moment I am near him. And as I say, Joseph hasn't helped.

Although he didn't want to start a new life with me, it seems he couldn't keep his distance either. When we shared our first proper kiss, we were little more than children. We met by the stream, hidden in the shade of the trees. As we shyly touched our lips together that first time, we both wondered what all the fuss was about, but we gradually understood. We grew, and we got bolder, and we explored the sensations our bodies could produce. Those few years of kisses were so precious, but they are so long ago now. I didn't know if I'd remembered them correctly. I thought perhaps my mind had built them into something they never were. However, that is not the case. Kissing Joseph today is as magical as it ever was. In fact, it is even better. I can barely cope with the sensations his lips create. And that is why he is making everything so much harder to bear.

Whether he planned for us to meet is something I'll never know. I couldn't really blame him if he had. He must be very lonely since Maude's passing and I had offered to leave my husband for him. Essentially, I'd given him an invitation. I often walk down the hidden steps onto the shore. They lead from the bridge that takes the road over the river. They are difficult to spot as the parapet at the end of the bridge almost hides them from view. I like to wander there because it is quiet and out of sight of the house. There are no expectations of Lady Constance out there. Anyway, as I sat one day, close to the steps, enjoying the play of the sunlight on the sea, Joseph appeared behind me. Not a word was spoken before we were in each other's arms, the years falling away as we held each other's gaze. Within seconds, his mouth was on mine and his hands wound their way into my hair. We were one again, just the way we should always have been. I experienced sheer joy in that moment. Then afterwards, I experienced pure pain because I realised this stolen moment wasn't a precursor of a relationship to come. It was all our relationship would ever be.

In my letter, I'd told Joseph I could live with an affair; however, I soon discovered that was yet another lie I'd told. I knew from that first touch I wanted more than snatched meetings and furtive kisses. I'd like to say that I was strong enough to turn him away. My mother might have shown me little affection, but she raised me to be a lady, and I know a lady should not behave in the way I have. Men have a weaker nature: they cannot help being led astray by temptations of the flesh. It is the duty of women to resist, but I have failed in that duty. Even worse than that, I know I will do it again. I have never arranged an assignation between us. I promised I wouldn't write to him again, and I have kept my word on that. But I have wandered the shore by the hidden steps almost every day since that meeting, wishing with every fibre of my being to see him there again. To both my shame and delight, those efforts have not been in vain. When Joseph described to James a lovely walk he had discovered, up in the hills behind the house, I carefully noted the route in my head, making sure to follow it the next day. It came as no surprise when I found Joseph waiting at the most secluded point along the track. So although I am not happy with this situation, I have certainly agreed to it, and I am grateful for whatever crumbs of affection he offers me.

And that is why life has not been easy since Joseph and his daughter came to Ardmhor. Our stolen moments are not enough for me, yet I live for the joy of them. I suffer through each evening that Joseph and Eliza dine with us, but on the nights he is not there, I am lost without his presence. I dream of his touch, and I live with the guilt of it. He won't say yes to me, but I can't say no to him. If I am honest though, as I am trying to be, I wouldn't choose to go back to the time before they arrived here. I would go forward to a time when Joseph is mine, but no matter how hard this is, I couldn't exist without him again.

CHAPTER EIGHTEEN

As the weekend arrived, Beth and Ali were still treading on eggshells around each other. Everything would have looked fine to an outsider, but the argument was still festering underneath the surface. Ali felt hurt that Beth possibly had more fun without him. Beth was hurt that Ali could even think she was hiding things. So they carried on, going through the usual motions of their lives together, and sometimes things even felt normal, but then Beth would catch Ali watching her as she responded to a text and remember his lack of trust, or Ali would hear Beth finish a conversation just as he walked into the room and wonder if she was hanging up because she had something to hide. They were silly little things, but they added up to a feeling that something wasn't right. However, neither of them could clear the air. For all that they wanted things back to normal, they were both too annoyed to make that first move.

"How come Eilidh isn't picking you up like she normally does?" Ali asked as he stacked the breakfast pots into the dishwasher.

He was trying his best to sound as though the answer didn't bother him, but with things as they were between them, they both knew it did.

"She's meeting Rich to watch a film in Inveravain afterwards, so it makes more sense for me to drive myself."

Beth was joining Eilidh and her parents, Claire and Alan, for lunch. It was something they'd done regularly since Beth had moved to Ardmhor, and she always looked forward to it. Alan was a builder and had turned their house from a dark, dank, abandoned cottage to the most spectacular home Beth had ever set foot in. It was almost wall to wall glass at the back and situated right next to the sea. At high tide, it gave Beth the impression she was on a boat. Although the factor's house was just across the road from the shore, you could only catch glimpses of the sea from upstairs, or from the sides of the bay windows, whereas at Claire and Alan's the sweeping bay with its scattering of islands was visible whichever way you looked.

"So you're not meeting anyone else as well?" Ali persisted.

"No," Beth replied. "I'm coming straight home, but it wouldn't make sense for Eilidh to bring me back here and then have to drive back out to Inveravain."

"You're right, it wouldn't," Ali agreed quietly. "It's just that Eilidh usually drives."

"I know. It's a shame really as we won't get as much chance to chat, and I feel like I've not spoken to her properly for ages. I'd best get a move on, actually. I hadn't realised it's already half ten."

She handed her empty mug to Ali for him to add to the dishwasher and set off to get ready, pausing as she reached the door to the hall.

"I thought I might…," she began, before stopping abruptly.

She had been going to say that she might ask Alan roughly how much the extension she kept dreaming about might cost, as opposed to the attic conversion that Ali was keen to push ahead with, but she thought better of it halfway through. What would she gain by bringing up another bone of contention between them?

"You thought you might what?" Ali asked.

"Oh nothing, it doesn't matter," Beth replied, turning to head up the stairs.

Ali watched her leave, wondering what else she was choosing not to share with him.

♦ ♦ ♦

Lunch was just as pleasant as Beth had expected. In fact, the time flew by. They chatted about local gossip and ate more of Claire's delicious cooking. Alan promised he'd call round to have a quick look at how straight forward Beth's extension plans might be, and Claire handed her a chocolate cake she'd baked—for Beth to take home and share with Ali and Rory. Then it was time to leave. There hadn't been time or opportunity to ask Eilidh how she was finding things at work now, or why she'd invited Jay to join them the other night.

"We need to have another catch up, just the two of us," Beth said to Eilidh as they walked back to their cars.

"I've got over an hour before I'm meeting Rich," Eilidh replied. "We could call for a coffee somewhere, if you've got time before you need to head home?"

They settled on a quick drink at Beth's favourite café in Inveravain. It had an amazing view over the harbour and an eclectic mix of brightly painted furniture. Claire had done too good a job of lunch for them to fit in any cake, but they were lucky enough to get the prized window seat and settled into it with satisfaction.

"So, what's going on with you? Are you happier with work again?" Beth asked, taking a sip of her hot chocolate and ending up with cream on her nose.

"Yeah, Jay's not so bad, now that he's settled down a bit."

"I've been meaning to ask you about Jay. When you told me about having to reorganise your work because of him, you sounded really annoyed, so I was surprised when he turned up at mine that night you came round. I'm assuming it was you that asked him."

Eilidh thought for a moment before she answered. "Yes, it was me. After moaning about him, I started to feel sorry for him. He was being really nice to me, apologising for interrupting my other work, and he was talking about not knowing many people round here anymore. So once I knew you were okay with Rich and Andrew calling in, I thought I'd text Jay as well. You didn't mind, did you?"

"No, like I said, I was just surprised. Ali wasn't that impressed though. I hadn't thought to mention it to him, but then Jay did, so he was pretty pissed off."

"What is it with those two? Ali's usually so laid back. I don't think I'd ever seen him wound up before, but now he's like a bear with a sore head around the office."

"Tell me about it," Beth grimaced. "I don't know why there's so much tension between them when they're together. When Jay's down in

London, they speak to each other fairly often and they seem to get on fine. But as soon as you put them in the same space, it's like they're a pair of jealous kids."

"They probably just need a bit of time to get used to being around each other again," Eilidh replied, pausing as the café owner stopped to top up her coffee, then absentmindedly taking a sip. As the now boiling liquid hit her throat, she wafted her hand in front of her mouth, as if it would somehow stop the burning. After a minute of huffing and puffing, she had recovered enough to speak. "Was Ali really upset about Jay coming to yours? It seems a bit of an overreaction."

"I don't know whether it was really about Jay coming round. I think it was more that I hadn't told him—he felt like everyone was in on something that he'd been left out of."

"I'm sorry Beth, I didn't mean to cause you any hassle by asking him."

"Don't worry about it, it's not your fault. Plus, I think he only reacted so badly because he also got told that I'd been in the pub with Andrew."

Eilidh slowly put her drink down on the table and regarded Beth with a mock serious expression. "I think this needs dealing with in two sections, Mrs Hutton-MacAird. Firstly, why were you secretly meeting Andrew?"

"I wasn't," Beth replied indignantly, even

though she knew Eilidh was only joking. "I just bumped into him when I was out walking. It turned out we were both at a loose end, so we called in the pub for something to eat."

"Hmm, well, the second issue is, if that's the case, why is Ali reacting like this?"

"I wish I knew," Beth sighed. "I think it's all because of Jay being back. He suddenly seems worried about being outdone, or being left out, which isn't like him. I had told him I was doing some marketing materials for Andrew and that didn't bother him. The problem is that I forgot to mention we'd discussed it at the pub, so now he's reading something into that because he thinks I was hiding it."

"I'm sure he'll calm down again soon. Like you said, Ali's not usually jealous or petty. I do sometimes wonder whether men are worth all the hassle they cause though."

Beth was grateful to move the conversation away from her and Ali. "What's making you think like that? Apart from the wedding planning stress, I thought everything was great between you and Rich."

"Yeah, things are fine, really. He just keeps irritating me. Things that he's been doing for years, like never shutting drawers properly, are suddenly making me want to murder him. I don't know, it probably is just wedding stress. That's why we've got our little cinema date today.

I'm trying to make more of an effort."

"It probably is just all the decision making," Beth agreed, "and if you've been finding work more difficult than usual, that might make you more irritable."

"I suppose, but work's fine now. That first day or so, Jay seemed so full of himself with all his big ideas. I think he just wanted to impress everyone, though, because now he's really down to earth. He always wants to get my opinion on things and his plans are brilliant. I don't know why no-one's thought about extending the accommodation options on the estate before."

"Just don't say that to Ali," Beth said with a rueful smile.

"I didn't mean it like that. Ali's been too busy with all his other ideas. I'm more surprised it hadn't occurred to any of the rest of us. Ali only needs to be jealous that Jay got all the looks in the family!"

"Which definitely isn't true," Beth stated loyally.

"I know," Eilidh grinned. "Both MacAird boys are pretty easy on the eye."

"It's probably safest to say Rory outdoes the pair of them," Beth replied diplomatically.

"I'm totally happy to drink to that," Eilidh said as she clinked her coffee cup against the side of Beth's hot chocolate, creating a spillage with her enthusiasm.

❖ ❖ ❖

As Beth climbed into her car a little while later, she checked her phone. There was nothing from Ali, but there was a text from Andrew. He wanted to know her thoughts on the photos he'd selected to go with the advertising blurb she'd written and was wondering whether it was best to meet up or if he should just email them. Beth knew that the sensible option would be to tell him to send them over. However, the part of her that was still cross with Ali didn't agree. That part of her was putting forward convincing arguments of its own. It was saying it'd be much quicker to call up to the activity centre and get it sorted straight away. After all, everything is easier face to face. So instead of heading straight home, she gave Andrew a quick call to check he was at the activity centre and told him she'd be there in about half an hour.

The annoyed part of her had been right. By going up there, they'd got the pictures sorted straight away, but despite that, she wasn't home for long before she regretted her decision.

"I thought you'd be back earlier than this," was Ali's greeting as she walked in the door.

"Oh, sorry. I went for a hot chocolate with Eilidh on the way back. We just fancied a bit of a chat."

"But hadn't you just had lunch together?" Ali

responded, not unreasonably.

"Well, yes, but it's not really the same with her parents there." Beth moved towards him, putting the chocolate cake down on the kitchen island. "Look, Claire sent us this. Doesn't it look amazing?"

Ali ignored the cake and pursued his earlier line of questioning. "So what did you need to talk about that you couldn't discuss in front of Claire and Alan?"

"I didn't really mean it like that. It was more that there were things we didn't get round to discussing. Also, Eilidh's been getting stressed out about the wedding and she probably wouldn't want to worry her mum and dad about that. That's why they're going to watch a film this afternoon. She wanted to make a bit more of an effort with Rich."

"Isn't the afternoon showing usually at three? If you've only just got back, she'd have been late, wouldn't she?"

That was when Beth wished she'd not gone to meet Andrew. It was all perfectly innocent, but she knew that by not telling Ali in advance it didn't look that way, especially when you considered the argument they'd both been so reluctant to discuss. When she went, she'd known it could lead to problems, but her anger with Ali had pushed her on. Now, she just felt mean. Whichever way she looked at it, she had taken a deliberate decision to wind Ali up, and she'd done that when she knew he was struggling. She knew there was nothing for it now except to tell him the truth, but she really wished she'd acted differently.

"I called at the activity centre as well, to finalise the photos for the marketing materials I told you about."

"Right," Ali replied quietly. "So you weren't just meeting Eilidh."

"I saw a text from Andrew as I was leaving Inveravain, so I thought I'd call up there quickly and get it out of the way." Then, in her guilt, she carried on digging a hole for herself. "I would have told you, but I didn't think it'd take long, and I didn't want you to overreact like you did before."

"It's fine, Beth. You can do what you like. You don't have to tell me anything," Ali replied calmly, but the look on his face told her it was anything but fine.

A loud knock, followed by Angela appearing at the window, saved them from any further discussion. Ali sighed and went to open the door.

"Hello sweetheart," Beth heard Angela saying to Ali. "Is Beth back? I've rushed round because I've found some things that I know she'll want to see straight away."

LETTER FIVE

March 1891

Dearest Joseph,
Oh Joseph, my love, the most special person in the world. A long time ago, I promised I would never write you another letter. I've kept to that promise, and I doubt I will send you this, but I need to explain how I feel. I need to put into writing the emotions swirling around me. It's the only way I can try to make sense of everything. I am just so angry with you. You have let me down time and time again, never caring enough to fight for me, or even to suffer any upheaval for me. Whereas I have loved you completely. I have settled for whatever scraps you have deigned to offer me. I have placed you at the centre of my life, even though I knew I was only at the edge of yours. But now, now for the first time, I cannot accept what you are going to

do. You cannot leave me again. I forbid you to do this. You cannot die. I will not allow you to go.

Yet I know you will. It is there in your hollow eyes and your shrinking frame, in your head now too heavy to lift from the pillow. It should have been obvious to me months ago, but I chose not to see it. That is why I am so angry with you Joseph, once again, you are going to ignore my pleas. Once again, you will not choose me, but this time there will be no tiny ray of hope. There will be no chance that you'll change your mind. There will be no crumbs of affection to sustain me. This time, you will leave me forever. Why can't you love me enough to stay?

It is almost funny that after a decade of clandestine meetings, this final abandonment means I can spend time with you openly. Everyone looks at the bountiful lady visiting the dying employee most favourably. What would people think if they knew of all the other times we have spent together? All those moments spent rushing down the hidden steps to the shore, furtively checking over my shoulder before reaching secret corners and melting into your arms. Now I find myself directed to the chair at your bedside by the nurse. I always wished to be allowed to have a place in your home. I should have been more careful with my wishes.

When I sit at your bedside, the anger leaves,

and I am filled with sorrow instead. There is so much sorrow. Some for you because of your pain at leaving Eliza alone. Certainly, sorrow that you are suffering. But also sorrow for me. A great chasm of sadness that I will never again feel the strength of your arms around me. Despair that I won't see the smile that lights up your entire face, the one that appears when I round the corner of the hill path and hurry into your embrace. Sorrow that I will have to exist without you.

But the sorrow I feel at the thought of losing you is hard to distinguish from the anger I feel that you won't stay. I know logically that you have done everything you can to carry on living, that you've done that for Eliza if not for me, but somehow the anger remains as strong as the sadness, and I fear that neither emotion will lead me to peace.

I hope you believe me when I say Eliza will always be welcome at Ardmhor House, that she will know she belongs in our home. Over the years, I've tried so hard to build a bond with her. I realise I've not been entirely successful in that, but I am confident in the bond I have helped to establish between her and Flora. Hopefully, their friendship will make what is to come easier for Eliza to deal with, but I still think it would be better to discuss these plans with her now. She is too intelligent to believe you when you say you will recover. It took me a long time to accept the truth, but Eliza is not so easily fooled. She may only have been a child when Maude was ill, but you need to remember she has seen this happen before. I am worried that if you don't tell her your plans, she will feel we have foisted them on her. If we all talked about them together, maybe she would feel more in control. It is a terrible feeling to realise everything you have known and dreamt of is gone, but I'm aware you know this too.

I'm also concerned about the idea of telling her she is to live with us as a companion to Flora. I understand that she already has a family, that she doesn't need a replacement for Maude or for you. It has been impossible to ignore how resistant Eliza is to me, and you obviously know her much better, so perhaps you are right. Perhaps she would feel patronised by the suggestion that she simply become part of my family, but what if she feels she is only being tolerated as Flora's companion? What if she believes that she only belongs with us for as long as she has a role to fill? I have always respected your wish not to tell her about my friendship with Maude. I know you thought it would be less painful for her if memories of her mother remained in the past. Don't worry, I'll respect that wish in the future as well; however, I can't help wondering if it has been a mistake. Perhaps she would have been more accepting of me and my frivolous ways if she had known her mother had tolerated my whims. Perhaps that knowledge could help us develop a better relationship in the future, but I will respect your wishes. And I promise you, Joseph, I will do everything in my power to make sure Eliza feels welcome and loved—you know I have strived my whole life to feel those things. So please do not worry for Eliza, don't add to your suffering because I promise you, I will care for her.

Although I have always longed to be your most important consideration, I hope you will not worry for me either. I don't know how I will bear your loss or say a last goodbye when the time comes. Even though I can explain regular visits to you now, there is still no way I can justify spending each day with you. I am afraid I might not see our last farewell for what it is. What if our final meeting is one of those times when the nurse never leaves? What if it's a visit when I'm not able to smooth the hair from your face and whisper how much I love you or gently kiss your lips? I am terrified that our final meeting might be a formal one between Lady MacAird and the loyal factor. Your loss will be the hardest thing I have ever had to bear, and that I will have to hide my grief makes it worse. However, I am going to bear it. I will bury my anger, and I will bury my sorrow. I will make you proud.

You might not have loved me enough to fight for me, you might not have loved me enough to make me yours, but I love you enough, Joseph. I will do all I can to love your daughter as my own. Finally, I will be a mother to your child, as I used to dream of when I was but a child myself. I will fulfil your wishes, even the ones I don't agree with. And I will carry you in my heart forever, as I always have. My mind will wander the secret shore with your arms wrapped around me. It will walk the hill path to find you and feel your lips meet mine. I will keep your smile tucked safely in my memory, and it will have to be enough. It will have to be enough because I will not fail you. My love is strong enough for both of us.

All my love,

Always

CHAPTER NINETEEN

It turned out they'd known where they could find more information about Constance all along. It was simply that neither Beth nor Angela had connected all the dots. Eliza's diary had suggested that Constance was censoring the post that arrived at Ardmhor; Eliza had wondered if that was why Alex never responded to the letters she wrote to him. A letter written by Alex, which Beth and Angela had then found hidden in the library, confirmed Eliza's suspicions: Constance had indeed been intercepting the Ardmhor post. Alex's letter revealed he had eventually discovered the stolen letters hidden in a secret compartment in Constance's desk. So they'd always known that Constance had a preferred hiding place. It was just that neither of them had thought to look if it still existed.

Ardmhor House was such a large building that even with a section open to the public, a decent sized museum, and a private apartment within it, there were still unused areas. These sections were kept at a suitable temperature to prevent damage, but other than that, they had essentially become storage areas and dumping grounds. The rooms that Lady Constance had used were in one of these unloved sections of the house. It was only when Angela was having a clear out in the family apartment, cursing the amount of junk an old house accumulates, that something triggered a thought in her head, 'Is Constance's desk still in those rooms?' Then she'd thought, 'If it is, is it possible her secrets are still in that hidden drawer?'

Angela had immediately abandoned her tidying and rushed to the other wing of the house. In the same way that Beth had felt propelled by an unseen force to uncover the box in the attic, it felt to Angela as if there was a presence telling her feet exactly where to go as she moved through the neglected rooms. She had only needed to remove one dust sheet to locate a desk, which was certainly old enough to have been there during Constance's time. The next challenge had been to find out if there was a secret drawer. Discovering a mechanism which allowed a hidden section to spring out from the base of the desk turned out to be easy. Although Angela had spent enough time surrounded by antiques to have a few tricks up her sleeve, this was more than that. It was as if her fingers were being guided by someone else's knowledge. A few quick jiggles of the tiny lever and her reward was a small pile of letters. Not the ones written by Eliza. Alex's letter had stated he'd removed them to his room, and they had disappeared somewhere in the intervening years. This handful of letters were all addressed to Joseph and signed by Always. It was the information they had wanted, the details that could help them fill in the gaps and explain how Constance had gone from a woman motivated by love to a woman deliberately thwarting its plans. The second the letters were in her hand, Angela had rushed out of the house to show them to Beth.

◆ ◆ ◆

"Have you read the others yet?" asked Beth as she finished reading and put the first of the new finds down on the table.

"No, I only glanced through that one and checked the names on the others. I know it's a distant link, but both Joseph and Constance are your flesh and blood, and I would never have thought to search that desk if you hadn't told me about the other letters. So I decided you should read them first, although you have to promise to tell me everything and not take too long over it!"

"You don't need to worry about that. You'll be hearing all the details. I'm surprised how sad that letter has made me though. It's not like I didn't already know that Joseph died young. After all, that's the whole reason Eliza ended up living with the MacAirds. I suppose it's like with the diary. I already knew the overall outcome, but it felt different once I got to know the people involved. You know how when there's a terrible story in the news, you recognise it must be awful for the people involved, but you don't know them, so you shrug it off and move on? Eliza's diary started after Joseph's death, so I didn't get to know him through it. He'd stayed like a stranger in a newspaper. Now, he seems like someone I know, and it feels much sadder."

"What do you think about Joseph?" asked Angela. "Now you know a bit more about him, do you like him?"

"Good question," Beth replied, stopping to think. "I don't know entirely. On the one hand, it's good that he wanted to protect his daughter from any more upheaval. It's nice that he doesn't fit the stereotype of a Victorian widower, remarrying in a hurry so he won't be troubled by dealing with his own children. I like that Eliza must have been very important to him. But I'm not sure about the way he treated Constance. I can't decide whether he actually loved her."

"I know what you mean. Do you think he's telling the truth about not receiving the letter Constance wrote after the ball? You found it with the other letters she sent him, so do you think he might have had it all along?"

"No, I think he's telling the truth about that. Everything suggests he really loved Maude, so I don't think he'd tell a lie that would make her look bad. I wonder if he found the letter in Maude's possessions after her death. It must have been hard for him to know how to react when Constance revealed Maude had said she'd delivered it. He wouldn't have wanted to admit to Constance that Maude had lied, and he might have been angry about what Maude had done. It must be difficult finding out something uncomfortable about someone you love, especially when they are no longer around to explain."

"That's true," Angela replied. "I'm sure it would be. You'd have thought Maude would have just destroyed the letter."

Beth paused again, trying to work out how to explain her thoughts. "I've been thinking about that. Maybe Maude had always felt guilty. Perhaps she kept the letter as a reminder, so she wouldn't forget what she'd done. She might even have put the letter somewhere she knew Joseph would find it. Maybe when Maude realised she was dying, she wanted Joseph to have a second chance with Constance."

"It's possible, although I don't suppose we'll ever know. Pretending to have delivered the letter was a horrible thing to do, but I suppose Maude might have seen it as her only chance. Perhaps she'd always been in love with Joseph and really believed Constance could be equally happy as Lady MacAird."

"It's just a shame it didn't turn out that way. Not only was she unhappy with James, but it also seems as if Joseph never fully committed to her."

"I know," Angela began with a sigh. "This letter suggests they were meeting secretly for most of the time Joseph lived here. That's ten years. I can't decide whether that means he must have really loved her—as carrying on an affair for ten years must take a lot of effort—or whether it makes me think he saw her as easy prey, and he was just using her because she was so obviously available."

"That's roughly what I've been thinking, and if it is the latter, then he definitely didn't deserve Constance's love and loyalty."

"But maybe it was the first," Angela said hopefully. "Maybe he loved her as much as she loved him. Perhaps he was just more practical and couldn't see a way around the obstacle of her husband. After all, it was very different then. I know Constance was suggesting they could make up new names and start again, but it wouldn't have been that simple. How could Joseph continue in his profession with a false name? Or get a decent job with no references? I don't think Constance could have adapted to living in poverty, no matter how much she loved him."

"I sort of hope it was just the impossibility of the situation that stopped him. I'm feeling quite sorry for Constance."

"Me too," Angela agreed. "Which is funny because I really hated her after reading the diary. I still can't imagine treating my boys the way she treated Alex, but I feel like there is a lot more to her."

Angela lowered her voice then, even though she knew they were alone; Ali had taken Rory out for a walk soon after she'd arrived.

"Speaking of my boys, is Ali okay? He seemed a bit subdued when he opened the door—whereas Jay is suddenly full of the joys of spring."

"I think he's just tired, what with his trip and Rory still waking up a lot. Plus, Jay being back has taken a bit of getting used to."

"I hope they can get over whatever's causing the problem between them. They used to be so close when they were little, but after they went away to school, it changed. I'm with Constance about boarding school. I never wanted them to go, but even at that point, it was still seen as what the sons of Lord MacAird should do. Obviously, it was different for me, Jay and Ali were teenagers by the time they went, it was a lot easier for them to come home, and we could speak on the phone whenever we wanted, but I still wonder if it was a mistake, the teenage years are such a sensitive time."

Beth thought for a minute, not wanting to make Angela feel bad.

"From what Ali says, I think he enjoyed lots of it. He just feels like he always had to compete against his amazing older brother. He hasn't said this exactly, but I get the impression Jay might have teased him to get a laugh out of his friends. I think that's why he's paranoid about Jay being back. In small doses, they're great together, but Jay being here permanently makes Ali feel like everyone will gang up against him."

"It's funny you should say that, Beth, because Jim and I have always thought that Jay is jealous of Ali. Ali makes friends so easily and he's always full of ideas, whereas Jay finds those things harder. I don't suppose it helped that I gave him that ridiculous nickname as a baby and then it spread to everyone on the estate. Being a teenager known as Tiny, when your younger brother is good at everything, must have been hard; I can see it's possible that Jay took the opportunity of already being established in the school to settle the score a little. But he wouldn't be like that now. He's always singing Ali's praises. Do you think I should have a word with Ali? Maybe I could reassure him a bit."

"It's hard to know," was as far as Beth had got in her reply when the front door opened, and a horrendous wailing filled the hallway.

It soon became apparent that the noise was coming from Rory. His face was bright red, and his arms were flailing angrily. Beth was on her feet in an instant.

"What's happened?"

"Not a clue," said Ali, shaking his head. "He started screaming out of the blue about fifteen minutes ago, and he just won't stop. We were having a little wander about on the shore. He was happy as anything, then he just screamed. I've cuddled him, offered him food, offered him a drink, cuddled him some more, but nothing's worked. We were only next to the pier, so in the end I thought we'd just come back."

"Do you think something has stung him?" asked Angela. "That happened to you once when you were little, Ali. It took us ages to work out what had happened."

They attempted to look for sting marks, but it wasn't a simple task with the flailing arms, which had now been joined by kicking feet. In the end, they found no sign of anything, and gradually the wailing abated, replaced by the occasional sniffle instead. Angela made drinks for everyone, and the tiny piece of Claire's chocolate cake they put in front of Rory turned his mood around totally. Beth looked across at Ali. Angela was right, he did seem subdued. He wasn't himself at all, and she hadn't helped matters by going to see Andrew. The problem was, she didn't know how to get him back to his usual self. If only chocolate cake could work on Ali as well as it had on Rory.

As if reading Beth's mind, Angela said, "You seem a bit fed up, Ali. Maybe I could babysit Rory tonight and you and Beth could have a night off. Perhaps you could go out for something to eat. You hardly ever get to take your time over a meal."

Ali and Beth answered together, but they gave totally different replies.

"I think I'm a bit too tired," said Ali.

Whereas Beth replied with, "That'd be brilliant."

Angela decided to take Beth's answer and arranged to come back in a few hours.

CHAPTER TWENTY

Ardmhor, 1891

I am determined to keep my promise to Joseph: I will do all I can to make his daughter feel loved—I have to because that promise is all that's preventing me from falling back into the darkness. Knowing that Joseph is no longer in this world, realising that the chance for him to truly be mine is gone, is like a physical pain. It is a blow that hits me again and again, catching me off guard in quiet moments. The darkness is ever present. It beckons to me when I wake in the morning. It whispers in my ear as I go about the household business. I feel it tugging at my hand as I lie awake each night. Sometimes,

I notice myself slip a little. It is so tempting to give in, to just accept the warmth and the nothingness and move into that world. But then I remember my promise. I must bite down the bitterness and the anger, and I must smile. For I need to show Eliza that she is loved. I have to take my one chance to be a mother to Joseph's child.

It is so hard though. Every day Eliza becomes more like her mother. I try to remind myself how much I loved Maude, constantly recounting in my head the things that we did together. I recall how people referred to us as sisters. But all the time I have to remember not to mention any of this to Eliza. Joseph didn't want her reminded of what she had lost, and I have promised I will abide by his wishes. So instead of being bonded by a love of Maude, it seems she keeps us apart. If I think of the good times, I must censor my memories to keep my promise to Joseph. But if I don't remember those better days, I only see how Maude betrayed me. Each time I look upon Eliza, I see Maude looking back at me, lying about my letter while stealing all I'd ever wanted.

Our grief cannot unite us either. How could I explain the depth of the loss I feel while keeping up the pretence that her father was only an acquaintance, just an important member of staff? I am trying desperately hard to keep my promises, but I sometimes feel I am thwarted at every turn. Even before Eliza moved into Ardmhor House, she was already questioning whether it was the best course of action. I had warned Joseph that if he didn't discuss his plans with her, Eliza might find them difficult to accept. However, he would not listen. He did not want any talk of his death in front of her, even though its approach was painfully clear. Therefore, it fell to James to explain the situation and then to me to pick up the pieces. I tried so hard to make coming to live in the house sound like an adventure, but her response was to talk incessantly about returning to England; she was so certain her mother had relatives she could go to. Once again, Maude was interrupting the plans that Joseph and I had made. I kept trying to focus on my promise, but I could feel the blackness and the anger creeping closer. So despite all my efforts, I had snapped at her before she had even moved in. I had to remind her these were her father's wishes and that she should be grateful he had planned so well for her future. I suppose that establishing authority is part of a mother's role, but it is not how I wanted our new relationship to begin.

I decided Eliza should share Flora's bedroom, thinking that the company would help her feel settled. I spent hours finding the perfect furniture and linens to add to the room, wanting her to feel she truly belonged. On the day she moved in, I gave her time to get settled. I'd wanted to help her unpack, but I was wary of smothering her. Over the years we have known each other, she has resisted all my attempts at friendship, so I realised I had to proceed cautiously. I couldn't just blunder in like I always had with Joseph, or like I'd done with Maude when we first met—I have learnt some lessons. When I finally allowed myself to check on Eliza's progress, the first thing I saw on entering the room was Joseph and Maude's wedding portrait. The simple shock of seeing Joseph would have been enough to bring me to my knees, but it was seeing how happy he looked, and seeing Maude next to him with a smug smile on her lips, that really took away my composure. It was like I couldn't move. I was rooted to the spot, just staring at the image. After a while, I remembered myself, but I couldn't look at that picture any longer. I picked it up and placed it face down on the dresser, telling Eliza it did no good to dwell on the past. That was Joseph's instruction, after all. However, Eliza then looked so crestfallen and unsure that it was as if I'd already failed. Then I did blunder in. I heard myself telling her that perhaps she should call me mother. Then I realised how insensitive that might sound, so I quickly changed it to calling me Constance. However, then I remembered Joseph saying that Eliza would react better to a more formal footing between us, which meant Constance wouldn't be suitable at all. Flustered, I settled on Lady Constance, but the damage was already done. I could see Eliza's eyes rolling at my stupidity, wondering why she had to be lumbered with me instead of the parents she should have had.

This pattern has continued. I try to make Eliza feel loved and wanted as I promised Joseph I would. I try to treat her as I treat Flora, and sometimes it feels as if it is working. However, then I remember Joseph didn't want me to be her mother. That is something I decided on for myself, something that wasn't part of his wishes. When I remember that, I pull back, and I try to make our relationship more formal again. That's when she looks at me with Maude's eyes and I can see her disdain. When Maude stole my dreams, it seems she made sure I could not replace her in them.

However, I must keep trying. The only way I can keep Joseph with me is by trying to fulfil the promises I made to him. When Alexander returned to us in the summer, the tension seemed to diminish slightly. It was as if Eliza softened. She blossomed somehow, as if she was finally happy to be here. During Alexander's time at home, I hosted a party for him and Flora, hoping to find them suitable matches. The night of the party was strange: as I watched Flora and Eliza walking down the stairs, I couldn't help but see two other girls laughing as they made their way into a ballroom, their hands clasped together and their heads full of dreams. I shivered at the thought that one night could change so many futures. For all her bookishness, Eliza was more caught up in the moment than Flora. For the first time, I felt genuine affection for her—perhaps it was because finally she needed me. As she stood at the side of the room, looking at the dancing couples, wanting to join in but not knowing how, I felt something change. She looked so uncertain that my heart twisted with affection. For once, I wasn't trying to love her—instead I felt that I really did. It was wonderful to help her with something, and her gratitude made my heart soar. For that one night, as my children whirled around me with laughter on their lips, I felt happy. For once, the darkness was far away.

It hasn't remained that way. Since Alexander's return to England, we have fallen back into our old patterns. I am too affectionate, trying to recreate the feelings of the night of the party, but then I see Eliza's reaction and realise that nothing really changed: she doesn't want that relationship with me. Then I go to the other extreme. I try to make everything more formal again, which simply results in more disdain. I just cannot get the balance right. It's then that Maude's eyes return to mock me, telling me I could never hope to replace her, saying that I didn't manage it with Joseph, and I won't with Eliza either. However, I can't give up. I made my promises to Joseph, and I won't let him down. The night of the party showed me I can do this.

No matter how hard it is, I can love Eliza. I just need to keep trying.

CHAPTER TWENTY-ONE

Twice now Beth had taken the 'special occasion' bottle of prosecco from the back of the fridge, and twice she had replaced it. She shut the fridge door and leaned against it with a sigh, wondering if accepting Angela's offer to babysit had been such a good idea. The moment Angela left, Ali had rushed outside to cut the grass, claiming he couldn't miss the chance of a dry afternoon to get it done. It wasn't like him to let a disagreement fester. In the past their arguments had been done and dusted in minutes. This awkwardness and avoidance was new territory.

Beth felt pretty rubbish about her decision to call and see Andrew earlier. Despite knowing Ali would interpret it badly in his current mood, she'd done it anyway, almost as if she'd been deliberately trying to provoke a reaction. It had felt justified at the time. After all, Ali was being ridiculous, but now, thinking about her conversation with Angela, she knew Ali's mood wasn't about her. At the moment, he wasn't the Ali she had met five years ago. He was a teenage version, away from home for the first time and feeling like everyone was ganging up on him. Beth felt terrible for adding to that, no matter how unreasonable his behaviour had been. She knew she needed to help him snap out of it. He'd done enough cheerleading for her over the years. Now she needed to suck it up about the unfairness of the argument and start evening out the balance.

She reached the bottle of prosecco out for the third time, and this time she didn't put it back. It was a beautiful afternoon, and she could see Ali was just finishing raking up the grass cuttings. She grabbed a blanket from the arm of the settee and shoved it into Rory's basket of toys. Balancing the prosecco bottle and two glasses on top, she arranged Rory on one hip and secured the basket between her other hip and her free arm. Then she manoeuvred everything through the front door and walked around the side of the house to the garden. Depositing the blanket, Rory, and the basket of toys on the freshly mown grass, she picked up the prosecco and headed across to Ali.

"I thought you might need some refreshment," she said, unwrapping the foil from around the cork. "And I also thought you deserved to be cheered up. I'm sorry you've been feeling so rubbish recently, and I'm sorry I haven't been very sympathetic. You know I love you more than anything, don't you?"

"I do," he replied quietly, his voice thick with emotion. "And I'm sorry too. I know you wouldn't hurt me intentionally. I've been acting like a total fool."

"Maybe just a bit of one," said Beth, glancing up at him with a smile.

He studied her closely for a moment, the way he used to when they first met, the way that had made her feel they'd always been waiting for each other. Then he leaned in and kissed her. As he pulled away, Beth was relieved to see him smiling properly. For the first time in a while, he looked like her Ali again.

The afternoon ended so differently from how it had started. The sun carried on shining, Rory played happily on the grass and Beth and Ali lay on the rug, sipping fizz and reminiscing, remembering why they worked so well together. Angela was relieved as she watched them set off down the road that evening. They were hand in hand and smiling happily. She decided she'd been worrying about nothing as she headed inside to run Rory's bath.

Originally, when Angela had offered to babysit, Beth had wondered about booking a table at a restaurant in Inveravain, but in the end they'd both decided on the Ardmhor Hotel. It was easier to stay local as it meant there was no need to worry about taxis, and it was also the site of their first date. They hadn't said it to each other, but they both knew it would be good for them to remember how special that evening had been. It was on that night that Beth knew she had met the man for her. She was used to doubting herself when it came to romance. She had a track record of going off people as soon as it seemed a relationship was on the cards. Also, when she met Ali, she was still getting over Alex: Alex who it turned out had been resident in Ardmhor churchyard since 1895, was the same Alex she'd been reading about in Eliza's diary, and was actually her great-great-grandfather. The first time Beth saw Ali, she had mistaken him for Alex. Ali had been standing at the viewpoint, with the winter light rendering him no more than a silhouette. Beth had been so certain it was Alex that she'd launched herself at Ali without taking the time to look at him properly. So she'd had more reason than usual to doubt her judgment, but somehow, on that first official date with Ali, she was certain. She knew he was the one she'd been waiting for.

Really, she'd known it before that, she'd known it from the moment she'd disentangled herself from that initial mistaken hug. They had talked easily that first meeting, which had surprised Beth, given how embarrassingly their encounter had begun. Then, when he'd reached for her hand to walk her home, it was as though a lightning bolt had struck her.

The last thing Alex had said to her was that he knew there was someone waiting for her, and that when she met him, she would have no doubt. She'd had the sensation of Alex repeating those words when she first looked at Ali properly. Later, when Ali had briefly touched his mouth to hers, just as the first flakes of snow swirled around them, she'd heard them again. Alex's words had joined the delicate patterns of ice floating through the air. The soft whisper of his voice danced around her until it felt she was surrounded by his presence. "You will have no doubt," he was telling her, and, almost unbelievably for Beth, he was right.

They had gone on their first date the next night: a drink at the Ardmhor Hotel. That drink had turned into a meal, and then a few more drinks, and then a star-lit stroll, before moving on to a seemingly endless discussion cuddled up on one of the viewpoint benches—and it had cemented in Beth's mind that she and Ali belonged together. They had talked non-stop about anything and everything, jobs, families, childhoods, fears and dreams, and Beth had confided the full story of the time she'd spent with Alex. She hadn't known what reaction to expect, being ready for Ali to laugh in her face and make a rapid excuse to leave, but he hadn't. He'd sat there enthralled, encouraged her to continue, and accepted every word. The only thing she'd left out were Alex's last words to her. Instead, it was Ali who gave voice to what she'd been thinking.

"Perhaps we're meant to be the end to Alex and Eliza's story," he'd said. "Maybe he led you to me last night. Maybe that's why it feels so right to be together."

Then he'd kissed her, not a fleeting kiss like the previous night, but a kiss that seemed both to last for an eternity and be over too soon. A kiss like none she'd felt before. It was after that she'd told him of Alex's last words.

"He said there was someone for me, someone not that far away, and that when I met him, I would have no doubt. It's like he's been whispering those words to me since we met yesterday. I didn't believe him when he first said them, but I think I do now."

"You think you do?" Ali had replied, studying her face in a way so reminiscent of Alex, yet also entirely new.

"No, I know I do. I realise this probably sounds more ridiculous than the whole Alex story, seeing as I've only just met you, but I have no doubt it's you—you're the person I'm supposed to be with."

"Well, if you're ridiculous, I am too. I knew something special was happening the moment you threw yourself at me."

"Technically, I was throwing myself at Alex," Beth pointed out.

"As I said," Ali had replied. "He led you to me. Which means we're meant to be."

The date that had started out as a drink hadn't ended until late the next morning, when they'd woken up in Beth's room, wrapped in each other's arms. From that day on, they'd spent every free moment together. Their conviction that they were made for each other had never wavered, and they'd been just as in love at their wedding a few years later. It was only now, after Rory's birth, with extra responsibilities and much less sleep, that their bubble seemed to have burst. It felt as though their closeness had almost disappeared. That was why returning to the scene of that perfect first date seemed the right thing to do. Beth was intending to take a detour past the viewpoint on the way home as well. She desperately wanted them to recapture the magic they'd been lucky enough to take for granted.

◆ ◆ ◆

The unspoken plan seemed to be working. They'd both ordered lasagne and chips, exactly what they'd had on that first night out together, and they'd talked. Obviously, talking itself wasn't a big deal. They talked all the time, little snippets of chat about what they needed from the shops, who should clean the bathroom, or who was going to get Rory ready for bed. But it was a long time since they'd talked properly, or even since they'd managed a conversation that lasted for more than a few minutes.

"I really am sorry about earlier on, and I'm sorry about the other night as well," Ali said, after their plates were cleared. "It wasn't about you. I was already sensitive about Jay and then when I found out he'd been at ours and you hadn't mentioned it, I just felt really left out. It reminded me of starting boarding school and how horrible that time was. But I know it was a long time ago and that I need to get over it, so I'm sorry."

"Hey, you don't need to be sorry. You can't help how you feel."

"But that's not the only reason I was annoyed. Before you got back, Alan rang to see if you were home yet. He'd realised he was going to be passing ours and wondered if he could call to look at the extension plans you'd been discussing. I thought we'd agreed we were going to concentrate on the attic..."

"I was just wondering what it might cost," Beth interrupted. "It'd be so lovely to see the sea from the house."

"I know, but the point in doing the attic was to have enough bedrooms for another baby. You always said you wanted two close together. It was what we'd agreed on. The fact you weren't sure about doing the attic anymore seemed like confirmation you'd changed your mind, even though we'd not discussed it. I suppose it seemed like yet another thing you'd decided not to talk to me about."

"Actually, I was wondering if we could afford to do both, and it's not like another baby would need their own room straight away." Then she stopped, knowing she had to be honest. "And I suppose I'm not totally sure I want another baby, at least not now. I feel like I can barely cope as it is. I sort of hoped you might feel the same."

Ali sighed before answering. "I do if I'm telling the truth. I know we're both too tired to even consider another right now, but I didn't know if you felt that way. You always put on such a good show of coping, and I suppose that's part of what's been upsetting me. You say you love me, but you won't trust me with how you're feeling anymore. I know I'm being paranoid about everything, but it's felt as if you're yet another person who doesn't want to talk to me. Everyone else leaving me out, I might just about be able to handle, but I couldn't cope with that from you." He paused for a moment. "I saw you the other day. You were walking back from your mum and dad's house, and you'd stopped to talk to Andrew. He was saying something, and you were laughing. But it looked like proper laughter. You threw your head back and held onto his arm, and I thought to myself that it's ages since you've seemed that happy with me. Then, when you said you'd seen him today, especially without telling me, it stirred it all up again. I know nothing's going on, but I can't seem to control how angry and left out I feel."

"I'm sorry Ali. You know I'm rubbish when it comes to talking about my feelings. That's not something new, and it's not your fault. It's just how I am. But you don't need to worry about Andrew, or anyone else I might end up bumping into. I have to look happy when I'm chatting with someone; it'd be rude not to laugh at their jokes, wouldn't it? But things like that don't mean anything. I mean, you basically flirt with everyone you meet, but I don't imagine you prefer them all to me." She looked him in the eye and held his gaze. "Unless, of course, you do..." she added, trying to make him see how ridiculous he was being.

"Okay, point taken. I just feel so paranoid about everything, and I don't like it. I want things back to normal, with us having fun again."

Beth took hold of his hand. "I know, I do too.

Do you think it might help to talk to Jay? Maybe he doesn't even realise how much he hurt you when you started boarding school."

"Maybe. But I don't know how I'd bring it up, and I don't know whether it would help. If he didn't notice how upset I was, then I think that'll make me angrier. But if he did notice, that means he just didn't care, and he'll think I'm even more of a loser for still going on about it. I think I need another drink. Do you want one?"

The pub door opened as Ali was at the bar, and in walked Eilidh and Rich. Normally, Beth would have been thrilled to see them, but the timing couldn't have been worse.

"Fancy seeing you here!" Eilidh cried, seeing Ali at the bar and kissing his cheek. "It's like a MacAird family gathering because we also found this one in Inveravain just as we were leaving."

Beth looked at where Eilidh was gesturing, and her heart sank like a stone. It wasn't just Eilidh and Rich who'd walked in, Jay was coming through the door behind them.

"Ali!" Jay boomed, wrapping him in a bear hug. Beth suspected he'd had a few drinks already. "I'll get these. What are you having?"

It was then that Eilidh noticed Beth sat at the other side of the pub. "Oh, are you two on a date night? Do you want us to leave you alone?"

"Don't be silly," Ali responded politely, although Beth thought his reply was lacking enthusiasm. "Come and join us. There's plenty of room."

So Eilidh, Rich, and Jay pulled chairs up to their table. Then, to top things off, a few minutes later, Andrew arrived as well. Ali entertained them with stories of the terrible hotel he'd stayed in up in Shetland, and most people would have thought he was back to his usual self as life and soul of the party—although he was getting a run for his money from Eilidh and Jay. They were bouncing jokes and digs off each other in between trips outside for sneaky cigarettes. It was only Beth that noticed the sparkle was missing from Ali's eyes. In the end, she didn't suggest a detour to the viewpoint. Jay had said he'd walk home with them and then accompany Angela back to Ardmhor House, so it wouldn't have worked. And anyway, the moment had already been lost.

CHAPTER TWENTY-TWO

The sharp snap of breaking branches echoed from ahead. Beth looked up just in time to see a flash of white as a deer ran into the distance.

"Look Rory! Can you see the deer running?" she said, angling herself so that he could look in the right direction from his position in the carrier on her front. Rory showed no sign of being impressed. Instead, he made his displeasure at his transport slowing down quite clear, letting out a loud wail.

"Alright, grumpy," she said, kissing the top of his head and inhaling the unique scent of his hair as she moved again. "You don't have to scare away all the wildlife."

They were on their way to meet her parents

at Ardmhor House, and she'd come the back way through the woods, rather than taking the pushchair up the road as usual. It wasn't sunny like the previous day, but although it was dull and windy, the rain seemed to be keeping away. The woods were alive with bluebells, and the scent of wild garlic was carrying on the breeze. Beth opened a gate in the deer fence that surrounded the gardens of Ardmhor House, securing it shut behind them. The deer might be a majestic sight, but they could wreak havoc in a garden.

The path led round the side of the staff accommodation block, before finally reaching the formal lawn in front of the house. Beth could see her parents in the distance, admiring the view. She unfastened Rory from the carrier and placed his feet down on the ground, holding onto both of his hands. He had suddenly developed the strength and balance required to walk with someone supporting him. Although it had only taken one and a half days of this new skill for Beth to realise how back breaking giving that support could be, she was nevertheless keen to show off her son's amazing abilities to his grandparents. They were suitably impressed, greeting his display of talent with praise befitting a gold medallist. Both Jean and David rushed to take their turn leading him around the lawn, leaving Beth laughing as they playfully shoved each other out of the way.

It was as she was trying to find the best angle to capture a picture of the three of them that Beth noticed Eilidh appearing out of the woods. Her head was thrown back in laughter, making her look so radiant that Beth moved the camera to take a picture of her instead. But before she got the shot lined up, she realised Eilidh wasn't alone. Someone else was also emerging from the trees, laughing and reaching out to pull her into their arms. Beth's first reaction was to look away. She didn't want to be spying on Eilidh and Rich's private time. She'd done enough of that when they used to share the staff accommodation together. However, just as she was adjusting her gaze, she realised it wasn't Rich taking hold of Eilidh's hand after all—it was Jay. Now Beth's attention had really been grabbed. Her mind whirred into action, thinking about the joking and banter between Eilidh and Jay at the pub the night before. She'd been too preoccupied with Ali to pay it much attention, but now she thought about it, Rich had barely got a look in; and then there was all that disappearing outside for cigarettes that the pair of them kept doing. Beth told herself she was probably mistaken, but she couldn't help feeling something was amiss. It was Sunday, but even if it had been a workday, they didn't look like two colleagues in the middle of a project. No, something wasn't right. She watched them turn back into the woods, making their way onto the higher path, and was glad they didn't seem to have noticed her.

"Shall we have a bit of a walk before we take him to the playground?" David called to her from across the lawn.

"Yes, let's head up towards the ponds," Beth suggested. She didn't want to risk bumping into Eilidh and Jay in the woods.

"What have you done with Ali today?" queried Jean, as they meandered along by the stream which led to the ponds. "I thought all three of you were meeting us."

Beth had thought the same, so it had been a surprise to find a note from Ali on the bedside table when she woke up, saying he needed to sort something out at work. She knew sometimes in high season it was all hands on deck every day of the week, but it was only the start of June. It was highly unlikely there was an emergency requiring him to work on a Sunday when they'd already made plans. It seemed obvious to Beth that Ali was still making excuses to avoid her. However, she didn't want to admit that to her mum.

"Oh, something came up that he had to sort out in the office." It was safer to stick to the party line than invite lots of questions. "Angela found some more of Constance's letters yesterday," Beth added swiftly, making sure the conversation moved onto safer ground. "It turns out they'd been hidden in Constance's desk all along."

Half an hour later, Beth had filled Jean in on the latest letter, and David and Rory had exhausted the potential of lying on their bellies with their heads stuck out over the pond, watching insects skim the surface. Beth fastened Rory back into the carrier so he could save his energy for playing. They were nearly at the turning to the play areas when a flustered Eilidh rushed up behind them.

"Have you got a minute?" she asked, placing her hand on Beth's arm. "I really need to talk to you."

"You go ahead, girls," Jean said immediately, reaching to take Rory. "We'll head into the playground, and you can find a bench for a chat. We can always ring if we need you."

"I've been looking all over for you," Eilidh said as they sat down on a bench to the side of the play area, screened from view by a row of trees.

"Are you okay?" Beth asked tentatively. She sensed this had something to do with what she'd seen earlier, but she didn't want to jump in with both feet if she was mistaken.

"Yes, well, no. Actually, I'm not sure. You saw us earlier, didn't you? Jay said you weren't looking in our direction, but I was sure you were."

"You mean when you were coming out of the woods and Jay was holding your hand? Yes, I saw you."

"Right," Eilidh replied quietly, pulling her knees up towards her chest and wrapping her arms around her delicate frame. "And?"

"And what? I think you probably need to tell me what's going on rather than the other way round," Beth replied, looking at Eilidh closely.

The pink crop she'd sported when Beth first met her had long since been replaced by a blunt bob and fringe, which framed her elfin face perfectly. It had been every colour of the rainbow in the time Beth had known her and was now a glossy purple. It always amazed Beth that there was never a hint of regrowth or fade, it just seemed to transition from one perfect colour to the next. None of Eilidh's usual confidence was showing now though. Beth had never seen her so uncertain and her heart went out to her. If there was something going on between Jay and Eilidh, Beth was in no position to judge. Until she'd met Ali, she hadn't been in a serious relationship, and she also hadn't thought twice about seeing two people at the same time. She'd been the other woman at least once as well, without giving a second thought to who might get hurt. At the time, she'd reasoned that it wasn't her problem —if someone wasn't concerned about being faithful, it probably just meant they weren't in a serious relationship. Now that she'd actually experienced love, her views had changed somewhat. Also, the fact she really liked Rich made this more awkward. However, she knew she couldn't afford to be on her high horse. Plus, Eilidh looked wretched, and Beth didn't want to make her feel worse.

"Of course, you don't have to tell me anything if you don't want to," she added after a minute.

"I think I need to, Beth," was Eilidh's reply. "Nothing's happened. We've not even had a proper kiss. I just really, really, like him. I want to be around him all the time, and he seems to feel the same. But then I think about Rich. We've been together so long, and I always thought we were totally solid. Basically, I don't know what to think, or what to do."

"How long has this been going on?"

"Not long. I mean, obviously it's not been long, he hasn't been here long. Although I think I realised I liked him more than I should almost as soon as he got here. When I asked him to yours that night, I was already really attracted to him."

"Do you think that's why you've been getting so annoyed with Rich?"

"Probably. I was stressing out over the wedding anyway, but the two things have coincided. That's why I've been trying to put more effort in with Rich. I want to make things work. I want to want him. But I can't stop thinking about Jay."

"You could have trusted me with this

yesterday, you know?"

"I know, but you're Rich's friend as well, and I didn't want to make things difficult for you."

"But I was your friend first," Beth replied, "and whatever happens with this, I'll still be your friend."

Eilidh unravelled herself a little and sighed. "Thanks, Beth. I sort of thought it wasn't worth mentioning either. Jay's a pretty flirty person, in the same way Ali is really, and Big Jim when you think about it. It's just the way they are, so I didn't think he felt the same. It was only last night, when we went outside for a smoke, that I realised he was being serious when he makes his daft comments."

"I noticed you disappearing, but I didn't really register it. It's not like it's unusual for you to forget you don't smoke when you've had a few drinks. So what happened? Is that why you've been skulking around the woods today?"

Eilidh shuddered. "Ugh, it sounds awful when you put it like that, but I suppose it is awful, really. We've been teasing each other a lot. I've been bantering about how he thinks he's God's gift and can't help himself when it comes to flirting. He's been saying it's only because I'm so amazing. But it was all just talk. I mean, maybe we both knew we were being serious, but we weren't going to admit it. Anyway, while we were outside last night, I'd made some silly comment and he'd given some daft reply about me being too gorgeous to resist. Basically, nothing different from any other time we've talked, but then suddenly he got serious. He sort of cupped my face in his hands and he just stared at me. I've been with Rich forever, so it's not like I'm always in that type of situation, but I knew he was about to kiss me, and I was so tempted, but then I caught the sound of Rich's voice drifting out from the pub and it brought me back to reality, so I pulled away and rushed back in. Then a minute later, you and Ali said you were leaving, and Jay said he'd go with you."

"So how come you were both here today, then?"

"Well, this morning there was a text from Jay saying he really needed to talk to me and could I tell Rich I needed to sort something at work so we could meet up."

It looked like both of the MacAird brothers had been using the work excuse that morning, Beth thought to herself.

"And you agreed," she began cautiously, "so does that mean you've decided you want something to happen?"

"No, because I know that'd really hurt Rich. But at the same time, I can't stop thinking about Jay and imagining what it'd be like. But I know I can't go there because it'd destroy everything. I wish I could magically make everything go back to normal, you know, when Rich was the only person I wanted."

"God, it's hard, isn't it? I know what you mean about wanting things back to normal. Me and Ali were always so loved up, but everything feels sort of broken now."

"But you're alright, aren't you? You and Ali are like ultimate couple goals. If you two can't sort things out, no one can."

"I'm not sure whether that's reassuring or not," Beth replied with a sigh.

"Sorry Beth, I know things aren't easy for you right now and I'm making this all about me, but seriously though, what would you do? I'm not going to take things further, but should I tell Rich what's happened? Would you tell Ali?"

"What? Would I say to Ali, 'sorry darling, I've developed strong feelings for your brother, and we haven't taken it any further, but we've been running round the woods together holding hands'? Of course I wouldn't say that! He'd be gutted, and I'd only be telling him to get rid of my guilt. Nothing's happened, so why cause all that hurt?"

"I don't know. I just feel awful keeping it from him."

"Yeah, but would you feel any better once you'd told him? Or would it just mean that you'd both end up feeling awful?"

❖ ❖ ❖

The problem was, they hadn't been as alone as they'd thought during the latter part of their discussion. Regretting his early disappearance from the house, Ali had been to the playground to look for them, wanting to fulfil their original plans after all. He'd found Jean and David pushing Rory on the baby swings.

"Beth's just over there with Eilidh," Jean had told him. "Why don't you go and surprise her? She seemed a bit disappointed you'd had to work."

So Ali had set off in the direction they'd indicated, tiptoeing through the trees and hoping Beth would be pleasantly surprised; he knew he needed to make things up to her. Unfortunately, the surprise had been his, and it hadn't been a good one. As he'd got close enough to pick out their voices, he'd heard his wife clearly state that she had feelings for his brother and that those feelings were reciprocated. It didn't matter that she'd also said nothing had really happened. The feelings were enough. He'd known Jay would ruin whatever he had, but he couldn't process that Beth had fallen for it. The only reason he'd been worried about her and Andrew was because he knew how hard she'd been finding things, and because he knew he hadn't exactly been helping. But he'd never thought she would have genuine feelings for someone else. He'd always believed they were literally made for each other, that they were meant to be. Jay doing whatever he wanted didn't surprise him. Ali expected that, but he couldn't take in the idea that Beth was part of it as well. He didn't reveal himself or listen any further, instead he hurried the other way through the trees. He couldn't face seeing Jean and David again, and he certainly couldn't face Beth after what he'd heard.

LETTER SIX

January 1893

Dear Joseph,

I do not know why I am writing this letter to you. There's no decision to be made now about whether to send it. You are gone and you can't respond to me. However, I still feel the need to write the words down, as if by doing so, they will somehow reach you. I have tried Joseph. I have tried so hard to make Eliza feel welcome, but I must admit I have failed.

I discovered the other day that Eliza is planning to leave us. I read a letter to her from your old business partner, Mr Hardwick. He was offering her a home with his family and a position within his firm. He could only have been suggesting this in response to an enquiry from her, so I know she has been looking for ways to leave Ardmhor. You may think I shouldn't have been opening post addressed to Eliza, but she is so private and guarded that I never know what she is thinking or feeling. I knew Mr Hardwick sent her birthday and Christmas greetings, but she had never mentioned a fuller correspondence between them, so when I saw his name on the back of the envelope, I couldn't resist looking at the contents. I wondered what reason he could have for writing so soon after his usual Christmas note, and I knew I would get no answers from Eliza. She has been so secretive recently, always rushing off and disappearing, finding any excuse to avoid my company. Now I know why. She hates me so much that without Flora here, she can no longer bear to stay.

I had been worried about the effect Flora's marriage would have on Eliza's happiness here. I must admit, Joseph, that I am angry with you about this. You were so insistent that Eliza's move into our household had to be formalised by her playing the role of companion to Flora, but Flora was always going to leave one day—what did you think was going to happen at that point? Why didn't it occur to you that Eliza would question whether she still belonged with us? If you had listened to me and discussed your plans for Eliza's future with her, perhaps she would have understood that she was welcome in our home as an equal, as another member of our family.

I understand why you thought you were acting in Eliza's best interests. Despite all my efforts, anyone could see that Eliza still regarded me with disdain at the time of your passing. I can see why you thought she would be insulted by me trying to become a sort of mother figure. Following that line of thought, it seems logical that she would have found a formal role in our home more palatable, but I still think it didn't have to be that way. If you'd given up on this ridiculous notion of never talking about Maude, Eliza could have been told of the friendship we had shared. Perhaps then she would have seen me in a different light. If you'd been willing to explain to Eliza that I had been your close childhood friend, she might have been able to see why I was so keen to care for her. But perhaps any acknowledgment of our childhood connection brought you too close to the uncomfortable truth of our later illicit one. Whatever your reasons, I think you were wrong, and it has led us to this point. Your failure to trust me cost us our dreams many years ago, and now it has made it impossible for me to fulfil my promise.

I think I was so angry when I read Mr Hardwick's letter and realised that Eliza was making plans to leave because I wasn't expecting it. I was almost becoming complacent about our relationship. It seemed we had grown so much closer. When she first moved in here, we had our struggles, we both found the change difficult.

However, as time has passed, we've shared some lovely moments. On her last birthday, I even gave Eliza the cameo brooch which my mother had given to me. That brooch is so special. You know how distant my mother could be, so when she gave me that cameo, with its image of a mother tenderly reaching towards her child, it was the most wonderful gift I'd ever received. Then I treasured it even more when you told me how well it suited me. You said the tawny colour of its background brought out the golden flecks in my eyes. No one else has ever commented on that gold. It's always made me think of you, so it seemed appropriate to give it to Eliza, and Flora has no shortage of my treasures. I knew I could never expect to enjoy the same relationship with Eliza as I do with Flora, but I had hoped we had become close enough to weather Flora's departure. By giving her something that was special to me, I hoped it would symbolise a connection between us.

Such was my complacency about our growing closeness that I was worrying about the wrong things, and I missed the problem that was right in front of me. I had been concerned that Eliza was becoming too close to Alexander. You saw for yourself how well the two of them got on. Once upon a time, I used to worry about Eliza taking Alexander away from me. I saw Eliza as the reason that I couldn't be with you and thought that one day she would take my precious son as well. As time has passed though, I've had to accept the inevitability of losing Alexander one day. I want him to have the sort of happiness I used to dream of sharing with you, and I realise that for that to happen, he must love someone else more than he loves me. So I wouldn't be against Eliza and Alexander falling in love. If they were to marry, I could keep them both here. It could be a wonderful solution.

My fear over Alexander and Eliza was now only that he wasn't the right choice of man for her. Eliza is so strong, forthright, and determined. I have always had my dreams, but I have brought none of them to fruition. Eliza is different. She studies, she learns, and she plans. She has your intelligence and Maude's tenacity. I know you don't like to be reminded of this, but I learnt the true extent of Maude's determination too late and to my detriment. However, Alexander is not like Eliza at all. You once said to me that you didn't believe I would have left James because you didn't think I could stand to be parted from Alexander. To an extent, you were right. I would have found it incredibly difficult to bear, but I would have done it because I've always believed the bond between Alexander and me would be strong enough to survive. As well as being gentle, kind, and caring, Alexander is a dreamer, like me. He inherited his father's intelligence. His plans for the development of the estate are quite exceptional. However, he did not inherit his father's confidence. He does not hold himself in high regard, and that tends to make him weak. I fear that Eliza could not be satisfied by a life with Alexander. Although he is a most wonderful man, he is not one to lead or take control. Eliza yearns for adventure, whereas Alexander has only ever wanted to be here. I worried that a relationship between them was doomed to fail, and I feared that the resulting distress might drive one, or even both, of them away. I was so preoccupied with that idea that I failed to see what was happening. Eliza was already planning to leave all of us behind.

My shock that her plans were already underway, that I had already failed you, meant that I reacted badly. I feel quite ashamed to write about how I behaved, but I somehow feel that I must. Who knows how our Lord's plans for the next life work? Perhaps you already know all I have done. I only hope that if that is the case, you can also see that my actions were from a place of fear. I hope you can understand that I was afraid I had let you down. The moment I read the letter, I stormed to the library. I knew I would find Eliza there. It is her favourite place to spend a spare moment. I don't know if I have ever displayed rage as openly as I did at that moment. It is almost surprising that Eliza comprehended what I was referring to, so hysterical was my behaviour. I shouted, I screamed, and I ranted at her: telling her she was ungrateful and that no matter how much love I showed her, she did not care. I said many hurtful things without even registering her reaction. Then suddenly, I saw she was afraid.

I handed the letter to her in the hope it would explain my behaviour, and I sat down to regain my composure. In order to explain my hurt more rationally, I tried to take myself out of that moment. I imagined myself away from the library, up in our spot on the hills. I tried to picture you holding my hand, giving me strength. But then James and Alexander rushed into the room. Seeing James walk in when I had been picturing you, knowing it will never be you, destroyed any composure I had regained. All I could do was sob that Eliza didn't love me or care for me. James sent her from the room before she had a chance to speak, but he didn't listen to me either. He ushered me to my bedchamber as soon as he was able. The display I had put on embarrassed him; I am embarrassed myself, and I think I have distressed Alexander. His expression was unreadable as he watched me being led from the room. How Eliza must view me now is something I don't want to think about. I haven't yet summoned up the courage to leave my room, and I really don't know how I will ever face her again.

I want you to know all this because I really have tried. Foolishly, I had thought my love was strong enough to do the impossible. I'd thought that I could finally win Eliza over. However, I was wrong. Simply loving someone isn't enough. It can't change reality. I just wish I hadn't learnt this so late, when I'd already made a promise to you that I couldn't keep.

All my love,

Always

CHAPTER TWENTY-THREE

While Rory had his afternoon nap, Beth had taken the chance to read through the next of Constance's letters. Rory's efforts with walking, and the fun of the play area, had worn him out, so he'd fallen asleep almost as soon as he'd finished his lunch. There was still no sign of Ali, Jean and David had mentioned seeing him at the playground, but he'd not arrived with Beth and he hadn't answered her calls either, so she assumed the work emergency had been real after all and that he'd been called back. With no one else around Beth had poured herself a mug of hot water, put the last slice of Claire's chocolate cake on a plate, and settled down to find out more about Constance. Reading these later letters had been a different experience to reading the others because they covered events she already knew about. The other letters had been written earlier, by a Constance Beth had no previous knowledge of, but these overlapped with the time of Eliza's diary.

Beth's heart had raced when she'd realised she was reading Constance's version of the library showdown. Beth had read Eliza's account of that day many times now. She knew off by heart that Constance had been so overwrought Eliza had struggled to understand her at first. Then, she'd calmed down to the point where she'd seemed cold and distant, before finally turning on the waterworks again when James and Alex appeared. Beth was interested to see that Constance didn't contradict Eliza's account at all. However, her explanations of the motives behind events were very different. When she'd read the diary, Beth had been unable to see the event from any perspective other than Eliza's. She'd been convinced, as Eliza was, that Constance's sudden coldness, after her initial outpouring of emotion, showed a level of control. It was at that point in the diary that Beth had decided Constance was conspiring against Eliza, rather than just being volatile. That Constance was picturing Joseph, trying to summon his love to support her, was not something Beth or Eliza could have known. Instead, Beth had been certain that Constance was trying to cast Eliza in a bad light when she'd dissolved into tears at the sight of Alex and James. She couldn't have comprehended that it was the return to reality, the confirmation of the loss of Joseph, which had made her cry.

Beth had to admit she'd also only seen Alex's reaction, or lack of it, from Eliza's point of view. She'd interpreted it as another sign of his weaker character. She had never really considered how it might have felt for him to witness this level of conflict between two people he loved. When her ideas of Constance and Alex had been solely based on Eliza's diary, it had been easy to dismiss any thoughts of actual affection between mother and son. She'd never thought about how torn Alex must have felt.

However, even with this greater understanding of Constance, it was still hard to see any justification for her final actions towards Alex and Eliza. Beth wasn't sure anything could excuse the deliberate lies Constance had told to separate them.

After finishing reading, Beth sat quietly, thinking about the difficulties caused by a lack of communication. If Joseph and Constance had actually talked to each other all those years ago, instead of relying on Maude delivering a letter, their story could have been very different. If Joseph had been more open with Eliza about her mother and their connection to Constance, perhaps Eliza would have viewed Constance in a more positive light. If Eliza and Alex had confided in Constance, perhaps she could have voiced her fears to them, and they could have persuaded her they were unfounded.

However, she recognised she was hardly in a position to judge. She couldn't really claim that she and Ali were excelling at communication. She was currently wondering how long a crisis at work could last for. He'd been gone since some time before half seven, and it was now almost three. She'd sent a couple of texts saying she hoped everything was alright, but she had heard nothing in reply. It was disappointing. Until Eilidh and the others had arrived at the pub the previous night, it had felt like they were really getting somewhere. Now, however, it seemed as if they were back at square one.

Beth was also feeling uncomfortable about Eilidh's revelations, and not just because she was also friends with Rich. As this involved Jay, she really wanted to tell Ali, but she'd promised Eilidh she wouldn't breathe a word to anyone. Now she felt caught in the middle. She didn't want to betray her friend's confidence, but she definitely didn't want Ali to feel she was keeping something else from him. No matter how long she thought about it, there didn't seem to be a solution. Telling Ali that his brother was currently ruining Eilidh and Rich's relationship was hardly going to help heal the rift between them, and Eilidh had said nothing else was going to happen between her and Jay. Therefore, Beth decided it was probably a situation where 'least said, soonest mended' should be applied.

She heard Rory stirring through the baby monitor and glanced at the clock—half past three. As she stood up to get him from his cot, her phone buzzed with a text. Finally, she thought as she pulled the phone from her pocket, some clue as to what's going on with Ali. But she was disappointed. It was a text from Andrew instead, asking if they could meet up later in the week. He'd finished adding the pictures to her advertising blurb and wanted a second opinion before committing to printing. She started typing a reply saying that was fine, but then thought better of it and put the phone back in her pocket. It would be better to discuss it with Ali first. She didn't know whether his disappearing act was really a work crisis or not, but she knew she didn't want to make things between them any worse.

It wasn't until much later, when Rory was having his nightly bath, that Ali came home. He appeared in the bathroom doorway, causing such a cacophony of splashes and squeals from Rory that Beth couldn't hear his opening words. Rory was determinedly grabbing at the bath handles, trying to pull himself up to get to his father. He wasn't quite capable of pulling himself to standing yet, but he thrust himself forward instead, face planting into the water before Beth could stop his fall. The resulting plunge left Rory crying in shock and Beth soaked from pulling him out. Ali quickly wrapped Rory in a towel, whispering soothing words in his ear as he took him from the room, and left Beth to sort out her wet clothes. It was well over an hour later by the time Rory had calmed down, had his bedtime feed, and finally drifted off to sleep.

Beth found Ali downstairs watching a wildlife documentary. Sitting in Rory's darkened room had left her tired, and the temptation to just grab herself a drink and head up to bed was strong. However, she knew she couldn't leave things to fester. They needed to sort out whatever was going on, before it led them down a path they didn't want to follow.

"Did you get everything sorted at work?" she asked, sitting down next to him.

"Yes," was all she got in reply. Ali didn't even move his eyes from the screen.

"What was the problem? I didn't expect you to be gone so long," she persisted.

"I didn't either," he said, still not moving his gaze from the documentary. "Do you mind if I finish watching this?"

"No," she said, realising she was getting nowhere. Then she remembered that she'd wanted to check with him about meeting Andrew. "Actually, there was something I wanted to speak to you about."

Ali sighed and pressed pause, turning his head slightly to look at her. "Andrew sent me a text asking if we could meet up on Wednesday to finalise his leaflets before he gets them printed. I thought I'd say I could meet him for lunch at the pier. Is that alright with you?"

"Fine. It's not like you've got feelings for him, is it?"

It wasn't what Beth had been expecting to hear, and she looked at him, confused. "Of course I haven't. I was only mentioning it because you said you'd felt as if people were keeping things from you."

"Well, it's good to know I can rely on you to tell me everything."

Beth tried to get him to meet her gaze, but he'd turned back to face the screen, determined not to make eye contact.

"What's going on?" she asked in frustration.

"Nothing. It's been a long day, and I'm tired, that's all. So, do you mind if I finish watching this now?"

"No," she replied again, although she most certainly did mind. It was frustrating to feel as though she was being punished for something when she had no idea what she was supposed to have done. Did he know about Jay and

Eilidh? Was he annoyed at her for keeping quiet? Various possibilities ran through her mind, but she could see there was no point in forcing a discussion now. They were both too tired for it to go well. Unfortunately, she also knew that no matter how tired she was, the day's events would be keeping her awake for hours.

CHAPTER TWENTY-FOUR

Ardmhor, 1893

Ever since the awful day when I read Eliza's letter and behaved so terribly, I haven't been able to relax around her. I have checked the post frequently, examining both the letters being sent out and those that arrive. It is not something I am proud of, and it is not how I expected I would behave, but I don't know if it is a habit I will ever be able to break. Through my vigilance, I have discovered that Eliza has replied to Mr Hardwick, asking if she would really be welcome to live with his family. I also learnt that he has responded positively to her enquiries. There is nothing to prevent her from leaving us now.

I so wanted to succeed at being a mother to Eliza. I know Joseph didn't necessarily want that, but he wanted her to feel secure and loved. He would never entertain the idea of anyone replacing Maude, and I had come to terms with the fact that he would not marry again; while it meant that we couldn't enjoy the life I dreamed of, it also meant I would never have to watch him with another woman. However, he also wouldn't entertain any criticism of Maude, and I found that much harder to accept. Even during our precious moments alone together, it would bother me that he viewed her as some sort of saint. Did he truly not see that it was her actions which had separated us all those years ago? Or maybe it was knowing that which made it impossible for him to talk about her? Perhaps reconciling the different sides of his beloved wife was beyond him, so she had to stay frozen in the past—never to be spoken of, but somehow always there. I cannot know Joseph's reasoning, but I know why I wanted to be a mother to Eliza. I wanted it for myself. My children have been the joy of my life. I might not have achieved closeness with my firstborn, but I have devoted myself to my relationships with Alexander and Flora. Before I married James, my dream was to live in a chaotic house filled with Joseph's children. Becoming a mother to Eliza was the nearest I could get to fulfilling that dream. It saddens me greatly to know I have failed.

I feel as if I am being pulled apart by worry. I spend hours thinking over every interaction I have with Eliza, trying to decide if I have said the right thing or behaved in the correct way. It is exhausting. Yet I cannot seem to leave her alone. Constantly I question her. Is she bored with my company? Does she want to be by herself? Why does she need to write to Flora so often? I want to ask her about her relationship with Alexander. I see them sneaking off together, and I am familiar with the actions of couples trying to hide their feelings. However, those questions I dare not ask because I am afraid of the answers. Eliza cannot intend for Alexander to leave here with her. She is a very shrewd girl, and it is obvious to anyone that Alexander belongs at Ardmhor. But if she is planning to leave without him, he will be heartbroken. Everything scares me. Everything is a sign I am going to lose one of them. So I overreact about silly things, and in doing so I push them further away.

This afternoon, Eliza offered to brush my hair. The gesture touched me, as I know it is not something she enjoys. When Flora was still here, we often used to while away the time, brushing and plaiting each other's hair. Eliza wouldn't join in, but she would sit quietly reading and watching, occasionally contributing to the chatter. I loved the intimacy of those moments, the soothing effect of the brush gliding through hair and the quiet words spoken in our little sanctuary. As Eliza picked up the brush today, I watched her reflection in the looking glass. Her face in concentration was so like Maude's. It transported me back to my youth, to all the times we had sat together, trying out the latest styles we'd seen on visits to London. For once, I remembered the joy we had brought each other rather than the betrayal. I watched Eliza's hands as she gently teased out a tangle and told her about my life before meeting James. It was a subject I had always wanted to broach but had previously avoided; I was fearful of ignoring Joseph's wishes and revealing our shared past. I was careful not to say too much, but I was soon carried away in memories of games by the stream, village fetes, and longed for summer balls. Eliza seemed enthralled. Her eyes were bright as she looked at me in the mirror, but as she asked questions, obviously trying to bring my descriptions into focus, I realised I could not answer her. I could not tell her more without betraying my promise to Joseph, and I will never betray him. That brought me back to reality. I remembered then that, no matter how interested Eliza suddenly seemed, she did not really want to know about me. After all, she had already made her plans to leave.

Tonight, at dinner, I suggested Eliza should move into one of the servant rooms. I honestly thought she might prefer it. She obviously does not consider herself part of our family, and my erratic behaviour must be difficult for her to live with. I thought the separation might make her see that she is her own person, free to leave if she wants, and that she doesn't need to keep her plans hidden. However, all I seem to have achieved is a greater rift. I suppose it was an ill-considered plan, yet another mistake of my unsettled mind. James said that the dinner table was not the time or place for such discussions. He said that under no circumstances could he treat Joseph's child in the same way as a member of staff. That James thought I needed reminding of Joseph's importance was almost laughable. If only he knew that a moment without thought of Joseph is not something I can imagine. Alexander said nothing, and his expression was unreadable. He must find it so hard to see the tension between Eliza and me. But how can I explain my fears to him when I am not supposed to know about their relationship?

My love for Joseph and my love for my children have been the only constants in my life. I thought that a combination of those loves would be all I needed to keep my promises to him. I feel that love so fiercely that I did not think it was possible for me to fail, but I have made such a mess of everything. Joseph is already gone. I know I have lost Eliza, and now I fear I am losing Alexander as well. I can feel the darkness coming for me again, and I can't see a way to make things right.

CHAPTER TWENTY-FIVE

Almost a week had gone by since Ali disappeared for the day, and Beth was no closer to getting any answers from him. She'd taken Rory to playgroup with her mum, she'd led a couple of school sessions in the museum, and she'd met Andrew for lunch. It had been a busy week, but she'd still spent plenty of time at home. Whereas Ali seemed to be avoiding the place. He was either at work or needing to meet someone. It was as if he couldn't bear to be around her.

On Thursday evening, Beth heard the front door open and Ali's footsteps on the stairs. She'd just cleared away Rory's tea, and he was crawling around on the floor, occasionally trying to pull himself up against the furniture. The footsteps made their way back down the stairs and Beth heard a jacket being pulled from the coat hooks. She was determined Ali wasn't escaping again. Regardless of anything else, Rory wasn't her responsibility alone. She rushed out into the hallway before he'd had time to reach the door.

"I thought you might want to put Rory to bed," she said, standing in his path.

"I can't. I said I'd meet Luke in Inveravain tonight."

"Wasn't it Luke you met on Tuesday?"

"No, that was Matt."

"Oh right, I assumed you were seeing both of them the other night. You usually see your primary school friends at the same time."

"I suppose I do," he said, moving to step round her. "Anyway, I'll be late if I don't get going soon."

"Ali, wait. What's going on? You've been out every night since Sunday. Rory's missing you, and so am I."

"I didn't think you'd have noticed, to be honest."

"What's that supposed to mean? What's wrong?"

"Nothing's wrong," Ali replied calmly. "Apparently, it's not even worth mentioning."

"I don't understand. Can you just tell me what's going on?" Beth asked, holding onto his sleeve, worried he'd leave before they sorted this out.

"As I said, apparently, it's nothing that matters. I thought we were supposed to be telling each other everything, but obviously some things just aren't that important."

"I still don't understand what you mean. I told you about meeting Andrew for lunch."

"I'm not talking about Andrew. I couldn't care less about that. It's Jay I'm talking about," Ali replied, anger clear in his voice now.

"Oh, so you know about that," said Beth, wishing she'd mentioned it after all. "Who told you? Jay or Eilidh?"

"What? It doesn't matter how I know. What matters is that you didn't tell me. You knew how much I was struggling with Jay being back, yet not only did you get drawn into his web, you kept it hidden from me as well. You discussed it with other people, but you kept it from me. It's like all my nightmares coming true. Maybe I expected too much of you. No one has ever been able to resist the pull of Jay, but it hurts even more than I'd imagined. It makes me feel like I'm nothing to you."

There was a catch in his voice that brought a lump to Beth's throat.

"I'm so sorry," she whispered. "I wanted to tell you, but I'd promised I wouldn't say anything."

"I should come before promises to anyone else, Beth." A tear slowly trickled down his cheek.

"I can't talk about this now."

Beth clutched his arm tighter. "I didn't think it mattered that much. Nothing really happened, and it's over now. I just thought telling you would make things even worse between you and Jay."

"Well, you were right about that," Ali said with a bitter laugh, snatching his arm from her hand and slamming the door behind him.

Rory crawled over to her and looked up, bemused by the raised voices and the noise of the door. Beth was just as confused. She'd realised Ali would be annoyed if he heard about Jay and Eilidh and found out she'd kept it from him, but she hadn't expected him to be so upset. Ali wasn't afraid to show emotions. Beth had always loved that he didn't subscribe to outdated ideas like men never crying, but at the same time, tears were rare for him. His laid-back nature just meant they weren't needed. His reaction seemed out of proportion with what had actually happened between Eilidh and Jay. Beth supposed it was more the fact that she hadn't told him, even after they'd discussed how important that was. It had been difficult to decide what to do with Eilidh's secret, and clearly, she'd decided wrong. She could see that now. What she couldn't see was a way to make things right.

◆ ◆ ◆

As she moved around the house the next morning, trying to tidy up and keep an eye on where Rory was, Beth felt drained. It had taken her a long time to fall asleep the previous night. Then at some point, the weight of Ali climbing into bed had woken her. She'd been relieved to know he was home, but the disturbance had set her mind whirring again. Ali's breathing had quickly changed to the gentle snores of someone who's had a few drinks, but unfortunately, Beth couldn't switch off so easily. The depth of her lethargy would have made it easy to believe she'd remained awake all night; however, she knew that couldn't be true because when morning had arrived, the other side of the bed was cold and empty. Ali had vanished again in the brief moments when sleep had claimed her.

Beth realised she'd sat down without noticing. She could feel her eyelids drooping. Rory, however, was full of energy, crawling around the floor and trying to pull himself up against the settee.

"Come on," she said to him, getting to her feet, shoving snacks into his changing bag, and gathering their jackets in case the weather changed. "We need to get out of here."

◆ ◆ ◆

Just half an hour later, she was sitting in the sunny living room of her parents' house with a mug of hot chocolate in her hand. The front of the room was all glass, from the floor right up to the pitch of the roof. Outside, clouds were blowing briskly across the sky and the waves were tipped with white. Although the interior of the house was now very different to how it had looked during Beth's childhood holidays, there was still a special feeling whenever she walked through the door, as if the excitement of all the people who'd holidayed there over the years had somehow seeped into the fabric of the building. From the hallway, old ladder stairs led up to two bedrooms with sloping ceilings. Beth could still hear her dad swearing as he hit his head on the roof getting out of bed, something he'd managed almost every morning they'd stayed there. They'd added a new bedroom and bathroom downstairs before they moved in, along with the extension they were sitting in now, so thankfully the bumped heads were consigned to the past. But despite all the building work they'd had done, the house still had a unique scent that hadn't changed. Usually, no matter how fed-up Beth felt, time spent here lifted her mood. But it didn't seem to be working today. She watched listlessly as Rory chomped on a biscuit, covering himself in crumbs.

"I think us boys are going to spend a bit of time with the train track," David announced after a while.

"Maybe us two should go for a bit of a wander then, Beth?" Jean suggested. "You look as if you need waking up."

Beth felt as if a quick nap on the squashy settee was what she really needed, but as Jean was already pulling her to her feet, she realised it would be easier to give in.

"Which way then?" Jean asked as they reached the end of the drive.

"I've been meaning to look for the hidden steps that Constance wrote about in one of her letters. You know the ones she talks about when she mentions a secret shore? Angela thinks there are some old steps near the side of the river bridge. We could look for them?"

"Okay, but surely the bridge over the river is much more recent than Constance's time?"

"Yeah, I think there was an older bridge before they improved the road, and the steps were connected to that. Apparently, they're still there, but they're overgrown because they don't really lead anywhere now."

"That sounds quite intriguing. Come on then, what are we waiting for?"

They walked along the road in silence. Beth was struggling to think of a conversation that wouldn't somehow involve Ali, and she really didn't want to discuss him with her mum right now. Jean was bound to realise something was amiss, and Beth wasn't ready for anyone to know that things between her and Ali were less than perfect. As they reached the bridge, they looked around for signs of steps to the shore. There was nothing immediately obvious, so they walked a little further from the road. On the first side they tried, all they found were impenetrable rhododendrons and overgrown tangles of brambles. The other side looked no better, and they were about to admit defeat when Beth's foot caught against something hard. She pushed the branches of another rhododendron to one side and realised that the ground dropped away in front of her. Taking a step forward, she saw she was standing at the top of a stone staircase. She called to her mum, and between them they pushed more branches out of the way, until they had descended to the bottom. To the side of them, the river rushed into the sea, spreading out as it crossed the shore to create shallow pools amongst the rocks. Behind them, they could just make out the shape of the bridge carrying the road over the river, but the sheer density of foliage almost hid it from sight. They both noticed a large, flat rock sat invitingly in front of them. It seemed to call them to take a seat and admire the view. Without speaking, they began picking their way across to it, treading carefully in case of slippery rocks in the river's spread.

"This must be the secret shore Constance meant," Beth said, once they were safely on the rock.

"It's certainly beautiful," Jean replied, looking around her.

"And secluded," Beth added.

"Perfect for a couple up to no good," Jean concluded.

"Is that how you think of it? That Constance was doing something wrong?"

Jean thought for a moment before responding.

"No, not really. I mean, she was married, and someone always gets hurt in an affair, but I suppose things were different then. It doesn't sound as if she or James MacAird married for love."

Beth was quiet for a moment, thinking of Eilidh and Jay's potential affair and the havoc that had already caused.

"I've liked Constance a lot more since reading these letters. But I hadn't really thought about the fact she was cheating on her husband. I'd been more annoyed that Joseph seemed to be stringing her along."

"It was all very different then," reasoned Jean. "I've sort of seen it as if Joseph is simply being practical. He was trained in the law. He'd have known it wasn't as straightforward as him and Constance running away and starting again."

"That's a good point. It's funny how we all end up seeing the same thing differently."

"Yes," Jean agreed. "No one ever has quite the

same perspective as you. Anyway, while we're talking about the letters, there's something I've been meaning to ask you. I've told you about my cousin Jackie in Australia, haven't I?"

"I think so," Beth answered, not sounding certain. "Is she Grandma's sister's daughter?"

"Almost. Alice, your grandma's big sister, moved to Australia in her early twenties and she had Patricia almost as soon as she moved there. My mum was in her thirties by the time I was born, so although Pat's my cousin, she's quite a bit older than me. Anyway, Jackie is Pat's daughter, so she's probably actually my cousin once removed or something like that."

"Okay, so anyway, why were you mentioning her?"

"Sorry!" Jean laughed. "I'd completely forgotten my point! So, Jackie is really into researching the family tree. She emails me a lot, and she completely loved the copies of Eliza's diary that I sent her. She hadn't known about the link to the MacAirds either, because obviously she'd based all her research on the official records. I've been emailing her about the letters as well and she wondered if you'd send her copies."

"Yeah, that'll be no problem. Just remind me."

"I will. Apparently, she's sorting through her mum's jewellery. She said she'll let me know if any exciting heirlooms turn up."

They sat for a while longer until Beth's phone buzzed, disturbing the peace. She reached it out straight away, thinking it might be her dad wanting some help with Rory. Instead, she found a text from Dan, her best friend Lucy's husband.

"Lucy's had the baby," Beth announced to her mum. "It's another girl, no name yet, but apparently they're both doing fine."

"Oh, that's lovely," Jean said happily. Then she looked at Beth again and her smile faded. "It is lovely, isn't it? How come you look so sad?"

"I'm not sad. It's great news. I suppose I'm just thinking that Ella's not even two and they've already got their second. I can't imagine ever having enough energy to have another."

"Well, it doesn't matter if you don't, does it?" said Jean, trying to be comforting. "You were happy enough as an only child, weren't you?"

"Are you saying I wouldn't be able to handle another?"

"No, I thought that was what you were saying. I was just trying to say it wouldn't matter either way."

"But you don't think I could cope?"

"I didn't say that. It was just you were saying how tired you and Ali are."

"I didn't even mention Ali. Has he said something to you?"

"No. I just assumed he must be tired because

you are. Calm down, sweetheart. You're getting worked up over nothing."

"I'm not getting worked up." Beth shouted, clearly quite worked up.

Jean didn't speak again, realising that anything she said would only add fuel to the fire. Instead, she walked a little further along the shore, giving Beth time to think. Beth sat silently fuming with herself. She was furious that she'd got annoyed with her mum yet again. However, Jean wasn't the type to hold a grudge. She came back a few minutes later, put her arm around Beth, and suggested that they head back to check on David and Rory. But no matter how much small talk Jean made on their return journey, Beth couldn't shake off her anger with herself.

◆ ◆ ◆

Much later, as Beth pushed Rory home, she was still berating herself for shouting at her mum. She was lost in thought when she heard a voice calling her name. Following the sound, she saw Jay sat on the wall by the side of the road. Realising it was his car parked in the layby, Beth tucked the pushchair carefully in behind it, where Rory could be distracted by the gulls arguing on the shore. She sat down next to Jay, feeling unsure of what to say. She hadn't seen him since the day of Eilidh's revelations.

"Eilidh said she told you about us," Jay stated,

breaking the silence.

"Yes, she said that nothing had really happened though, and that nothing was going to."

"The thing is, Beth, I don't think that's possible. I can't look at her without wanting to touch her. She's on my mind every minute. I just don't know what to do."

"I don't want to get dragged into this, Jay. I don't know what to tell you, and I know all the people involved."

"But I really need to talk to someone," he said pleadingly, taking hold of her hand.

"I'm sorry, Jay. I want to help you, but I can't. Maybe you could try talking to Ali. I think he'd appreciate you asking for his advice."

"Do you think so? He seems to have been angry with me ever since I moved back. I can't imagine him wanting to sympathise with my problems."

"I think he's finding it hard to adjust. You announced you were staying with no notice and then waded in with all your big ideas. If you tried spending some time alone with him, showed him you're interested, perhaps talked to him about what he's already achieved here, he might feel a bit more like you respect him, and maybe things would get easier."

"Well, I suppose it's worth a try. I really need to talk to someone. And, regardless of whether Ali wants to listen to me banging on about my relationship woes, I probably haven't paid enough attention to his feelings since I've come home. Thanks, Beth, I know we've put you in a difficult position, and I'm sorry," he said sincerely, before pulling her into a tight hug.

LETTER SEVEN

April 1893

Dearest Joseph,
 I have often wondered what happens after death. The Bible tells us of a perfect life to come, but I have always struggled to see how that would work. Sometimes I like to indulge in a fantasy of us whiling away eternity together, finally able to be open about our love. However, a fantasy is all it is. I can't maintain the thought for long because it is flawed. How could you spend eternity with me when you're already there with Maude? For the first time, I can see a positive to the fact that eternity was never to be ours because it means that what I must tell you can't really matter. There was never going to be a happy ending for us.

I don't know if you'll be able to forgive me

when you hear what I have to say. I can picture you and Maude, sitting on your cloud, discussing my flaws. Although, if you are there together and you can see what happens down here, I suppose you must have had a fair amount of explaining to do when you first passed through those pearly gates. Was Maude angry with you for the time you spent with me? Has she finally confessed to her role in keeping us apart? Anyway, I'm straying from my point. I think I am nervous. I know you can't read these words, but the act of writing them feels like an admission that I have done something wrong.

I've had to send Eliza away. There I've said it. I've had to send her away alone, knowing that her heart is broken. It is not how I wanted things to be, but in the end, I had to protect my son. If you'd let me be a proper mother to Eliza, perhaps things could have been different, but you wouldn't listen. You never allowed me to share with her the things that could have united us. Your wishes made it so I was always guarded in the stories I told, always wary of my actions. It meant that we could never become truly close. Perhaps that was your intention. Maybe you didn't want us to be close because of some sort of loyalty to Maude. Whatever the reasons, it meant that when it came down to a choice between Eliza and my son—I had to choose Alexander.

Eliza was going to leave us. I've told you that

before, so you already know how worried I was. You know it broke my heart that I had failed you. However, I knew I had to accept that. My greatest fear was that I would also lose Alexander. I feared that Eliza's departure would destroy him. He has such a gentle heart, and I didn't think it could survive breaking. However, the reality of Eliza's plan was worse than I'd feared. She wasn't planning to leave Alexander behind; she was intending to take him to Manchester with her. I would have been left here with nothing. I know what you must be thinking. How could I stand in their way after all I have said of Maude's interference? Well, it isn't as simple as that. Maude knew we belonged together and prevented that purely for her own gain. This situation was very different. I know Alexander is not strong enough for Eliza. She would have tired of him eventually, and he would have been broken. The only option was to end things swiftly now, before any more hurt could be caused.

Alexander has always belonged here at Ardmhor. I struggled to adapt to life here, but Alexander was literally born to it. He wilted like a plant without water each time he went away to school, only to revive on his return when he saw the estate come into view. He would have wilted again as soon as he arrived in Manchester, whereas I know Eliza will bloom. She is more like me in that respect. She never really wanted to be here, always pining for the English childhood that she barely remembered. I wish I could have shared that side of me with her. Anyway, Eliza would have come into her own in England. She would have been glorious, and Alexander would have gradually shrunk by her side. All the things that make him special would fade away in a city he could never feel at home in. Eliza would have been left with just the shell of him, and how could that be enough for her? Alexander would have seen her disappointment and been destroyed. I couldn't allow that to happen to him. I had to stop things before they went any further.

I am certain that things couldn't have worked between them. Alexander could never match Eliza's strength. He couldn't even control himself around her. Even though he prides himself on his gentlemanly behaviour, he couldn't resist the lure of Eliza's bed. And really, if he had truly loved her, if he was honestly strong enough for her, nothing could have kept him from her side. A few words from me couldn't have separated them.

I didn't say that he couldn't leave with her. All I did was point out some flaws in his plan. I may have added some embellishments to strengthen my arguments, suggesting that he hadn't been the only man Eliza had shared her affections with, but he was adamant that he did not believe me, so those fabrications cannot really be held to blame. The reason he didn't leave with her was because he knew he'd be holding her back. He knew deep down that she needed a different sort of person; that was what had prevented him from being open about their relationship. He already knew that things weren't right. I only helped bring those fears to the surface. If they hadn't already existed, if Alexander had really believed in them as a couple, I could not have convinced him to stay.

So, I have said it. I have told you what I have done, and I hope you believe me when I say this is not the outcome I wanted. It gives me no pleasure to imagine Eliza alone in Manchester, believing that Alexander never cared. In fact, the opposite is true. She left a parcel for me on the table in the hall. It contained my cameo brooch, carefully wrapped in tissue. That tiny parcel told me she considered our relationship over, our connection gone. As I saw that symbol of all we should have become lying discarded on the hall table, I felt another crack open in my heart. If I could have chosen an outcome, I would have chosen for them both to remain here. I would have told Eliza the stories of our childhood from the moment she arrived. After your passing, I would have confided in her about my love for you. I would have opened her eyes to the unseen ties that bind us. Eventually, I would have made her realise she could learn to belong here, just as I have. But I wasn't able to choose, and this was the best I could do for both of them.

I know Eliza will move on. She will find a love that is everything she needs, a love that will challenge her and complete her. I hope that one day Alexander will do the same. Mostly though, I hope I am wrong about the life to come. I hope that there is a way for us to be together, and I pray you want that too.

All my love,

Always

CHAPTER TWENTY-SIX

After stopping to talk to Jay, Beth had continued home. She'd hoped Ali had already made it back from work as his car was on the drive, but the house was empty. Rory had fallen asleep in the pushchair, so rather than disturb him, she'd grabbed the next one of Constance's letters and settled on the bench outside the front door to read it while he slept. The combination of the contents of the letter, her disagreement with her mum, and her brief chat with Jay had made her more determined than ever to sort things out with Ali. Constance might have been right in some ways: Eliza had grown to love her husband William, perhaps more than she had ever loved Alex, but that didn't mean Alex and Eliza couldn't have been happy. Their relationship could have worked if they had discussed their plans openly. She knew she needed to talk to Ali properly. They had to be honest with each other. They couldn't let everything they had fall apart.

She needed to make Ali see how sorry she was for not telling him about Jay and Eilidh. It should have been obvious to her how hurt he'd be about being kept in the dark. And she also needed to make it clear to him that she wanted another child. She'd always pictured them as one day being a family of four. She'd just been scared about how they'd cope. But mainly, she was determined to make him see he was more important to her than anything else. She was going to make him feel the way he had when they'd first met, back when they'd annoyed everyone with how sickeningly happy they were, but first she needed him to come home.

◆ ◆ ◆

By the time she heard Ali's key in the door, Rory was already tucked up in bed. The sound of stumbling from the hallway suggested Ali had been in the pub. Beth bit down her annoyance that he'd once again left her to deal with bedtime alone and took another sip of her wine. Now wasn't the moment for that discussion. What she needed was to bring Ali back to her, not start another fight. She was certain that if they could just be open with each other, everything else would follow. She poured a glass of wine for Ali and went out to the hall to greet him.

"I've poured you a drink," she offered as her opening line. She didn't ask him why he was late, or where he'd been. She didn't want to risk annoying him before they'd talked.

"Actually, I thought I'd head straight up to bed," he replied, his feet already on the bottom step.

"Please, Ali," Beth said, working hard to keep her voice even, determined not to show any signs of frustration. "I've hardly seen you recently."

He relented with a sigh, following her into the kitchen and picking up his glass of wine. They perched on the stools at the kitchen island for a while, Beth telling him what Rory had been up to that day while she put off the more serious conversation. It seemed a shame to bring up issues she knew would cause upset when they were finally talking again, but as Ali downed the remains of his wine and moved to stand up, she knew she couldn't put it off any longer.

"Ali, don't go. We need to talk properly."

"I'm tired, Beth. I don't think now is the right time for a serious conversation."

"Well, when is then? You've been avoiding me all week and there are things I need to say to you." She was exasperated now, and she couldn't stop the sound of it seeping into her voice.

"Beth, please, just leave it. I don't want to hear this right now."

"No, Ali, we have to talk. I can't carry on like this. I don't understand what's happening to us, and it's scaring me."

Ali gave a snort of derision. "You're scared? You don't understand what's going on? Come off it, Beth. If anyone should feel that way, it's me."

"I'm so sorry I didn't tell you about Jay. You know I wanted to, but I'd promised I wouldn't. I wish I could go back in time and do things differently."

"Really," Ali replied, his voice still scathing. "Exactly what would you change?"

"I'd be open with you from the start. I never meant to hurt you. Honestly, it's the last thing I'd ever want to do."

"Well, you've done a pretty good job of it."

"I know, and I'm so, so, sorry. That's why I need to tell you everything now. I saw Jay today and…"

"No," Ali hissed over the top of her. "I told you I don't want to hear this. Sorry, Beth, I just can't… I'm leaving."

"What do you mean?" Beth asked, stunned, but he didn't reply. He simply walked into the hall, shoved his feet into his shoes, and shut the door behind him.

Beth rushed to follow. She thought she'd heard

the car door slam as she fumbled with the latch, but when she finally got the door open, the car was still next to the house. However, there was no sign of Ali. She tiptoed to the end of the drive, wincing at the sharpness of the stone chippings through her socks, calling his name as loudly as she dared, but there was no response. Now she was stuck. She couldn't go any further and leave Rory alone, so she had no choice but to make her way back inside. She couldn't comprehend how things had gone so wrong, and she was worried about where Ali would go. He'd obviously had a drink already and clearly wasn't in the most rational frame of mind, but she reasoned he knew many people in the area who'd be happy to put him up for the night, and the pub wouldn't have called last orders yet, so he'd probably just head back there.

A couple of hours later, she lay in bed, unable to sleep. Her mind was frantically inventing terrible, tragic scenarios. She pictured Ali stumbling off the pier and being too drunk to save himself, or she saw him falling into the road and not being noticed by a tired driver until it was too late. She contemplated phoning the police, or at least ringing his parents and some of his friends, but she felt too embarrassed to make the calls. What would she say? How would she explain what was going on? And then she felt terrible that she was putting her own fear of looking silly ahead of Ali's safety. She wept to herself because everything had been perfect and now it had gone so wrong. And then she wept some more because the only person she'd ever fully admitted her worries to was Ali. He was the only person she'd feel safe turning to for help, and he was gone.

At some point, she'd fallen asleep. The faint light of dawn now showed around the edge of the curtains, but Ali's side of the bed was untouched. She went through the motions of getting showered, dressed, and taking care of Rory. She messaged and called Ali's phone repeatedly, but there was no answer. Eventually, she decided there was no option. She had to be brave and confide in someone. Making sure Ali was safe was what mattered. She took a deep breath, picked up her phone again, and called Angela.

"Hi Beth. Are you okay? Are you coming up to the museum today?"

"I'm not sure yet," she stammered, caught off guard by the questions. "Is Ali with you?"

"No, Jim took him to the station ages ago. I think his flight was leaving Inverness at ten, so he needed an early start. I said to him he'd have been better off not having so much to drink, but at least he was thoughtful enough not to disturb you by coming back from the pub late and then getting up again at the crack of dawn. And I suppose as he was getting the train across to the airport, it's not as though he needed to worry about being over the limit this morning."

Beth desperately wanted to give the impression that she knew what was going on. She didn't want to admit to Angela that she had no idea what she was talking about. Where was Ali flying to? And why? She wondered if she could just play along. Now that she knew Ali was safe, did it matter if she didn't know all the other details? She wasn't just being secretive to save her own embarrassment, she reasoned. Ali probably wouldn't thank her for involving his mum in their troubles either.

"Do you know what time his return flight is?" she ventured, hoping to work out the other details from there.

"Hang on a second." Angela's voice became a bit more muffled, but Beth could still hear her talking to Jim, asking what time Ali's flight got back from Shetland. Then Angela's voice was clear again. "Jim says he's picking him up from the station the day after tomorrow. It'll be around lunchtime. Unless you want to get him, of course."

"I'm not sure," Beth replied, wondering if meeting Ali would be a good way to force him to talk to her, but also unsure about what sort of reception she could expect.

"Well, just let us know which is easiest. We can always have Rory for you if you want to go."

Beth had never been more grateful for her

chatty mother-in-law. Without having to answer any awkward questions she now knew where Ali was, and she knew when he was coming back. Unfortunately, she still had no idea what was going on in his head.

CHAPTER TWENTY-SEVEN

Ardmhor, 1893

I still believe that I acted correctly when I convinced Alexander to stay. It was only possible to persuade him to let Eliza go because he knew he wasn't the right man for her. He knew she needed someone stronger. I know I lied to him about Eliza being involved with other men, but those lies made no difference, so they should not need to be accounted for on my day of reckoning. It was the truth that made him stay. Alexander knew he'd disappoint Eliza if he left with her. If he'd believed otherwise, I would not have been able to stop him. It is not easy to see how much Alexander is hurting, but it proves to me that I acted correctly. Their relationship unravelling in its infancy has gravely wounded him. It would have destroyed him if this had happened after things had progressed further.

However, I am less sure of my actions since then. Choosing this path was easy, remaining on it has been more challenging. To ensure Alexander's suffering has not been in vain, I have had to make some difficult decisions. I have had to do some terrible things, and I fear that although my motivation has been good, when my deeds are finally weighed, the balance may no longer go in my favour.

As soon as Eliza left, I realised I would need to offer Flora an explanation of events. The two of them had kept up quite a correspondence since Flora's marriage, so inevitably, Eliza would pour out her heartbreak to Flora. I had to make sure that she would not be sympathetic to Eliza's words. If Flora got involved, perhaps trying to convince Alexander to go to Eliza and try again, all my efforts would have been in vain. Alexander would have suffered this sadness for nothing. So I had to prevent that from happening. On the day of Eliza's departure, I wrote a long letter to Flora. I told her that Eliza had been taking advantage of Alexander's kind nature to secure her position in society, explaining that she had coaxed him to the point of proposing marriage, whilst also enjoying more physical liaisons with a variety of other men. I was careful to suggest the name of Angus here, the young gardener that Flora had always very much admired. It was essential that she should not be sympathetic to Eliza's plight. I explained that when I had stumbled across one of these dalliances, Eliza had run away to Manchester, leaving Alexander heart broken. I made it clear that Flora should be careful not to mention her again. There is no pride to be had in my careful planning. It is a terrible thing to lie to your own child, but once I had set these events in motion, I had to commit to ensuring their success.

Within a few days of Eliza's departure, the letters started arriving. It didn't seem so hard to intercept them by then. I'd already taken the step of reading other people's letters, so it wasn't much of a leap to hide them instead. The only difficulty was making sure I was always the first person to see the post. However, it didn't raise any suspicions when I requested that all correspondence be handed directly to me. Sadly, mistrust of servants is common enough that my instruction surprised no one. I don't know whether it is better or worse that I read the contents of the letters I hid, but I read them because I still care for Eliza, and I needed to know if she was settling into her new life. The contents are always similar. She tells Alexander that she loves him and that she is sorry she had to leave. She tells him she wishes he was with her, and then she tells him of her new life. Whether Eliza herself will have been able to see this, I cannot know, but reading her letters as an outsider, it was clear to see that although she missed Alexander—she was becoming increasingly settled. It was reassuring, confirming I'd done the right thing. It seemed both Eliza and Alexander would recover, and with far less damage than if their relationship had progressed.

I knew my actions were something I would never boast of. I still feared that I might be judged harshly for them, but my conscience felt clearer. However, that was before I discovered a secret that changed everything. It is my actions because of that secret which keep me awake long into the night. Eliza's letters were dwindling slightly by the middle of May. The envelopes still arrived, piling up in the hidden drawer of my desk, but they did not arrive every single day. I hoped the end was in sight and that Eliza had given up. I thought perhaps I could relax, but then the number of letters increased again. Sometimes two would arrive on the same day. The pile grew, taunting me. Some of the earliest ones found themselves consigned to the flames of my fire, but I couldn't bring myself to destroy them all. Then one day, I opened the letter that revealed the reason behind this new intensity: Eliza was expecting a child. It is my actions since then that I fear have gone beyond simply protecting Alexander.

My first thought was that maybe the child wasn't his, but despite what I have tried to make others believe of Eliza's character, I knew this would not be the case. I truly believe that Eliza would have grown bored with Alexander and frustrated by his weaker nature, but I know she loved him at the time of her departure. I know there will have been no one but him. The child changes everything. Alexander still wouldn't have been enough for Eliza, but they would have had to marry, regardless. She would have pretended for the sake of her child. I've told myself this pretence would not have been fair to Alexander, but if I am honest, I know that is not true. I think that any semblance of happiness with Eliza would have been enough to sustain him. So I had a choice: let Alexander know the truth and let him go to Eliza or continue down the road we had already begun travelling, the road on which he was already recovering.

I chose to continue. How could I tell him the truth? Even if I'd tried to pretend this was the first letter, it would have been obvious from its contents that this was not the case. One or two letters going amiss might be explainable, but there have been at least forty. If Alexander was to know about the child, he would also have to know about my deception, and then I would have lost everything. Flora is gone, Little James was never mine, and Alexander would not be able to forgive me. I love him so much, but not enough to lose him.

So this time I cannot claim that my actions were to protect Alexander. I know that all I have done recently has been solely to protect myself. These are the deeds I fear will condemn me to an eternity far worse than any darkness I have experienced before. I concealed the letter from Alexander, and I have concealed all those that have followed. I feared Eliza might travel back here to speak directly with Alexander, so I explained to the servants that under no circumstances was she to be allowed into the house. Fortunately, on the day my fears proved justified, Alexander and his father were away in Edinburgh. Telling the servants to keep her out would not have been a sufficient precaution had Alexander been here, for she ran around the house crying out his name. I know I am the cause of her pain, but my heart still ached for her. I remember how it felt to lose Joseph, the dreadful realisation that he wasn't coming to save me, but panic quickly overrode my sympathy. She waited on the lawn until I feared she was intending to wait forever. I was sure I could guarantee the servants silence, but if Alexander was to return and find her here, well, I knew I would never see my son again. I watched her all day, until I was quite frantic, but at the last minute I was saved. As it neared the time Alexander and James were due to return, she finally disappeared. I asked Mr Harper to follow her and ensure that she had got on the train. He has worked here for so long that I knew I could rely on his discretion. I tell myself that the fact she left after just one day proves I was right. For all her determination, even in what must seem a dire situation to her, she gave up.

But in my heart of hearts, I have to ask myself, what lengths did I go to when I believed Joseph had abandoned me? He is the love of my life, but I put up no fight for him. I simply accepted that he didn't want me, and then I married someone else. However, I cannot allow those thoughts to take root. I dare not think of the fate of Eliza and her child, my grandchild, a child with the blood of the two most precious people in my life flowing through their veins. It would be foolish to think that way. I cannot doubt my actions now. The path I chose was the one I believed to be right, and it would be dangerous to even consider that my choice was wrong. My aim was to keep my beloved son safe, and I have done that. Now I must do everything in my power to make sure he never learns the full extent of my actions. I must cling to Alexander now. I must devote my life to his happiness. It is the only way I can keep the darkness at bay.

CHAPTER TWENTY-EIGHT

It was grey and misty as Ali's train made its way to the west coast. The mist obscured the views, and the train felt cold and damp. It was as if the drizzle had permeated the structure of the carriage, settling into its seats alongside the slightly sodden passengers. The weather matched Ali's mood, and he wondered if the trip had been a mistake. He'd known about it for over a week before he was due to go, but he'd somehow not mentioned it to Beth. Really, he'd done a good job of avoiding saying anything to her over the last week or so. He knew it had been wrong to leave with no explanation. The number of texts and missed calls from her told him she was worried, but he was managing not to care. He hadn't used the two days away as a breathing space to help him organise his thoughts. He'd used them as an opportunity to crystallise his anger, to turn it into something very solid and very real. To be betrayed by his brother yet again was hurtful, but for that betrayal to include Beth, the person he'd believed was made for him, that was more than he could bear.

When he'd first heard Beth telling Eilidh about her feelings for Jay, he'd thought he could learn to cope. Obviously, he'd been devastated. It was the confirmation of what he'd long suspected, that in a comparison of himself and Jay he'd be the one found lacking, but he'd also heard her say that nothing had happened, so in the end he'd decided not to confront her. There was an all too real possibility that challenging her might make her realise she wanted a future with Jay after all. He'd concluded that Beth and Rory were his world, and he didn't want to risk losing them. So he'd decided the only option was to pretend that he hadn't overheard Eilidh and Beth's conversation. He'd hoped that eventually he'd be able to believe the pretence.

It had proved harder than he'd expected though. He couldn't talk to Beth properly; he could barely even look at her. He couldn't meet her gaze without wondering if she was wishing he was Jay. So he'd tried to avoid her, hoping that as time went on the betrayal would become easier to live with, hoping that eventually Jay wouldn't be the first thought in his head when he saw his wife, but that hadn't worked. It had been obvious he was avoiding spending time at home, and when she'd confronted him, he'd ended up blurting out what he knew. That was the point when he'd questioned whether he could do this, when it finally dawned on him that maybe this was the end for him and Beth.

He'd expected her to deny it. When he'd realised they were about to have that conversation, that they were actually going to discuss what had happened, time had slowed down. His mind had raced through all the films he'd seen where lovers confronted each other about indiscretions. He'd thought there would be crying and pleading, shouting and recriminations. What he hadn't expected was for her to act as if it didn't even matter, as if her feelings for his brother were of absolutely no consequence, as if they hadn't shaken the foundations of his world. Her first words after he'd told her he knew weren't words of apology; she'd simply wanted to know who'd told him, as if that mattered more than her betrayal. Then she'd said that because nothing had happened, she hadn't thought it was worth mentioning, believing it would only make things worse between him and Jay. He'd told her she'd been right about that, but her blithe tone and her assertion that this wasn't even worth discussing made him angrier than he could ever remember feeling. It was as if she was trying to say he was the one being unreasonable. It was too much to take, and he'd had to walk away. After he'd stormed out of the house, the anger had dissipated, and the hurt had surfaced again. She'd said she hadn't told him because she'd promised not to say anything, not because she didn't want to ruin their marriage or because what they shared was too important to risk destroying; the reason she hadn't told him was because she'd made a promise to Jay. It had hurt enough when no one at school had wanted to talk to him, when Jay had laughed as he'd told stories about what a loser he was, but when his own wife was the one choosing Jay over him, that didn't just hurt—that was devastating.

He hadn't gone to meet an old school friend as he'd told Beth. That had only ever been an invention to avoid spending time at home. He'd made his way along the shore instead. The wind had picked up, and the waves had crashed against the rocks, as if the sea was mirroring his emotions. He wondered what it would be like to not go back. Would anyone miss him? Would they all be perfectly happy as long as they had Jay instead? But he knew deep down that wasn't the case. Whatever happened between him and Beth, there was Rory to consider. Rory made his love plain every single day, every time his pudgy little arms crept their way around his neck, or when he squealed with joy as he walked in the door. Ali knew he was one of the two things that formed the centre of Rory's world, and he couldn't let him down. He stayed out for hours, knowing he couldn't face talking to Beth, but he also knew that eventually he had to go home and try to make things work. He had to do that for Rory.

He'd thought maybe he could do it. The alternative, a life without Rory and Beth in it, was definitely worse. On the occasions when he let his thoughts drift to that different future, a future where his wife and son lived with his brother instead, he knew he had to do whatever he could to avoid it happening. But then he saw them together.

He was driving home from work. The only reason he'd been so early was because he'd wanted to make more of an effort. He knew he'd been leaving everything up to Beth while he worked through his feelings, and that was not going to save their marriage. He was only a minute away from home when he spotted them. They were on the wall at the side of the road. Maybe they thought Jay's car hid them from view, or maybe they just didn't care. They were locked in an embrace. Beth had said it was just feelings, that nothing had happened, that it was all over, but from what Ali could see, that clearly wasn't the truth.

Abandoning the car on the drive, he'd quickly packed a bag. He knew he had the flight to Shetland in the morning, so at least he had a reason to disappear for a few days. After dumping the bag in the car, he'd stalked off into the hills, needing to think. Eventually, he'd stopped walking and gone to the pub, sinking a couple of drams of single malt while trying to decide what to do. A couple with a young child came up to pay for their meal while he was at the bar. The child was almost asleep. His cheek rested against his father's neck, and his eyelids flickered as he battled to stay awake. The child's dimpled hand clasped around the fabric of his father's top, clinging to him, trusting he was safe if his father was nearby. The sight brought Ali's thoughts back to Rory. He had to put his own feelings aside and be there for him. He'd finished his drink and set straight off home, hoping he'd be in time to put Rory to bed. The silence that greeted him as he opened the door told him he'd left it too late. He heard Beth in the kitchen and stumbled in his hurry to get away. He really couldn't face talking to her. She'd insisted though. She'd appeared in the hall and refused to take no for an answer. To start with it'd been alright, they'd talked about Rory and he'd been able to block out everything else, but then she'd wanted to talk properly, she'd said there were things she had to tell him, and that was when he'd left. He'd known what she was going to say, she was going to tell him she was leaving, that she'd made her choice and she'd chosen Jay. He could see his world collapsing around him and he couldn't handle hearing her say the words, so he'd told her he was going, grabbed his bag from the car, and headed back to the pub.

The early flight to Shetland had been a convenient excuse for staying in his old bedroom at his parent's house, but the trip hadn't helped him to calm down at all. He'd swung between sadness and anger until the emotional pendulum had settled on cold, hard hatred. A feeling that was now as real to him as the noise of the packed train. He reserved most of his anger for Jay. Beth took her share as well, but Ali accepted he couldn't really blame her; it was inevitable she'd see Jay was the better option. With Jay, it was different. Jay was his big brother, and that meant he was supposed to look out for him; he certainly wasn't supposed to turn up and destroy his life. Ali knew he could never forgive him.

◆ ◆ ◆

"Do you want dropping off at home first, Ali?" his dad asked as they set off out of the car park at Inveravain train station.

"No, I need to go straight to the office. Thanks though."

"Are you sure? It's no bother for you to go home and relax a bit. You must be worn out."

"I said I need to go to the office," Ali snapped back.

Jim didn't bother responding. He reasoned Ali was tired and that it was best to leave him be. He glanced at his youngest son, who was staring pointedly out of the window, and turned the radio on to make the silence less obvious.

◆ ◆ ◆

Ali didn't know what his plan had been for when he got to the office and saw Jay, but as it happened, events took their own course. Jay was walking out of the door as Ali approached it.

"Ali!" he exclaimed, smiling broadly. "I didn't think you'd be back yet. Have you got time for a chat?"

Jay wasn't perceptive enough to register the look of pure hatred on Ali's face. He didn't notice the movement as Ali clenched his hand, his knuckles turning white with the strain, and he certainly wasn't prepared for the pain of Ali's fist connecting with his face. He stumbled backwards, only the wall of the office preventing him from falling to the ground.

"What was that for?" he shouted at Ali's retreating figure, as confused as he was shocked.

"I know," Ali shouted back. "I know what's been going on."

Ali continued to walk away. Jay followed, still dazed, trying to make sense of his words.

"Ali, wait," he called out. "Slow down, mate. I

don't understand."

Ali showed no sign of complying with the request, forcing Jay to run after him until eventually he was close enough to grab Ali's arm and spin him round. Ali tried to shake him off, but this time, Jay had the upper hand. He shoved Ali towards the trunk of a nearby tree, pinning him against it, finally forcing him to look in his direction.

"What's going on?" Jay demanded. "You can't just punch me and then walk away."

"Why not, Jay?" Ali spat back at him. "It seems as if you think you can do whatever you like."

"I really don't know what's happening here, Ali. You're going to have to give me a clue," Jay said, exasperated, still holding Ali tight against the trunk of the tree.

"I've told you. I know. I know what you've been doing. Beth…"

Jay interrupted before Ali could finish, relaxing his grip slightly, a look of understanding spreading across his face.

"Oh, so Beth's told you. I suppose I should have expected that. I still don't get why you punched me though. I know you get on, but I didn't know you were that close. Unless…" He paused for a second, the understanding his face had shown a moment ago now turning to surprise. "Unless you like her too?"

Jay still had hold of Ali's arms at this point,

but he had no defence against the kick Ali landed hard on his shin. He also wasn't ready for the knee that connected with his stomach as he reflexively bent to rub his injured leg.

"You total bastard," Ali said, stepping away from where Jay had sunk to the ground. "Of course we're close. Of course I like her. She's my wife. Does that not mean anything to you? Did you think we've just been tolerating each other until someone better comes along?"

"Ali, stop," Jay said, panting as he struggled back onto his feet. "I think we're talking about different things. I thought you meant Beth had told you about me and Eilidh."

"Eilidh, what's Eilidh got to do with anything?" Ali shouted, rounding back on Jay.

"I've been seeing her. Nothing has really happened, but Eilidh spoke to Beth about it. I assumed Beth had told you."

"What? You've been seeing them both?"

"No! Of course not. I've been seeing Eilidh. Beth's lovely, but she's your wife and she's besotted with you. Also, I may do daft things, but even I can't handle two illicit relationships at once."

Ali seemed to deflate in front of Jay. The righteous anger disappearing to be replaced by confusion.

"But I saw you together the other afternoon. You were at the side of the road with your arms round each other."

"I'd asked her for advice about Eilidh. She said she didn't want to get involved. She suggested I should talk to you. That's why I wanted to chat now. Beth pointed out that I haven't made much effort to spend time with you since I've been back, and she's right. I hugged her because I was grateful to her for listening, and I felt bad for putting her in a difficult position."

Ali still wasn't convinced. He'd spent the last week allowing his hurt to permeate through his being and the last few days solidifying his anger. That he might have been wrong was a lot to take in, no matter how much he wanted it to be true.

"But I heard her talking to Eilidh. She was saying she had feelings for you."

"I think you got the wrong end of the stick, Ali. It's Eilidh who's got feelings for me, like I have for her." He paused for a second, weighing up whether a joke would take the tension out of the situation or make things worse, in typical Jay style he decided to go for it. "Obviously, it is possible Beth has feelings for me as well. I mean, she'd be daft if she didn't."

This time Ali's punch was gentle, the sort of tap on the arm they'd been giving each other since the moment they were old enough to wind each other up.

"So there's honestly nothing going on between you?" Ali asked again, quietly this time. He sank down to rest his back against the tree Jay had pinned him against just a few moments before.

"Of course not, mate," Jay said, lowering himself slowly to sit beside him. "It wouldn't be possible because as far as I can tell, Beth only has eyes for you. Also, no matter what you might think of me, she's your wife, and I wouldn't do that to you."

"You've treated me pretty badly in the past though. You've turned people against me before, so you can't really blame me for thinking it was happening again."

"Do you mean when you started boarding school?"

"Yes," Ali replied, not turning to look at him, not wanting to meet his gaze. "I mean, there have been plenty of other times where you've tried to make me the butt of the joke, or prove that you're better at everything, but that time at school was more than that. I felt so alone, and the one person I should have been able to rely on was the person making everything worse."

"But you never said anything," Jay countered. "You just kept carrying on, not reacting. I was enjoying finally being the one in control. I loved everyone laughing along with me, and you didn't seem bothered. You just kept going to your classes, turning up to all the clubs. I thought it couldn't be that bad. I thought that if you were really upset, you'd have said something. I figured you just didn't care what me and my mates thought."

"Of course I cared. Everywhere I went for the first few months, people laughed at me. Whenever I went in a room, people stopped talking and whispered. It was hell. I was desperate to phone Mum and tell her to come and get me, but I didn't want her to know what a loser I was. How could I have talked to you about it? You'd have just told everyone, and it'd have got even worse."

"Shit, Ali. I'm so sorry. You're always so good at everything. Everyone loves you, and you make friends within seconds. When I went away to boarding school, for the first time, no one knew my amazing little brother. Finally, I was the popular one with the good ideas. Then, when you started, I wasn't ready to give that status up. I thought I'd just spread a few rumours, make you look silly, make things a little harder for you. You'd never had to put up with being called Tiny instead of your own name, for God's sake. I thought you deserved to suffer a bit, but you never reacted once, so I just kept on with it. Then, after the first couple of terms, I'd got used to you being there, and I sort of got bored with it all. I honestly thought you cared so little about what I did that the teasing had washed over you."

"Well, it hadn't. It was the most hideous time of my life. I thought I was over it, but you coming back here has just raked it all up again. I started imagining people laughing at me all the time, everyone preferring you."

"I really am so sorry. I've always believed it hadn't bothered you, that you're so confident the teasing hadn't mattered. Or maybe I've just convinced myself of that so I didn't have to feel guilty about how I treated you. If I could go back and do things differently, I would. I was completely in the wrong and I'm sorry."

"Well, I'm sorry for punching you. I should have talked to you first."

"The punch was probably the least I deserved. I came back here because I've spent my whole life trying to be like you. You might be the youngest, but you're the one who always knows what you want to do. I saw your life with Beth and Rory, and it looked amazing. I thought if I came back home, I could find that too, but all I've done is make a gigantic mess."

"So, what is going on with Eilidh? Is she planning on leaving Rich?"

"No, she doesn't want that. She thinks she was panicking about the wedding and the commitment, and she just got carried away with the excitement of something new. Anyway, she's going to tell Rich what's happened, which is nothing really, just a couple of kisses. She says it's him she loves, and she wants them to make a go of things. I, on the other hand, can't stop thinking about her. I'm even dreaming about her."

"So, what are you going to do?"

"When I left the firm, they tried to persuade me to stay. They offered me a position in the Edinburgh office as a halfway measure, but I was adamant I wanted to leave and come here. I spoke to them yesterday to see if there was still a job available in Edinburgh."

"And?" Ali pressed him. "What did they say?"

"They said they'd be delighted to have me back, and I'm going to go. Coming here was maybe too big a change. I'm hoping that Edinburgh might be less pressured than London, but with a few more distractions than here. I'll have more opportunities to come home and see you all, but I won't be treading on your toes."

"But like you said, whatever I might feel, this is your home too. We'd get used to being together again. After all, we survived at boarding school after that terrible first year."

"Thanks. That means a lot. It really does, but I can't stay here now. I can't work alongside Eilidh and not be with her, but she's made her choice and I've got to leave her alone. I really think I love her, so I've got to respect her wishes. The only thing I can do to help is leave."

"I'm sorry," Ali whispered.

This time, when he moved unexpectedly, it was to pull Jay into a hug, something he hadn't instigated between them for years.

"Me too," Jay replied. His voice was muffled by Ali's jumper, but the emotion in it was clear.

CHAPTER TWENTY-NINE

Seagulls squawked and shouted overhead, before swooping down to devour the chips a tourist had thrown for them. Eilidh shook her head in dismay, rolling her eyes at Rory, who giggled to her from his highchair. Seagulls could be a menace and feeding them only made them worse, but visitors still persisted in doing it. It drove Eilidh mad. They were outside the café at the end of the pier. Although it was overcast and a little chilly, the inside of the café was full, so they were crossing their fingers that the earlier drizzle didn't return.

"When will they ever learn?" Eilidh said to Rory with an over-exaggerated shake of her head. He giggled again and grabbed a chunk of her glossy purple hair in his sticky jam covered fist. "Ouch!" she yelped, trying to disentangle herself and limit the spread of jam.

"When will you ever learn, is a better question," Beth said, laughing. "You know he can't resist your hair when you get too close."

"Well, that's me all over," Eilidh sighed sadly. "Totally irresistible."

"Hey, come on." Beth pulled Eilidh into a hug. "Jay is going to be fine. He's a big boy, he'll get over it."

"He just looked so sad when I told him we couldn't see each other anymore. I know he's going to meet someone else soon enough and then I'll be raging jealous, but honestly, it was so hard walking away from him."

"Hard because you felt sorry for him, or because you still want to be with him? Are you totally sure you don't want Jay? Are you certain you want to marry Rich?"

"I'm totally certain I want to marry Rich. Jay isn't the man for me. Rich is. He has been since the day I met him. I think the wedding just threw me into a panic. I've always known me and Rich are forever, but making that official, saying that's it, no-one else, not ever, that still feels like a big deal. Jay coming along, being so flirty and gorgeous, it turned my head. Jay looked at me like I was the most beautiful thing he'd ever seen, and when he kissed me, it was just so flattering and exciting. Me and Rich are lucky if we kiss each other goodnight nowadays, but when I really thought about it, when I tried to imagine telling Rich I was leaving, I couldn't do it. I tried to imagine living with Jay instead, but I couldn't picture it. I can't imagine a future with anyone but Rich. So if I'm being honest, it was hard ending things with Jay because I'm still really attracted to him, and knowing he feels the same is incredibly tempting, but I know walking away is the right thing to do. It's Rich that I love, and I always have. I just feel terrible for leading Jay on."

"Jay knew you were engaged to someone else right from the start, so I don't think you need to feel too sorry for him. He was well aware of what he was getting into, and it didn't stop him from pursuing you. Rich is the only person who deserves any sympathy here." As she spoke, Beth saw Eilidh's face crumple. "Not that I'd have behaved any better. Feelings aren't that easy to control," she added hastily. "Anyway, have you decided whether you're going to tell Rich what's been going on?"

"Yes, and I'm dreading it. I know it might mean the end, but I have to tell him. You're right, he's the only person who's done nothing wrong here. I can't let him go through with marrying me without him knowing the truth."

"Oh Eilidh, that sounds tough."

"Well, I've only got myself to blame, and it's not just my personal life that I've messed up. I don't know what to do about work either. I can't face working alongside Jay anymore, and I can't imagine Rich being too pleased about it after I tell him what's gone on."

"You're not thinking of leaving your job, are you?"

"I might have to. I've made such a mess of things"

Beth hugged her again. She couldn't think of any words to make things better. She couldn't even offer the reassurance that Eilidh wasn't the only one making a mess of things. It was impossible for Beth to confide her own relationship issues because she didn't actually know what the problem was or how she and Ali had got into this situation.

She headed home after leaving Eilidh, hopeful Ali might arrive back soon. Jim had said he'd bring him straight home from the station after picking him up. Beth hadn't volunteered to collect him in the end. She hadn't wanted him to feel cornered, and she couldn't be certain she wouldn't get angry and end up making things worse. However, she wanted to make sure she was there when he got home. Rory was rubbing his eyes sleepily and settled into his cot without too much of a struggle, leaving Beth free to focus on Ali. Staring out of the window had done nothing to make him materialise though, and her mind was busy turning over everything that had happened. She couldn't help but be angry with Ali. She couldn't think of an excuse that was good enough for him storming off without explaining what the problem was. If all this was just a reaction to her not telling him about Eilidh and Jay, it was unreasonable, no matter what had gone on between him and Jay in the past. He'd ignored every contact she'd made, not bothering to let her know he was safe, not even asking how Rory was. No matter how he felt about her, he had obligations as a parent that he was completely ignoring. So a huge part of her was seething, ready to rip Ali to pieces and feeling like she'd be totally justified in doing so. But she also knew this behaviour was totally out of character; she knew he must really be struggling, and she just wanted him home safe. In the end, she reached for the last of Constance's letters. Maybe that could take her mind off things.

◆ ◆ ◆

While Beth was reading Constance's letter, waiting for Ali, Ali was rushing to get home. He knew he had to put things right with Beth. She'd made so many calls and sent so many texts over the last two days, and he'd ignored every single one. He thought of the way he'd avoided her over the last week or so, the way he'd deliberately stayed away from home, leaving everything up to her, completely abandoning all his responsibilities. Now, after speaking to Jay, he was finding it hard to believe he'd leapt to such wild conclusions. He could see how foolish he'd been, and how badly he'd treated Beth. He could only hope that she'd give him another chance. If she didn't, he wouldn't blame her. What kind of man had so little faith in his wife? His mind was so focused on Beth, he didn't notice Rich rushing up the path towards him until the moment of collision.

"Watch it!" Rich shoved Ali out of the way, causing him to stumble.

"Hey, are you alright?" Ali registered the anger radiating from Rich and thought that for the first time in weeks he was reading a situation correctly. Eilidh must have told Rich about herself and Jay, and Rich was here for revenge.

"I'm fine," Rich muttered, shaking Ali's hand from his arm. "Or I will be as soon as I've gone in there and sorted out your brother. I assume he's in there."

Ali moved in front of Rich, putting his hands on either side of him, trying to get him to make eye contact. "Come on Rich, this won't help."

"Oh, it will Ali. It'll help me no end," Rich replied, once again shaking himself free.

"Rich, just wait a minute. Hear me out. Jay's leaving. He's been a total bastard, and he deserves to be taught a lesson, but he's leaving anyway, and this isn't how you act. You haven't got a violent bone in your body, don't be someone else because of him. Eilidh chose you. She wants you to be you, not some macho man running round sorting things out with his fists."

Rich made a sound somewhere between a groan and a scream and punched the tree trunk at the side of him. Then he visibly sagged.

"Does everyone know?" he asked quietly.

"Not as far as I'm aware. I only just found out. Jay hadn't told anyone and Eilidh only spoke to Beth."

"I feel so ridiculous. I knew things weren't right. They haven't been for ages, but instead of doing anything about it, I've just carried on looking at invitations and talking about colour schemes. As if I even care about any of that. I could have lost her, and the thought makes me feel sick."

Rich slumped down at the side of the tree, just as Ali had earlier.

"You haven't though," Ali reasoned, moving to sit down next to him. "You've both realised how much you need each other, and you're going to make things work."

"We have to. When she told me what had been going on and I thought of a life without her, it was like getting hit by a truck. There's no way I'd survive."

"I know how you feel," Ali stated simply.

"No offense, Ali," Rich laughed bitterly. "You're

a mate and everything, but you haven't got a clue how I feel right now."

"I thought it was Beth," Ali said quietly. "A bit ago, I overheard her and Eilidh talking. I thought it was Beth that had feelings for Jay, and I reacted the same as you. Just like you did, I came here to confront him, only no one stopped me."

He lifted his hand to show Rich his damaged knuckles.

"To be honest, my fist hasn't come off any better from the tree," said Rich with a rueful smile. "You can't seriously have thought your brother would be carrying on with your wife though."

"That's the problem. I could believe it too easily. There's a lot that's gone on between me and Jay in the past. The daft thing is, having confronted him today and having actually talked properly, we're probably in the best place we've been for years. But I was so quick to doubt Beth. I didn't talk to her or give her a chance to explain. She won't have had a clue why I've been treating her so badly. I've ignored her, been horrible every time she's tried to talk to me, and I've left her to deal with Rory on her own. I knew she was close to breaking from the lack of sleep, but I didn't care. I just hope she can forgive me."

"I'm sure she will. You two are made for each other. You can get through this."

"Well, I'd say the same about you and Eilidh."

"Then we both need to do everything we can to make things work, don't we?"

"Yeah, you're right, we really do," Ali replied, already wondering how he could possibly make up for what he'd done.

LETTER EIGHT

March 1895

Dear Joseph,

This is the last letter I will ever write to you. Perhaps it is the last I will write at all. I am finding it increasingly difficult to express my thoughts on paper. The pen won't stay in my hand properly, the words jump about and don't form the phrases I want. The last letter I wrote prior to this was cruel and hurtful, although I thought it was necessary. Perhaps my punishment is to never write easily again.

I always thought of my love for you as something that sustained me. Those stolen moments with you were the moments I lived for—your arm around my waist as we strolled along the furthest reaches of the hill path, your fingertips subtly catching against mine as we walked into dinner, your eyes searching for me as you gazed around the church each Sunday, our lips meeting when we sat hidden on the edges of the secret shore. I always thought those were the moments when I truly lived, that those were the moments when the sun came out, the moments that seemed to keep the darkness at bay. But I wonder now if I was wrong. Was my love for you what led me to the darkness in the first place? Perhaps my love for you is the darkness, and it was everything else in my life that prevented me from being engulfed by it. However, I have nothing else left. Flora has her own family. My husband James and my son James were never truly mine, and my precious Alexander is dead. Just as I finally understand that loving you has been my undoing, it seems it is all I have left. Yes, my love for you is the darkness, but I still cannot give it up.

If you had loved me enough, if you had been willing to fight for me all those years ago, it would have been different. Had you not fallen so easily for Maude's trick, had you not married her, everything would have been alright. If you had not married Maude, Eliza would not have existed. She could not have broken Alexander's heart, and he would not have made that wearisome journey to see her when his body was already weak with illness. He would not have had his heart broken again by seeing her new happiness, and he might have had the strength to recover.

If you had been stronger, if you had married me instead, Alexander would have been our son, and he would be alive with me now. If you had been strong enough to return my love, I too would have been strong. I might not have seen danger and loss waiting around every corner. I might instead have seen everything tinted in a different light. My world has always been edged with black, the light a harsh glare, like the cold light of the northern windows. Perhaps with love, it could have been lit with the soft glow of the stained glass in the hallway. I think a person living in that warm glow would make much better decisions, kinder decisions. My unrequited love for you left me always in that cold light, and trying to run from the darkness led me to act cruelly. I can see it now, but I still have to accept responsibility for what I have done. My need for you led to Alexander's death. My love for you has taken away the most precious thing in my life, and I will accept the punishments that I deserve. However, you also need to accept your share of the blame. There is no doubt in my mind that your weakness set these events in motion. So, just as I am guilty, you are too. We are both responsible for Alexander's death.

I have set about removing all traces of Alexander from the house. It is taking a long time and each day I achieve less, but I must carry on. I do not deserve to see his image or remember his existence. I failed him. I cut short his life and denied him his chance of happiness. It is only right that I should find no comfort in memories of him. I told James that Alexander's gravestone should not bear any reference to me. How can I still claim the right to be thought of as his mother? My views were ignored though, there are still appearances to keep up. I know they are all concerned for me. Flora has written, asking if she should come and stay. Little James has sent many letters from London. Even my husband has shown touching concern, coming to sit with me on the days when I cannot make it from my bed. But I do not want or deserve their concern. I need to take my punishment. I want to take my punishment.

I was wrong to think my love for you was glorious, that it was something pure and worthy of celebration. I can see now that it wasn't. It was selfish, it was immoral, and it led to cruelty. I was always running from the darkness, the hideous pit of despair which constantly threatened to engulf me. I thought you could save me from it, but now I understand the darkness was simply a manifestation of my need for you. If only I'd realised sooner. How different things could have been. However, I cannot change what is done, instead I must embrace the results of my deeds. I must welcome the darkness and the suffering, for it is my just reward. This darkness is what we created, Joseph, and now it is all mine.

All my love,
Always

CHAPTER THIRTY

The final letter hadn't improved Beth's mood, but it had certainly taken her mind off her own worries for a while. It was so tragic that Constance believed her life was now worthless, that her choices had all been mistakes, and that she deserved to suffer. Beth wondered if the cruel last letter Constance had referred to was the one she had written to Eliza, informing her of Alex's death. In that letter, Constance claimed Alex had been aware of Eliza's pregnancy. She said he knew that Eliza had given birth to a daughter named for him but had never believed the child to be his. Eliza had not accepted this, and Beth had found a letter written by Alex, which proved this was not the case. He hadn't known of his daughter, Alexandrina, until long after her birth. He only discovered her existence because Constance became ill and could not intercept Eliza's letters, but the news had thrilled him, and he had immediately set out to see his child. The sad thing was that Eliza had never known this: on seeing her and realising how happy she now was, Alex had decided not to intrude on her new life. Tragically, he had become ill on his journey home, and he died before he had chance to send the letter he'd written explaining everything.

When Constance had written those lies to Eliza, Alex was already dead. So even after losing her beloved son, she had still been determined to follow through with her plans to keep Eliza away from him. Beth couldn't decide whether the fact Constance regretted her actions went any way to redeeming her, but she knew she didn't want this to be the end of her story. It seemed such a sad fate for the excited girl from those early letters. If Constance had never moved on from the depression expressed in this last letter, it seemed such a terrible waste of a life.

Beth could already hear Rory stirring from his sleep, his shuffling and sighs gradually turning to babble. There was still no sign of Ali though. He must have asked Jim to drop him off somewhere else instead. Maybe he'd gone straight to the office, or perhaps he'd gone back to his parents. That was, after all, where he'd gone on the night he'd stormed out. Beth decided what to do. She wasn't going to sit here wasting the day waiting for him. She was going up to Ardmhor House. The letters Alex's brother had written, shortly after Alex died, referred to Constance's emotional state, so she wondered if they could throw any more light on what had happened next. Plus, maybe Ali would be there, and maybe he'd finally be ready to open up about whatever was going on.

◆ ◆ ◆

Angela was delighted to see Beth and Rory walking up the path towards the house. She was already opening the door to the private apartment before they'd had time to ring the bell.

"What a lovely surprise! Two of my favourite people," she exclaimed, opening the door wide.

"I've finished Constance's letters," Beth explained, filling Angela in on the bleak tone of the final one. "I wondered if you fancied a little trip into the archive to look at the letters written by James MacAird? They might tell us a bit more."

Angela didn't need asking twice. Within the space of minutes, they had the letters in front of them. Rory was contained in his pushchair in the corner, turning a soft book over and over in his hands, determinedly trying to make it rustle and squeak.

"They don't give us a lot more detail, do they?" Beth sighed in disappointment.

"No, but they confirm the truth of what Constance was saying," Angela replied. "She really was trying to remove any reminder of Alex from the house. What a shame she wouldn't let the rest of the family help her. Maybe she could have got through the grief if she'd opened up to them."

"Maybe." Beth paused for a minute, considering what she was trying to say. "It sounds like it goes further than grief, really. All those references to darkness and how she's always had to keep it at bay, they make it sound as though she was struggling with depression."

"Well, she was certainly lonely and desperate for affection in all the letters. It wouldn't surprise me if she was depressed."

"The entire story is really sad, but I'm sort of relieved she got too weak to continue her mission to destroy all traces of Alex. Those lovely pictures of them all outside the front of the house wouldn't have survived if she'd been able to carry on."

"That's true, but it would be even better if there had been a happy ending to her story," said Angela. "Unfortunately, she died in May 1895, only a few months after Alex's death, so I think we can safely assume she never pulled herself out of this low."

"Oh, that's awful," Beth gasped. "I hadn't realised she died so soon after that last letter."

"Yes, it was just a couple of months later, and she was only forty-five. I don't know whether she hadn't fully recovered from the illness she'd had when she was too weak to hide the post or if she simply succumbed to the effects of grief. I mean, it must have been quite a severe illness. She had to take to her bed, and it seems likely that the same infection led to Alex's death. Both her letter and James's letters say that she was finding physical activity increasingly difficult, but it's hard to know if that's down to illness or her mental state."

"I'd never thought about how young she was when she died. I've spent so much time thinking how tragic it was that Alex died at just twenty-five, but it hadn't registered that Constance was only twenty years older than him. Her story is almost as tragic as his. In fact, maybe it's more tragic."

"In what way?" queried Angela.

"Well, at least Alex saw Eliza and saw that she was happy. He was at peace with the idea of moving on and starting again. Although he was disappointed in himself, he didn't seem angry. In that last letter he wrote to Eliza, he said he didn't know if he'd be able to forgive Constance, but he didn't say he couldn't. He certainly didn't hold her totally responsible for the breakdown of his and Eliza's relationship."

"That's true," Angela agreed. "I remember he made that little joke about trying to persuade Constance to start up her matchmaking parties again."

"Exactly! It's not the sort of thing you'd say if you totally hated someone. I hadn't really thought about it until I got to know more about Constance, I think I was just too wrapped up in the end of Alex and Eliza's story, but it sounds as if he'd come to terms with the situation and still loved his mother. Would Constance have known that though? Or did she die thinking he hated her for what she'd done? Is that what pushed her into the darkness she describes?"

"I don't suppose we'll ever know," Angela said sadly. "Even if she knew he didn't hate her, she'd still have to live with the fact that he wouldn't have made that rushed journey to see Eliza and Alexandrina if she hadn't been hiding things from him. If he'd always known of Alexandrina's existence, there would have been no need for him to travel at that point, and he might have survived the infection. I just really hope she found some sort of peace at the end."

"Me too," Beth agreed.

When she'd first read Eliza's diary, she could never have imagined feeling sorry for Constance. She'd hated the idea that they were related. Now she wished she could have known her, she wished she could have helped her, and she wished she could have shown her some of the love she so desperately craved.

"I think I'd like to visit her grave," Beth said after a while. "Do you want to come?"

◆ ◆ ◆

Half an hour later, they were by Constance's grave—three generations of MacAirds. The oldest, a MacAird by marriage, just as Constance was. The youngest, a MacAird by birth. Beth was both, although she had only known of her distant birth connection to the family for a short while before she married into it. The MacAird family graves were in a walled section of the churchyard. It was a peaceful setting. The white painted church with its tall, arched windows stood to the side and the sea lay beyond. Although the day's weather had picked up from its murky start, it hadn't turned sunny. The air seemed too still to move the clouds, but there was a brightness to the sky now that made the church glow. A pair of buzzards wheeled overhead, their haunting cry adding to the melancholy of the moment. There was a mixture of graves in the MacAird family plot, from simple headstones to elaborate monuments. Constance and James MacAird's memorial was amongst the latter. The base with its inscription was relatively plain, but a magnificent angel with its wings aloft soared above it, marking it out from the memorials of the lesser branches of the family. The first inscription was for Constance. It read, 'Lady Constance MacAird of Ardmhor. Beloved wife and mother. 1850–1895'. Beneath it was a quotation, 'It always hopes, always perseveres. Love never fails.' Finally, there was a memorial for James MacAird, added after his much later death in 1920.

"Do you recognise the quotation?" Angela asked.

"I think so. It's from the Bible, isn't it? Is it Corinthians? I'm sure it's part of the reading that lots of people have at weddings."

"Yes, it is. I think it might have been adapted slightly, but that's definitely where it comes from."

"It seems perfect for her, doesn't it?" said Beth. "Her love for Joseph might not have brought her much happiness, but she certainly persevered with it. She was definitely hopeful about it, and even at the end, when she was so distressed, it never failed."

"Maybe James understood more about his wife than we've been giving him credit for."

"I suppose I've not thought about him much at all, to be honest," Beth admitted.

They stood quietly for a while. A gentle breeze seemed to come from nowhere, rustling the leaves of the trees behind the graves.

Just two generations were side by side now. The third was crawling happily around the grass after squirming to be released from the constraints of his pushchair. The older two were both lost in their own thoughts, although those thoughts were very similar: sorrow for the sadness and loneliness Constance seemed to have experienced throughout her life, a little guilt for the man whose feelings they had barely considered while learning her story, and hope that wherever Constance was now, she was finally experiencing some peace.

CHAPTER THIRTY-ONE

Ardmhor, 1895

I know I haven't got long left. It feels like the end of summer. It reminds me of that subtle change just as the nights start drawing in. It's like the moment when you look back at those first warm days, when endless light and possibilities stretched out ahead, and you wonder why you didn't appreciate it all more, why you didn't seize every single second. Everything you should have done becomes so clear once the opportunity has passed.

Now is my winter. The moments of each day when it is bright enough to think are increasingly short. But think I do. I think of the dreams I had and the reality I have lived. I think of the people I have loved and the hurt I have caused. I think of the closeness I longed for and the fact that I am alone. There is not enough time left to atone for my sins, and I know I cannot reach those I have harmed the most. My only comfort is that I deserve this miserable end.

I lie here with my memories and my regrets, hardly knowing where day ends and night begins. The darkness has tightened its grip on me, but I notice now that it has a warmth to it. Each day, it becomes more difficult to remove myself from its clutches. It wraps around me, clinging tighter, suffocating all else. And there is peace in its warm embrace. I find I no longer want to escape. But escape I must. I do not deserve peace. Suffering is what I deserve.

I've tried to punish myself by removing all mementoes of Alexander from the house. I've burnt the letters he wrote, the photographs we had, his clothes, and his treasures. Reading the words he had written to me when he was a scared child at boarding school, remembering the total faith he'd placed in me, was painful. He'd believed I could right all wrongs for him, yet it was my actions that brought him to his death. It was painful to read those words and realise how I had failed him, but it was more painful to watch them burn. How quickly his letters and his photographs disappeared. Like Alexander himself. It was the right action to take. I do not deserve to be comforted by his memory, but I am struggling to complete the task. My weakness increases by the day, and I cannot ask anyone for help.

I know James means well. For the first time in our marriage, he actually pays attention to me. How sad that it took the loss of our child to bring that about. But I don't deserve attention or sympathy. I have asked him to tell Little James and Flora to stay away. No matter how much I would like to be comforted by their presence, I must accept the pain. I must pay my penance if there is to be any hope of redemption.

Accepting my suffering is one small thing I can do; what feels impossible is making amends. It is too late to make things right with Alexander, but I must try to correct the wrongs I have done to Eliza and her child. At the very least, I want Eliza to know that I recognise the pain I have caused. However, I don't know how. If only I could write, but I no longer have the strength to hold a pen and bend it to my will. I wish with all my being that I hadn't written that terrible letter to Eliza in the days after Alexander's death. How could I have tainted his memory in that way? How could I have claimed such terrible thoughts were his? I would gladly give my last breath to strike that letter from existence, but it cannot be undone. When I am capable, I think about how I can convey my regret to Eliza. I know my apologies would mean little, even if I could write them. I may have believed I was acting in Alexander's best interests, but there was never any doubt my decisions would cause Eliza pain. Why should she accept an apology for actions that I knowingly carried out? But I would like her to know that I realise I was wrong. She should know that I acknowledge her child as my grandchild, that I recognise Alexandrina as one of us. She should know that Alexander would never have disowned her. Also, I would like her to know that I truly wanted to care for her. I knew deep down that I could never be her mother, but I wanted us to be close. When I learnt of Eliza's child, I should have rejoiced. Finally, there was a tangible connection between us, but I destroyed that link. If only I had told the truth as soon as I knew Eliza was with child. If I'd taken the risk and told Alexander what I had done, perhaps they could have forgiven me, perhaps I'd have the three of them alongside me now. But I was too scared of losing him. My desire to keep him close was stronger than any sense of right or wrong. I need Eliza to know that I recognise my mistakes, but I don't know how. Maybe it is another part of my penance to think endlessly about this impossible task.

The moments of light are so brief now. I feel it will not be long until the darkness is all I know, and I am not scared of that. In the darkness, there is no pain. If anything, it feels as though an eternity of emptiness is too good for me. However, I am fearful that, once I can fight it no longer, the darkness will change. Perhaps once I am trapped in its eternal embrace, my thoughts will find their way in, ready to torture me for the rest of time. Perhaps the emptiness is but a trick to tempt me to accept its solace. There can be no hope of heaven, but I am still terrified of accepting my fate. The pains of hell are what I deserve: I should experience the sort of suffering that my desires have caused others. I know this, yet I am still afraid. But the darkness is so powerful and so warm, and so hard to resist.

CHAPTER THIRTY-TWO

"Would you like Jim and me to babysit tonight, so that you and Ali can catch up after his trip?"

It took Beth a while to register that Angela was speaking to her, never mind come up with an answer. She'd got the pushchair stuck on a something just inside the churchyard gate. So far, she'd freed it twice, only to get it stuck again as soon as she moved. Eventually, she escaped the churchyard and came up with a response.

"I don't know. I haven't seen him yet, so I don't know if he'll be too tired to go out."

"That's a good point, actually. Jim had been expecting to drop him off at yours, but he insisted on going straight to the office, so maybe he will be too tired, especially as he had such a heavy night the evening before he went. You can just give me a ring if you decide you want to though. It'll be no bother to have Rory."

Beth's mind had immediately gone back to the night before Ali's trip. His reaction to her asking to talk had been completely unexpected and totally out of proportion, and he hadn't responded to any of her calls or texts since. She knew it wasn't like him. He was usually so straightforward and open, which told her he must really be struggling with something. However, knowing this didn't make it any easier to deal with. It hurt to be shut out, and it hurt to know he'd rather go straight to work than risk seeing her.

"Are you alright, love?" Angela queried. "Do you want me to take the pushchair for a bit?"

Beth realised that not only had she missed most of what Angela had said, she'd been so lost in thought she'd totally stopped moving. She couldn't handle any more discussion of Ali right now. She needed an escape.

"No, it's fine," she finally answered. "I think I might call in and see my mum and dad, actually."

"That's a good idea. It makes sense, seeing as you're almost at their house. Plus, being at Constance's grave makes you think, doesn't it? It's such a special connection between mothers and children, but it doesn't always work out how you want. I feel like I want to give both of my boys big hugs right now. I'd hate to think they didn't know how much I loved them."

Beth smiled at her. She had been thinking about complex family dynamics, just not parent and child ones. Angela was right though; Constance's story was a reminder that family shouldn't be taken for granted. She needed to make sure she didn't let the irritation she kept experiencing with her mum overshadow all the love that had gone before.

"I don't think you need to worry about that, Angela, everyone in your family can see how much you care. I'm always so grateful for everything you do for us."

"Aww Beth, that's lovely, thank you," said Angela, pulling her into a big squeeze of a hug. "Right, I'll get off then, but don't forget to call if you decide you want a babysitter." She kissed the top of Rory's head, tickled his tummy, and set off on her way.

◆ ◆ ◆

"This is a nice surprise," Jean exclaimed as she opened the door to find Beth and Rory. "Your dad's just in the byre if you want to let him know you're here."

"I might take Rory out to see him in a while. I wanted to talk to you about Constance. I finished the last of her letters."

"Oh right, let me stick the kettle on then," Jean

called over her shoulder as she set off into the kitchen, leaving Beth taking her shoes off in the hall. "I hope things picked up a bit. She hasn't exactly been happy in the last few."

"In fairness, she hasn't really been happy in any of them, apart from that very first one, but no, this one doesn't get any better," Beth said as she joined her mum in the kitchen.

She put Rory down on the floor, watching as he crawled off towards the enormous windows at the front of the room, drawn by the light and the gulls arguing on the lawn.

"That's a shame, although I suppose I should have known, really. The last letter you told me about was written after Eliza left and it's not really that long after that when Alex died." She handed Beth a mug of hot water and settled on to the settee next to her. "When was this last one written, then?"

"It's just after Alex died. I hadn't really put two and two together before, but Constance died in May 1895. That's only three months after Alex's death. It seems like she never got over it."

"Well, she wouldn't have in that time, would she? I don't know if I'd ever recover if something happened to you, maybe eventually I'd accept it and get used to it, but in three months I doubt I'd have got anywhere." Jean stopped speaking for a moment, and her voice cracked as she started again. "Even thinking about losing you makes me tearful. I can't imagine what the reality would be like."

"I know," Beth whispered. She'd not realised until Rory's birth quite how bound up your existence could become in someone else's. When she'd met Ali, she'd had an inkling of it. She couldn't imagine a future without him, but since Rory was born, death had become a terrifying prospect. The idea of something separating her from him, or even worse, the idea of her being unable to protect him. Well, those thoughts were almost unbearable.

Eventually Jean filled the silence again. "What did Constance write after Alex's death, then? I can only imagine how awful it must have been for her."

"That's exactly how it sounds, awful. She's furious with herself. Alex wouldn't have gone to Manchester when he was probably already ill if she hadn't kept him and Eliza apart, so she thinks it's her actions that caused his death. She's angry with Joseph as well because if he hadn't married Maude, Eliza would never have been born. And she's angry with herself for loving Joseph so much and ending up with nothing. It's just all really tragic."

"Poor Constance. I think anger is a very common reaction to grief."

"I suppose that makes sense, but Constance isn't just angry, she feels really guilty too. She keeps talking about how she deserves to suffer. She talks about writing a really cruel letter and how she's being punished for it. I presume she means the last letter she wrote to Eliza, where she said Alex had wanted nothing to do with her and her child. So she obviously knew that was wrong and felt bad about it."

"Yes, I think she probably did. I imagine very few people act rationally after the death of someone close."

"True, and I think Constance always struggled a bit. She mentions her life not being what she expected quite a lot, and she talks about a darkness that's always surrounded her in her last letters."

"Hang on a minute." Jean got up and moved across the room to where her laptop stood on the kitchen worktop. "There's something I want to show you."

She carried the laptop back over to the settee, clicking away until she found what she was looking for.

"I think you're right about Constance feeling bad about how she treated Eliza, and I think Eliza might have known that, too."

"Really?" Beth was intrigued. She'd thought the last letter was the end of Constance's story.

"You remember I told you about Jackie? My cousin in Australia who's into the family tree."

"Yes, she's related through Gran's big sister.

You mentioned her when we found the secret steps."

"Oh yes, that's right. It was just before I upset you by saying the wrong things about having a second child." Jean gave Beth a little smile, showing she was gently teasing rather than being serious.

"I'm sorry about that. I just get annoyed really easily at the moment."

"Don't be sorry. You're tired, Beth, you haven't slept properly for months, and everything's changed. You made this fantastic life here, and you made it sound so good that me and your dad followed you, so now you have to get used to being a mum and having your own mum around again. No wonder you're finding it all a bit much."

"I do like having you here," Beth offered, not really sure where she was going with this.

"I know you do, sweetheart, but that doesn't mean we can't find each other irritating from time to time."

Beth reached across to give her mum a hug but was constricted slightly by the laptop balanced on Jean's knee.

"I was never trying to say that I didn't think you could cope with another child. You know that, don't you?" Jean continued. "I think you've been amazing with Rory so far. When you were born, I struggled. Even though I loved you more than anything, I found being a mum incredibly hard to adjust to. I could barely get out of bed. Each day I'd be counting the minutes until your dad came home from work, and I cried almost constantly. I'd always wanted two children, but in the end, we decided against having another. It was too big a risk. I couldn't face feeling like that again. So I would never judge you about anything to do with Rory. I know how hard it can all be."

"I always thought you only wanted to have one child."

"I think I just found it easier to say that. It avoided awkward questions. Also, I didn't know how to explain that having one child put me off having more, without making it sound as if I regretted having you, which isn't true at all. I always knew I loved you. I just wasn't very good at being a new mum."

"It sounds more like post-natal depression than not being good at it."

"It probably was, but things like that weren't talked about as much back then. I thought if I admitted I wasn't loving it all, to anyone apart from your dad, they'd think I was a monster and take you away. If I'd had you today, when people are more open about struggling with mental health, maybe you'd have loads of siblings."

"I'm glad I don't have to share you," Beth said. "But I am sorry you went through all that without being able to talk to anyone. I'm desperate to escape from Rory some days, but at least I've got all these willing grandparents surrounding me."

"That's why we're always offering to have him. We love seeing him anyway, but I didn't want you to have to ask for help, in case you felt you couldn't, like I did. Really, I should have just spoken to you about it properly, but it's not that easy to talk about. I can remember how sensitive I was, so I thought this way would be better. I can see now that I was wrong."

"I don't know whether I'd have been in the right place to listen before now. I'm glad you've told me though. It's good to know it's not just me who's found it hard. Now he's finally sleeping a bit more; I'm beginning to imagine having another. I'm hoping it'll be different if we do it again because I'll know a bit more about what to expect, and I'll know not to be worried about asking you for help."

"You're always too hard on yourself, Beth. No one can do everything perfectly. We want to help you whenever we can. Please don't ever feel worried about asking." Jean's voice sounded choked again as she squeezed Beth's hand. "Anyway, I was trying to show you this email from Jackie. You know how I said she was sorting some of her mum's jewellery out? Well anyway, she found a brooch and because she'd read a copy of the diary, she thought we'd want to see it."

Jean turned the laptop round so that Beth could see the screen properly. On it was a photograph of a cameo brooch. The image on the cameo was a woman reaching towards a child. It was so finely rendered that you could sense the love between the pair. The background was a tawny colour, not bright enough to be considered amber or orange, but certainly not a brown. It was exactly as Constance had described the brooch given to her by her mother, the brooch she had in turn given to Eliza and which Eliza had then returned to her when she left Ardmhor.

"This can't be Constance's brooch, can it?" Beth said, amazed. "Eliza gave it back to her, so how would it have ended up in our family?"

"Well, have a look at this." Jean clicked onto the other attachment within the email. It was a photograph of a scrap of paper, the writing on it was spidery and the ink was faint, but it was just possible to make out the words. They said, 'This brooch belongs to the daughters of my family. It should belong to you and your daughter. C.M.F.'

"Oh wow," Beth exclaimed. "Constance's maiden name was Forsyth, C.M.F has to be her. It's hard to tell if it's the same writing as her letters, but she had said she was struggling to hold a pen. Do you think she sent it to Eliza to show her she was sorry?"

"It makes sense, and it fits with what you were saying about Constance feeling guilty."

"I suppose the brooch is a piece of jewellery that says a lot," Beth mused. "With it being passed down the women of Constance's family it shows she is acknowledging Eliza's child as part of that. It says she knows Alex was the father. If she was struggling to write, sending this to Eliza would express a great deal without many words."

"Exactly," Jean replied. "And the fact that Eliza kept it and then passed it on to Alexandrina, who must have passed it to her eldest daughter, your great aunt Alice, shows she must have accepted and understood the sentiment behind it. If she had felt no forgiveness towards Constance, she'd surely have sent it straight back, or just thrown it away."

"I like the thought that Constance experienced a bit of forgiveness," Beth said with a sad smile. "Even if she didn't know how it was received, perhaps just sending the brooch to Eliza gave her some hope. I hate to think of her dying wracked with guilt. It isn't like she gained anything from her actions, and wrong as she was, her motivations weren't evil, just misguided."

"It's funny, really," Jean began. "The diary had us all convinced that Constance was horrible, and that Eliza couldn't stand her. Reading the letters made us question what we thought about Constance, and now, seeing this makes me think Eliza mustn't have hated her either. Maybe after Alexandrina was born, Eliza started to see Constance and Alex's bond differently. Perhaps she could see that Constance's actions, although wrong, were about trying to protect Alex. It's so hard to know what someone else is thinking."

"Tell me about it," Beth said with a sigh, thinking how little she understood about what was going on in Ali's head at the moment.

"That sounded ominous. Is everything alright?" Jean asked.

For once, Beth decided maybe she should open up and ask for help. Her instinct was always to deal with things alone. She felt that if she admitted she needed help, it was like admitting that she was a failure. But her mum had been honest with her this afternoon. Perhaps she should try to honour that by being open as well.

"It's Ali," she said, and then she told her mum everything that had been going on.

Jean listened without comment until Beth had got everything off her chest, including how hurt and angry she was feeling right now. Then she finally gave her response.

"You need to talk to him, Beth. I know you already know this, but there really is nothing else you can do. There has to be something behind all this, but until you talk about it properly, you won't know. His behaviour has been awful, and if I thought it represented him at all, I'd be telling you that you're best off out of it, and that maybe you should think about walking away. But this doesn't represent the Ali that I know at all. He adores you. The pair of you make an amazing team, and clearly you want to sort this out. So your only option is to swallow your pride and talk to him. Put your anger, which is totally justified by the way, to one side and get to the bottom of things. If you let this fester any longer, it might become too big to get over."

"You're right, I know you are. Angela said he went straight to the office when Jim picked him up, so maybe I'll go there now."

"That sounds like a plan. Do you want me to drive you there?"

"No, we'll walk. I could probably do with some thinking space on the way. It's been an emotional afternoon."

"It has," Jean agreed, pulling Beth into another tight hug once they'd finished fastening Rory into the pushchair. "But I'm so glad you felt you could talk to me. I love you so much."

"I love you too," Beth replied into her mum's hair.

CHAPTER THIRTY-THREE

Ardmhor, 1895

I feel as if my time is almost at an end. I don't have long in the light now and ghosts are creeping in. I'm afraid of what will happen next. I'm terrified of how death will come for me. Even though I know I deserve to suffer, I am so frightened by the thought.

For a time, my every thought was about how I could express my regret to Eliza. Even when I was insensible, trapped in the darkness, she was there in my mind. It was her presence that kept pulling me back. I knew I had to focus. I knew I had to put things right, but I didn't know how. Thoughts would chase each other round, like a dog chasing its own tail. I should write to her, but I couldn't write. I had to explain, but what explanation could I give? I'd wanted to love her, but I'd got everything so wrong. I'd thought we were becoming close, but then I made it all fall apart. I'd given her my mother's brooch, and she'd handed it back. The thoughts repeated round and round, round and round, until finally it became clear. I had the answer. I knew how to convey everything I needed Eliza to understand. The brooch was the answer. It was supposed to be handed down amongst the daughters of my family. Before I destroyed all hope of a relationship between us, my intention was to love Eliza as a daughter. Alexandrina is my granddaughter—she carries my blood along with Alexander's. She is without doubt a daughter of my family. The brooch could say everything I needed Eliza to know, and Flora has no need for it. She has never had reason to doubt my love.

I knew I had to act quickly. The times when I have the strength to control my thoughts are so fleeting now. Whether it was night or day when I finally pulled myself from my bed, I do not know. I do know that the old and unkempt woman reflected in my dressing-table mirror shocked me. At first, I wondered if she was another ghost come to visit me. I thought perhaps she had been sent by death himself. Then I finally realised the woman was me. I am so changed. The evil I have done is written across my face. It stands to reason there could be nothing lovely about a woman who could willingly cause such pain. The shock almost caused me to lose sight of what I was trying to achieve, but somehow my body knew to keep going, to keep moving towards the desk, the place where everything lay hidden. I'd placed so much in the secret compartment over the last few years that my hands knew how to work the mechanism without needing to involve my mind. Without that knowledge buried in my fingertips, I would have failed in my mission, for I could already feel the darkness seeping in, turning my world into a comforting nothingness, an empty warmth.

It was the maid that found me on the floor with the brooch tightly clasped in my hand. She helped me hold the pen and scratch out the few words needed to send it on its way. 'This brooch belongs to the daughters of my family. It should belong to you and your daughter. C.M.F.' Those words were all I could manage. It was important to me to include the F for my maiden initial as well as the M for MacAird. I wanted Eliza to know I don't just see her child as part of Alexander's legacy, she is a part of mine, too. She embodies the connection I always dreamt of. At last, a child exists that links my blood with Joseph's. Alexandrina is the most precious of children, a combination of those I held most dear. If only I had seen that from the start, how different this ending could have been.

I feel some comfort to know that the brooch is on its journey, but I do not expect to live to find out whether it has succeeded in its quest. My terror of eternal damnation will not abate, but the ghosts give me some solace. I dare not let myself believe that the presence of Joseph and Alexander means I will be forgiven. To hope for that and then find it was simply a trick of the mind would be worse than never having hoped. But I can't help hoping. I don't have enough control over my thoughts now. The ghosts come and go unbidden by me, and they whisper for me to come. They tell me all will be well. They tell me they know how truly I loved. They tell me my mistakes are forgiven, and that they are waiting for me. I try not to hear them. I try not to hope. I do not deserve to hope. But the thoughts will not stop. They whisper for me to come. They whisper it again and again. And I will. I don't have the strength to resist.

CHAPTER THIRTY-FOUR

After trying all afternoon, the sun finally broke through while Beth pushed Rory along the road. As the breeze chased away the remaining clouds, the sea changed from dark grey to vibrant blue, and the sunlight played across the distant hills, highlighting the peaks and the valleys. Beth decided to call at the viewpoint on the way to the office. She didn't know how easy this conversation would be, and the outlook from there never failed to soothe her. Also, it would do no harm to remember the magic of that first ever meeting with Ali before talking to him.

She walked up the drive to Ardmhor House, passing where she'd stayed on the holiday which had led to her life at Ardmhor. She waved at

Callum in the ticket office as she made her way through the gates and continued towards the viewpoint. The path skirted the playground, which Beth had helped to build as part of the volunteer group, and then headed along the front of the main lawn, before edging around the woodland. Every part of the walk held memories, and every one of them was good. She stopped beside the plaque Bob and Mary had attached to the play equipment on the last afternoon of the volunteer holiday and thought about how lucky she was. Five years ago, when she'd first arrived here, she was unhappy and unfulfilled. Every part of her life had been disappointing in some way. Now things were so different. She had a job she enjoyed, and she lived in a place that never ceased to amaze her with its beauty. And that wasn't all. She had both friends and family nearby, people who'd do anything to support her. Somehow, she'd fallen into the trap of only noticing the things that were going wrong. She'd been too tired to see anything other than what was directly in front of her, but when she really thought about it, her life was exactly as she'd always wanted it to be. All that time ago, Constance had dreamt her dreams, but her reality had fallen short, and it had led her to a dark and lonely place. Beth felt a renewed sense of determination. She was going to get to the bottom of whatever was going on with Ali, and she was going to make things right. She already had what she'd dreamt of, and she would not let it slip away.

Beth cursed inwardly as she reached the viewpoint clearing and saw that it was already occupied. Making polite small talk was the last thing she wanted to do. She wanted to sit quietly and replay every moment of that first meeting with Ali in her head. After the embarrassment of mistaking him for Alex, she'd known immediately that Ali was something special; she'd known that he was made for her, and he'd felt it too. The viewpoint had remained 'their' place. Despite it being open to the public, Beth couldn't help resenting the unsuspecting visitor already enjoying the view. She approached as loudly as possible. Often, when it was quiet, people would take the arrival of another person as their cue to move on. The visitor turned their head as they heard the pushchair crunching through the gravel, and it was then that Beth realised she'd been mistaken again. It wasn't a visitor, it was Ali.

He'd ignored every attempt at contact over the last few days and now here he was, exactly where he'd been on the day they'd met. She didn't rush into his arms as she had then, instead she stood and considered him for a while. She knew she still felt angry with him, but mainly she felt love. Over the past five years, he had become almost as familiar to her as her own reflection, but she had to admit he had become no less attractive for it. He was still the most beautiful man she'd ever seen and knowing that the beauty went deeper than the surface only made him more appealing. So she knew she needed to put the anger to one side for now. She didn't want to make things worse for the sake of proving a point.

She clicked the brake into place on the pushchair and took a step towards Ali, just as he took a step towards her.

"I'm so sorry," he said, reaching out to her.

"It's okay," she replied, taking hold of the hand he offered. "I knew you were struggling, but I was too wrapped up in how tired and miserable I was feeling to pay much attention. I've got so used to you supporting me, I started taking it for granted. When you finally needed me, all I thought about was how much harder you were making my life. I'm really sorry, Ali, and I want to help, but you have to tell me how."

"No, none of this is your fault, Beth. I got everything wrong. You tried to be understanding about Jay, but I wouldn't talk to you. I ran away, leaving you to deal with everything, and then I overheard something and leapt to conclusions. What I'm trying to say is, you don't need to apologise for anything. To be honest, I don't know if you'll be able to forgive me."

"Right, you've totally lost me now." Beth moved away from him and took a seat on the bench. "You need to explain everything properly from the start."

Ali sighed and sat down next to her. "Well, obviously you know I rushed off on that work trip as soon as Jay announced he was staying. I just wanted to get away from him and I was feeling loads better about everything when I got back. But then, when Jay mentioned you'd all been hanging around together, I felt like I was right back at the start of boarding school, where everyone else was in a group and I was on the outside."

"I explained it wasn't an organised thing though, didn't I? It'd have gone on the same if you'd been home, apart from it'd have been better."

"I know, but it made me paranoid, and then when someone else made a joke about seeing you with Andrew, I completely overreacted to it. I realised as soon as you walked off that I'd gone too far, but I was too wound up to back down. Then the next day when I saw you laughing with him, even though I knew there wouldn't be anything going on, it just sowed a tiny seed of doubt. It seemed like you were always too tired, or too busy, to want to talk to me, but then you were fine to call and see Andrew on the way back from Alan and Claire's, even though you'd said you were coming straight home."

"But all that happened before we went out to

the pub that night your mum babysat. We talked about everything then, and I thought you were fine with it."

"I was, but when everyone turned up halfway through the evening, you all seemed to be getting on so well that I started to wonder if you'd planned it."

"You were the centre of attention though, telling stories from your trip. If anyone was left out of the conversation, it was me."

"Maybe, but I've been so paranoid that it didn't feel like that. We'd been having such a lovely time and then suddenly Jay and Andrew were there, and I felt like I couldn't compete."

Beth looked at him. "And that's what this is all about? I still don't understand why you stormed off to Shetland without telling me, but it doesn't seem unforgiveable."

"I've not got to the worst bit yet. The night we went to the pub, I didn't sleep a wink. I was so churned up that my mind couldn't switch off. I ended up getting up really early and making an excuse about needing to work. Anyway, I did go to the office, but after a while I felt guilty. I knew we'd been supposed to meet your mum and dad, so I came to find you. I found them at the playground with Rory, and they told me you were with Eilidh and pointed me in the right direction."

"Yes, I know you saw my mum and dad, but

you didn't come and meet me. I thought you must have been called back to work. You didn't get home 'til really late."

"I know. I didn't meet you, but I heard you. You were telling Eilidh you had feelings for Jay. Then it all made sense. I'd known nothing was going on between you and Andrew, but I suppose the thought had been planted that there could be someone else. When I heard you say that about Jay, something just clicked in my head. Of course he'd be trying to take you away, that's what he does, and it sounded like it had worked."

"It's Eilidh that has feelings for Jay," Beth said, aghast. "We were just talking about what she should do and whether she should tell Rich."

"I know that now, but I didn't think to question it then. As I said, it just seemed to make sense."

"So that's why you were so angry when you said you knew about Jay." Beth stopped, horrified. "I couldn't work out why you were so upset about him and Eilidh, but you thought it was about me and him. How on earth could you have thought I'd tell you something like that didn't matter? Surely you must have realised you'd got things wrong?"

"I was just so convinced, and the fact that you were so dismissive confirmed it for me. In my head, you'd already moved on, Jay was already more important than me. Then I saw you together. You were by the road, and he had his arms around you. I had thought maybe we'd be able to work things out, but when I saw that, I knew we were over."

"It was a two second hug, Ali. I'd told him I didn't want to get dragged into things with him and Eilidh, and I'd also told him he needed to sort things out with you. You know how tactile your whole family is. He was thanking me for telling him to get his act together."

"I know that as well now, but at the time, it just seemed so obvious. He'd won again and everyone would be laughing at me. I should have talked to you though."

"Yes, you should have. You should know I would never treat you like that," Beth replied, not entirely sure whether she should be angry or relieved.

"I know, and I'm so sorry. I've been a total fool."

"You have, and you should at least have credited me with enough intelligence to know that if I was having an affair, I wouldn't carry it out in full view of the main road."

"Well, yes," Ali said sheepishly, "there is that too. Honestly, I'm so sorry. I should never have doubted you and had I been thinking rationally, I never would have. My mind was just so messed up, but I know that's not much of an excuse. Can you forgive me?"

"Of course I can, you've been as daft as they come, but I know for definite there've been plenty of times when I've been pretty ridiculous too."

"Thank you, thank you so much," he sighed, wrapping his arms around her, holding her so close she could hardly breathe. "I'll make it up to you, I promise. I'll do everything in the house forever. I'll send you off on nights away so you can finally get some sleep. I'll...."

"Alright," Beth said with a laugh, pulling away slightly so she could catch her breath. "Don't start making promises you can't keep!"

"Seriously though, I'll do anything to make things right. Before you got here, I was thinking about the night we met. I honestly don't think I could bear losing you."

Beth smiled at him. "I came here for the same reason, to think about when we met. I was on my way to the office to force you to talk, and I thought it might help. How did you work out you'd got it all wrong though?"

"I punched Jay."

"What?" Beth gasped.

"I went to confront him at the office when I got back, but as soon as he spoke, I saw red, and I just lashed out."

"Oh," was all Beth could come up with. She wasn't really sure what the appropriate response was. "Is he okay?" she asked after a minute. "I doubt he expected that."

"No, he definitely didn't, but he's fine. In fact, we both are. We finally talked properly about everything, and I think we've sort of reached a peace. He's leaving though, taking a job in Edinburgh. He says he can't stay here and see Eilidh if he can't be with her."

"That might be for the best. She really wants to make a go of things with Rich."

"Rich does too. I spoke to him as well earlier. He was doing exactly the same as I had, heading up to the office to teach Jay a lesson. But we talked, and Jay avoided his second beating of the day."

"I'm glad about that. I mean that Rich still wants to work things out. Eilidh was so worried about telling him. Obviously, I'm glad Jay didn't get punched again as well. It sounds like he's probably suffering enough."

"Yeah, I think he is. It'll need a lot of water to pass under the bridge before he feels comfortable spending much time here again."

"Poor Jay. I can't believe you thought I'd prefer him to you though," Beth said, shaking her head.

"I know, and I'm sorry. Can we never mention this again, please?"

"No way," Beth said with a grin. "I'm bringing this up at least once a day forever."

"Seriously though, I'm so sorry."

"Seriously though," Beth repeated, "I know you are. I'm just glad we're okay. Promise me you'll always talk to me in future."

"I promise," Ali said, standing up and helping Beth to her feet, pulling her into his arms.

They stood there for a while, holding each other tight, in exactly the spot where they'd met. Except this time, they weren't alone. Now there was Rory as well. This was where their family had begun. Perhaps one day it would grow further. But whatever happened, they both knew there was nowhere they'd rather be.

CHAPTER THIRTY-FIVE

One year later...

The midday sun covered Ardmhor churchyard in its warm glow as the happy couple emerged from the church. It was a perfect day. The air was warm with only the slightest hint of a breeze, and the sky was a brilliant uninterrupted blue. The sunlight glistened off the sea and the distant hills were visible in all their glory, creating a magnificent backdrop for the photographs.

Eilidh made a stunning bride. She looked like a film star from a bygone age. Her dress was a 1950s style concoction with a full satin skirt, covered in layers and layers of polka dot net. The net swept up over the satin bodice to create delicate cap sleeves, and she wore a short frothy veil of the same net in her hair. True to form, there was nothing natural about Eilidh's hair colour that day, but she had swapped her previous bright blue for the softest shade of pink, matching the flowers in her bouquet. She whispered something into Rich's ear as the guests showered them with confetti, and the pair of them smiled at each other, completely wrapped up in the moment. There had been times over the last year when Beth had been unsure whether Eilidh and Rich would reach this day. When Eilidh had confessed what had happened with Jay, it had changed the dynamic between her and Rich. They'd been together for so long that their relationship wasn't something they'd really had to think about, it just was. Eilidh's revelation had changed all that. Neither of them had been sure how to act around the other at first, but they'd been determined to make things work, and they'd emerged stronger than ever. They both looked at each other in a different light now. They no longer took each other for granted, and on their wedding day, they honestly felt like the luckiest couple alive.

They weren't the only people feeling lucky that day. Rory was winding his way between the bushes at the front of the church, squealing with delight.

"Aster, aster," he chanted.

He didn't have many words yet, but he was perfectly capable of getting his point across, and right now, Uncle Jay wasn't running as fast as he should be. For Rory, the best part of playing chase with his uncle was getting caught and whisked up high into the air. Jay didn't mind being bossed around by his nephew. Rory might have been a tiny tyrant, but he looked adorable in his pale pink shirt and his little shorts. A year ago, Jay couldn't have imagined being able to be in the same room as Eilidh, let alone a guest at her wedding. When he'd left to start his new job in Edinburgh, he'd been heartbroken. He'd fallen for Eilidh in a way he'd never experienced before. His previous relationships had all been quick flings, so his intense connection with Eilidh that never progressed beyond a few stolen kisses was unchartered territory. He'd genuinely wondered if his only chance at happiness had passed him by. Wanting to respect Eilidh's wishes, he'd made no attempts to contact her and had instead thrown himself into his work. He'd worked such long hours that he'd barely had time to think, and after a few months he realised Eilidh had retreated slightly in his mind. When he'd braved his first visit back to Ardmhor, Jay had run into Rich and Eilidh as he'd known he would. The forced politeness had been awkward for all three of them, but they'd survived, and Jay was pleased to realise he didn't feel any worse for the encounter. The Eilidh he'd seen that day seemed totally in love with the man whose hand she was holding. She wasn't the same person he'd felt that sense of belonging with. He wondered whether the futility of their situation had led him to build it into something more than it had been.

The month after that, he'd bumped, quite literally, into his neighbour while looking at his phone rather than where he was going. He'd been spending so much time at work that he hadn't yet met many of the people living in the flats surrounding his. When he'd offered to buy Sophie a coffee to make up for the one he'd spilt in their collision, it was because he was genuinely sorry. He hadn't initially registered the brilliance of her smile or the way her hair fell in long, chestnut waves. It was only after the coffee turned into dinner that he realised how beautiful her deep brown eyes were. It was during their drink after dinner, when Sophie told him she'd moved to Edinburgh after her fiancée called off their wedding, that he realised he hadn't thought about Eilidh once that evening. In fact, it was only the parallels between his and Sophie's situations that had called her to mind, not the wistful longing he had become used to being assailed by. Somehow, his life and Sophie's became intertwined. They were both wary of being hurt, so after a drunken kiss that first night, they'd agreed to remain just friends, but that hadn't lasted long. Within two months of meeting, they were spending every night together. By the third month he'd taken her to Ardmhor to meet his family, something he'd never considered doing with any previous girlfriends. Sophie had loved everything about that first trip and on their second visit, they had braved an evening in the pub with Beth and Ali. As expected, Eilidh and Rich had made an appearance and, to Jay's surprise, it was fine. After an initial moment of silence, everyone had relaxed and by the end of the night it was almost as if nothing had ever happened. In fact, the evening had been enjoyable enough that they'd all gone for a meal together on their next visit, and again on their next. So the invitation for them both to attend Rich and Eilidh's wedding hadn't been completely out of the blue, even if it was the last thing Jay would have expected when he initially left for Edinburgh.

Jay looked up from chasing Rory to see Sophie stood with Beth. They were laughing together as they watched uncle and nephew's haphazard progress between the shrubs. When he'd first moved back to Ardmhor, Jay had been dreaming of a relationship where he felt a genuine connection. He'd been imagining being surrounded by family, feeling like he belonged. It might not have happened as he'd expected, but he felt incredibly lucky to have everything he'd wanted.

Beth walked over to where Ali was chatting with Andrew and Leonie. After Leonie had dumped him, Andrew had realised the thrill of the chase was no longer as thrilling as it used to be. It dawned on him that Leonie was right, that moving in together might not be such a bad idea. He'd had to work hard to persuade her to take him seriously, but they'd been living together for six months now, and Andrew could honestly say he'd never been happier. Ali smiled as he saw Beth approaching and held out his hand to her. Beth's heart melted at the sight of him. She always found him attractive, his strong lean build, his tousled hair, and his dark eyes came together in the most pleasing way, but today, all scrubbed up in his suit, he was simply beautiful, and he was all hers. Ali was thinking something very similar about Beth. He still couldn't get over how close he'd come to throwing their relationship away. All because he hadn't talked to her, letting suspicion take hold instead. It was hard to believe that they had got to that point. Their relationship had been so close and so intense from the moment they'd met that it had seemed impossible it could fall apart. However, it almost had, and Ali would be eternally grateful that they'd sorted things out. Beth and Rory really were his world, and it was a world that only got better. He pulled Beth close to him and they smiled at each other, in the way that couples do when they have a secret. It was too soon to tell anyone, but Beth had done a pregnancy test the day before and, all being well, there would be four of them living in the factor's house after all. They both felt a little trepidation at the thought of a return to sleepless nights. They hadn't handled sleep deprivation at all well last time, but at least they knew what to expect now. Also, they reasoned they had made it through to the other side once already, even if the road had been bumpier than they'd expected. As Jay deposited a squirming Rory at their feet. Ali was also considering just how lucky he was.

Beth looked across the churchyard to where Eilidh and Rich were posing for photographs with their families. Claire and Alan were radiating pride as they stood alongside their daughter. Beth thought about a wedding held at this same church many years before, when Flora MacAird had married Algernon Rutherford, with Eliza as her bridesmaid. Had Constance felt the pride Claire seemed to be feeling now? Or had she been too sad at the thought of her daughter moving away to feel truly happy? The sunlight caught the wings of the magnificent angel that topped Constance's memorial. Beth hoped she'd finally found some peace. Over by the corner of the MacAird family plot, Beth could see her mum and dad busy chatting with Angela and Jim. Along with herself, Ali, Jay, and Rory, both Jim and her mum carried Constance's blood in their veins. Beth wondered if Constance could somehow see them here, stood together near her final resting place. Would it please her to see the happiness those future generations shared, to know that in the long run her actions had prevented nothing? After all, Eliza and Alexander's descendants had eventually made their way back to Ardmhor and into the MacAird family.

Beth had never felt Alex's presence at the churchyard. He'd once said to her he didn't believe people remained where their bodies lay, but that they instead clung to the things they had loved, and for Alex, that had been the grounds of Ardmhor House. Today, though, as she watched the people she loved moving around that sunlit churchyard, she could almost hear him. He'd loved to tell her that this was where she belonged, and he'd been right. She couldn't think of anywhere she'd rather be. She leaned back against the wall of the church and enjoyed remembering the sound of Alex's voice. Then, amidst the bustle of the crowd, she sensed a different presence, a less familiar one, one that was saying all was as it should be. The wings of Constance's angel seemed to move as Beth looked across at it, as if it was finally ready to take flight. She allowed herself the fantasy that it was Constance she could feel, that it was Constance who had led her to the letters in the attic and guided Angela to the others hidden in the desk at Ardmhor House. She let herself believe Constance was pleased to have finally been understood, that her soul was flying away as the angel seemed to want to. The churchyard was emptying as Beth looked at the memorial one last time. Then she moved away, hurrying to catch up with those she held most dear, knowing how lucky she truly was.

FROM THE AUTHOR

Firstly, I'd like to thank you for reading this book. I have always wanted to write, but it took a long time to build the courage to have a go. It then took even longer to have something ready to share with others, and I am hugely grateful to every single person who takes the time to read my work. If you have enjoyed this book and are able to leave a rating or write a review, that would be fantastic! If you would like to know more about me, my books, or any new releases, you can find information in the following places;

Website - leaboothbooks.com

Facebook - Lea booth books

Instagram - leaboothbooks

Secondly, thank you to my family for putting up with me and my funny ways.

In particular, thanks to P, E, and R for letting me ignore you, trying to teach me grammar, and constantly encouraging me. I think I used up all my luck getting each one of you in my life, but you are worth never winning anything else!

Thank you to the Jeans, my amazing mum and mother-in-law, for reading my drafts and being so positive.

Thank you to my sisters, Rae and Bags, for all your feedback and ideas.

Thank you to Lindsey; I am possibly the most useless friend ever, but you've stuck with me for over a quarter of a century, and I couldn't be more grateful.

And finally, thank you Mum and Dad for giving me a love of Scotland and giving all these characters places to go!

BOOKS BY THIS AUTHOR

The Holiday At Ardmhor

Always, Ardmhor

What Was Hidden At Ardmhor

The People Who Ruined My Life

Printed in Great Britain
by Amazon